There was something compelling, seductive even, about his voice. And his eyes. Something in them that made her want to believe what he was saying

'I don't want to have to hurt you,' Maggie said.

'Then put the phone down,' Drew said calmly. So persuasively. 'You know they won't listen to me. They'll come here with their dogs and their sirens and their shotguns, just looking for an excuse to kill me. You know that. You know how this works. Put the phone down, Mrs Cannon, so we can talk.'

Was it true? Had her ex-husband made a deal to save their daughter's life? A deal with the devil? And what would happen to her daughter if Maggie undid whatever had been done to send this man—this stranger—to prison?

'I don't have a choice,' she said, her eyes falling to the phone. And then suddenly, he was there. Right in front of her, reaching towards the gun. Somehow he had managed to close the distance between them, moving in almost total silence…

W9-BBY-050

Dear Reader,

Welcome to this month's romantic suspense novels from Silhouette Intrigue®!

May sees fantastic writer Gayle Wilson bring us another one of her breathtaking SECRET WARRIORS in *Renegade Heart*. Gayle returns in August with her next strong, sexy SECRET WARRIOR, the hero of *Midnight Remembered*.

We have another hunky hero driven by honesty and integrity in this month's LAWMAN LOVER, *The Second Son* by Joanna Wayne. Sheriff Branson Randolph is the first Randolph brother, and next month Joanna is back with *The Stranger Next Door*, featuring Langley Randolph…

Intrigue newcomer Ann Voss Peterson's *Inadmissible Passion* is a steamy, passionate drama—lovers have to reunite in order to stay alive. And in BJ Daniel's magnificent *Intimate Secrets*, Clay Jackson's search for the truth results in his learning the woman he never stopped loving was keeping the biggest secret of all…a baby!

Enjoy them all,

The Editors

Renegade Heart

GAYLE WILSON

SILHOUETTE

INTRIGUE

*First published in Great Britain 2001
Silhouette Books, Eton House, 18-24 Paradise Road,
Richmond, Surrey TW9 1SR*

© Mona Gay Thomas 2000

ISBN 0 373 22578 4

46-0501

*Printed and bound in Spain
by Litografia Rosés S.A., Barcelona*

ABOUT THE AUTHOR

Gayle Wilson is the award-winning author of twelve novels for Intrigue™. She has lived in Alabama all her life except for the years she followed her Army aviator husband—whom she met on a blind date—to a variety of military posts.

Before beginning her writing career, she taught English and world history to gifted students in a number of schools around the Alabama area. Gayle and her husband have one son, who is also a teacher of gifted students. They are blessed with warm and loving families and an ever-growing menagerie of cats and dogs.

You can write to Gayle at PO Box 3277, Hueytown, Alabama 35023, USA.

Gayle Wilson on…

What she loves most about being a writer:
'Connecting with readers.'

Besides writing what other talent she'd love
to have:
'I'd love to be able to sing in key (I can't).'

The most romantic meal she's ever had:
**'Brunch in the courtyard at The Court of Two
Sisters, New Orleans.'**

SECRET WARRIORS

by

GAYLE WILSON

**Men with new identities and hidden
agendas—sworn to loyalty and
tamed by love!**

Her Private Bodyguard
(February 2001)

Renegade Heart
(May 2001)

Coming soon:
Midnight Remembered
(August 2001)

Don't miss this dramatic and dangerous mini-
series by best-selling author Gayle Wilson

Only from Silhouette Intrigue®

Prologue

When Drew Evans regained consciousness after the wreck, two things were apparent: the prison transport bus was on fire and the man he was chained to was dead. Neither seemed promising.

At least *he* wasn't the one who was dead, Drew told himself as he tried to inch upright despite the weight of the dead body lying on top of him. And he'd been in worst fixes. He couldn't remember any of them offhand, but he was sure there must have been at least a few during his years with the CIA.

The smoke was getting thicker, even here at the other end of the bus, away from the ruptured gas tank. There was a lot of cursing and screaming, and the sound of glass breaking as people kicked out windows to get out. The fire was close enough that Drew could hear the hiss and crackle as it ate through vinyl seats and scorched metal framework, turning the overturned vehicle into an inferno.

He tried not to think about any of that. Tried to keep his mind off the fire and concentrate on his search of the dead deputy's pockets. It was not until he reached the last one, working through them strictly by feel, that he found the key. After that, getting the lock undone was a matter of seconds.

He rolled the dead deputy off him and onto his back. Then Drew pushed up off the floor, surprised to find that other than a knot the size of an egg on his head, he didn't seem to be injured. Blind luck, he thought, seeing the carnage around him.

The other deputy was slumped over the back of the seat in front of the one in which Drew had originally been sitting. Drew bent over him, finding the artery in his neck. There was a pulse, thready and uneven, but definitely there.

Son of a bitch, Drew thought, glancing back at the fire. He bent, crawled between the seats, and got his shoulder under the deputy. Using the muscles in his thighs, he pushed up, managing to lift the man into a makeshift fireman's carry despite the fact that the guy must have outweighed him by fifty pounds.

Adrenaline surge, maybe. Or the realization that the metal of the seat the deputy had been draped over was already getting hot. He wouldn't have to carry him far, Drew told himself. Just get him off the bus. Out of the path of the fire.

He could not only hear it roaring behind him now, he could feel the searing heat, as if he were too close to the heart of a blast furnace. And it was sucking all the oxygen out of the air around him. Replacing it with deadly toxic fumes.

Drew glanced behind him toward the curtain of flame. There were other bodies between him and the approaching fire, but he couldn't do anything for them. Nothing except pray they were already dead. He turned and, staggering under his burden, climbed out through the emergency exit someone had already kicked open.

Drew carried the deputy as far away from the burning vehicle as he could, expecting at any moment to hear sirens in the distance. Or to have someone stick a shotgun against his spine and order him into formation. Expecting something.

None of those things happened. Drew laid the deputy down as carefully as he could under one of the tall mountain pines like the one that had finally stopped the headlong descent of the bus. And then he stooped beside the guard, ignoring the commotion around him.

Even in the dim glow provided by the fire, Drew knew when he looked into the man's face that he was gone. He put his fingers against the artery again, just to be sure, then used them to close the vacant, staring eyes. Finally he straightened, looking around at a scene out of a nightmare. Or out of Dante's *Inferno*.

The bus was completely engulfed in flames now, sparks rising from its shell to float upward into the night air. He could hear men all around him, but he couldn't really see them. They were shadows, their movements hidden by the thick smoke and the night.

Someone was moaning, but he couldn't tell from where. And finally, in the distance, came the sound Drew had been dreading since he'd regained consciousness.

The lonely wail of a siren whined through the darkness. Coming this way. Coming for him, he thought. Coming to take him back to prison to serve the rest of the life sentence he'd been given for a crime he hadn't committed. He had already spent two years in hell because of one man's lies and the CIA's treachery. He wasn't about to spend another.

Drew Evans had once been a government agent who had a healthy respect for the judicial system of this country. No longer. That had been burned out of him, just as the fire had gutted the transport bus.

If he stayed here until those distant sirens arrived, he would never be able to prove his innocence and take back his life. *His life.* When he had been Drew Evans. When he had been a member of Griff Cabot's elite External Security Team. When he had been a man and not an animal kept in a cage.

He began to back away from the garish light of the burning bus and to fade into the shadows. He knew where he was. He knew these mountains and their thick forests. And he knew that by using the knowledge and the skills the CIA had taught him, he could disappear into them. Maybe long enough to do something he hadn't been able to do when they had convicted him two years ago.

Like a miracle, Drew Evans had been given another chance to prove his innocence. Last chance. He took one final look at the burning bus, and then he turned, the distant sirens growing louder and louder, and vanished into the thick, dark woods of the Appalachian Mountains.

THE HAND OF FATE, Drew thought. Or luck. And he was way overdue for some of that. Balancing carefully, one foot on either side of the flat rock that bisected the mountain stream he was wading up, he paused long enough to look behind him.

Although he had heard the faint yap and bay of the dogs all morning, there was nothing back there now. Nothing but deeply shaded woods, their silence unbroken except for the incessant insect noises and the drip of water from low-hanging branches.

His clothes, drenched by the recent downpour, had already begun to steam in the late-afternoon heat. He slapped at a mosquito that settled to feast on his neck, feeling his breathing ease a little, now that he'd stopped running. He knew he couldn't afford more than a short rest. Just long enough to catch his breath.

Despite the physical cost of what he was doing, staying in the middle of the stream was his only chance. He stepped carefully onto the next rock, which was under the surface of the clear, rushing stream. It was slick from algae despite its frigid temperature. His feet had long since gone numb from the icy, spring-fed water, and he had fallen more than once.

He was determined, however, that the hounds wouldn't have a scent to follow. Before he left the stream and headed toward his destination, he needed to put a lot of distance between himself and that mangled transport.

If his luck held, it would take the authorities time to sort through the remains and make positive identifications of those who had perished in the flames. For a while at least, the bulletins they issued on the escapees wouldn't be too specific as to details and descriptions.

Maybe when they discovered that the prisoner listed as Martin Holcomb had no dental records—actually no records of any kind, at least before he'd moved to Tennessee just over two years ago—their confusion would be compounded. That would depend on how careful the CIA had been in erasing an agent named Drew Evans and creating his alternate identity as Martin Holcomb.

The agency was usually efficient in doing something like that. In this situation that efficiency might work to Drew's advantage. It hadn't, of course, when he'd been on trial for murder. Martin Holcomb hadn't even been able to provide a credible character witness for his defense.

Not that a hundred character witnesses would have made any difference, Drew thought bitterly. Not with Tommy Cannon lying through his teeth on the witness stand.

Last chance, he told himself again as twilight began to fade from under the thick canopy of trees. As darkness closed in around him, Drew Evans still struggled upward. And he repeated the phrase like a litany, using it now to drive his aching legs, which trembled with exhaustion. *Last chance.*

"...AND ARE CONSIDERED to be extremely dangerous. Anyone with any information—"

Without looking at the radio, Maggie Cannon turned the dial until the sound of the announcer's voice faded off into a soft click. The motion was unhurried because her gaze, resting on her daughter, had assured her that Laurie wasn't paying the least attention to what was being said. Her small blond head was bent over the puzzle Maggie had laid out on the coffee table in the other room, chubby fingers hesitating indecisively over the placement of the next piece.

Maggie's lips curved into a smile as she watched. There were very few things that gave her more pleasure than watching Laurie, especially when the little girl was totally absorbed and unaware of anything around her. Actually, Maggie couldn't think of anything that even came close to the joy looking at her daughter gave her. The joy of knowing she was in the next room. Of being able to glance up and see that small frown of concentration on her face. Of hearing her laugh.

Each moment spent with Laurie was so infinitely precious that gratitude sometimes welled up in Maggie's heart, overflowing into her eyes. Tears came too easily, she acknowledged, when she thought about how close she had come to losing her daughter, too. And Maggie Cannon wasn't a crying woman. She had been raised in the quiet stoicism of her Scottish ancestors, who had settled in these Tennessee mountains more than two hundred years ago.

She swallowed against the unwanted thickness in her throat, brusquely raking the summer squash she had cut into thin slices off the cutting board and into the pot on the stove. She put the lid on the boiler and turned down the flame. Then, by force of habit, she dried her hands on the apron she wore over faded jeans and a pale blue T-shirt.

Considering how old both garments were, the protection of the apron was certainly unnecessary, but when her grandmother had taught Maggie to cook, she had begun each lesson by putting on this same apron. Of course, in her grandmother's case, it had been used to protect one of the starched and ironed cotton dresses the old woman had donned every day of her long life.

Even on the day she died, Maggie remembered. Her grandmother had drifted off to an eternal sleep, sitting in the rocker that was still in the same place on the cabin's narrow front porch. From there, she could look over the panorama of the mountains spread before her, a view Maggie had known and loved all her life. An endlessly varied landscape that, no matter the season or her mood, never failed to take her breath with its beauty.

"All done," Laurie announced.

Maggie looked up to find her daughter's eyes focused expectantly on her face. Obligingly, she walked over to the table and looked down on the finished puzzle.

It was an old wooden one, its colors faded with age and wear. She had picked it up for a quarter at a yard sale yesterday. Money well spent, she thought, seeing the pride of accomplishment in the little girl's eyes.

"You sure are," she said, reaching out to brush an errant strand of straight flaxen hair back onto the correct side of Laurie's part. "It's wonderful, buttercup. You did a good job."

She resisted the urge to unfasten the barrette that was supposed to be holding the baby-fine hair in place. Laurie hated to be fussed over, probably as a result of having been sick for so long. She and Tommy had done a lot of fussing over her then.

And a lot of the other kind of fussing, Maggie acknowledged. Having a chronically ill baby was an enormous strain on any marriage. Having no money and no resources to fight that illness was an even greater one.

She took a breath, fighting only memory now. And an endless regret. There wasn't any use crying over spilt milk, her grandmother used to say. There certainly wasn't in this case.

"You need to wash up for supper," Maggie said, unable to resist one last caress over the fair, silken head.

"What are we having?"

"Vegetables and cornbread," Maggie said.

"Again?" Laurie asked, her voice plaintive.

"And just what were you expecting?" Maggie asked, smiling at the protest of the sameness of their lives. A sameness she welcomed.

"Some night we could go to McDonald's," the little girl suggested. "You said we could."

"We will. I promise. Just not tonight. Tonight we'll eat supper here, and then I'll read you a story before bed."

"Two," Laurie bargained, like any normal three-year-old.

"Only if you're a good girl."

"I'm *always* a good girl," Laurie countered, a touch of indignation in her voice.

She really was, Maggie agreed, watching her skip across the room toward the bathroom. Uncorrupted by exposure to the things that made children acquisitive and whining, Laurie was still sweetly grateful for what she had. And that was really quite a lot, Maggie told herself reassuringly. Plenty of room to play and the infinite variety of the mountains.

There wasn't a better life for a child. After all, this was where Maggie herself had grown up, and she hadn't turned out so badly, she thought, smiling a little at her blatant attempt at self-deception. Because there was no denying she wanted far more for her daughter than she had ever had. More opportunities, more education, even more of the material things, but...

She took a breath, pushing the old arguments and indecisions from her mind. Maybe later. When Laurie was old enough for Maggie to have to worry about a school. Time enough then to make that decision. More than enough time.

And until that day, they would live here, safely protected from the evil that stalked the outside world. Protected by the mountain's isolation and the rugged nature of the terrain that surrounded the cabin. Safe, she thought again, looking at the windows that ran across the front of the room. And in the midst of that familiar reassurance, she remembered the announcement she had just heard on the radio.

She walked to the window and pulled the curtains over the glass. She hadn't realized how late it was. The sun was sinking and the shadows lengthening, lending a subtle mystery to the land she knew as well as she knew the contours of her own face.

It was past time for supper and nearly time for Laurie to be in bed. This used to be her favorite part of the day, Maggie admitted, unable to deny the rush of remembrance. Tommy would be home from work, and the house would be full of his laughter and his teasing. And then, after Laurie's illness had begun, his laughter and the jokes had stopped. And now...

Now, she waited for night to fall over her mountain with a touch of despair. With Laurie asleep, these were the loneliest hours of the day. The work was done, and there was a long stretch of time to be gotten through somehow until she finally gave herself permission to cut off the lights and go to bed.

She turned away from the window and walked back to the kitchen to check the vegetables simmering on the stove and to peek at the cornbread browning in the oven in her grandmother's cast-iron skillet.

She would have to be sure she remembered about the hamburgers. Maggie didn't make promises lightly. That wasn't the way she had been raised, either. Once you said you would do something, you did it. That was a kind of code most of the mountain people still abided by. If a man couldn't be trusted to stand by his word, then he couldn't be trusted in anything.

And a trip to McDonald's was little enough for Laurie to ask for. This weekend, she decided, dishing the steaming vegetables she had grown in the garden behind the cabin onto two plates and carrying them to the table as Laurie settled into her place across from hers.

Surely there was enough in her grandmother's china sugar bowl to manage a night out on the town for the two of them. And if not, there should be enough produce from the garden or eggs from the henhouse to make up whatever was lacking.

Little enough to ask, she thought again, her throat closing

suddenly at the sight of Laurie's head, bowed as she solemnly asked the Lord for His blessings on their food and for His presence in their lives.

Two years ago Maggie had used up all the prayers she had a right to pray in this lifetime. And they had been answered. She had promised the Lord then that if He would spare her child, she would never ask Him for another thing as long as she lived. That, too, was a promise she hadn't broken. And she never intended to.

"You don't make bargains with the Lord," her grandmother used to warn. Maggie Cannon had gone against that wisdom, and it was a decision she could never regret, she thought, adding her own soft amen to Laurie's.

Her daughter was alive, and that was the only miracle she ever expected to receive in this lifetime. More than she deserved. And only He knew how grateful she was that He had granted this one.

Chapter One

Damn it, Drew thought, frustration threatening the elation and anticipation that had carried him so far throughout this difficult journey. Damn it to hell, he repeated bitterly.

There was still no sign of Tommy Cannon. And there hadn't been in the two and a half days Drew had spent watching the cabin below from his carefully chosen vantage point.

Drew rolled onto his back, put his entwined fingers over his forehead, and closed his eyes against the force of that useless anger. When he regained control, he opened them again, looking up at the twilight sky, his mouth set against the curses he wanted to scream into the approaching darkness.

Every day he was forced to spend keeping watch here brought him one day closer to recapture. One day closer to hearing those iron doors slam closed behind him again, this time forever. He could feel the incredible chance he had been given to clear himself slipping through his fingers like so much worthless sand.

He couldn't confront the man who had sent him to prison unless he could find him. And so far, he had seen no one around the cabin except the woman, whom he was assuming to be Cannon's wife, and the child. Was it possible Cannon had heard about the escape and gone into hiding, knowing that the first place the man he'd framed would head was here? If so, Drew's options might be very limited. Especially since he would expect the authorities to make that same assumption.

There had been no law enforcement officers calling on Mrs. Cannon, however. Not while he'd been watching. Maybe they'd come before he'd gotten here, but in that case, he had thought they would have the place staked out. Drew had spent several hours on the afternoon he'd arrived determining that they hadn't. And it worried him.

After all, a lot could have happened in the two years since the trial. Things Drew would have no way of knowing. Tommy Cannon might no longer be living in the community he had mentioned that day in court. He and the woman Drew was watching might have gotten a divorce. It was always possible, he supposed, that Cannon might even be dead. And if he were…

Drew released the breath he hadn't been aware he was holding, blowing it out softly between his lips. Nothing had happened to Tommy Cannon, he told himself. Fate couldn't be that cruel, not after giving him the chance to get out of that hellhole and confront his accuser.

Cannon was the only one who could clear him, since it was his testimony and his alone, that had put Drew behind bars. And Cannon was the only one who could finger the people who had paid him to lie. Somehow, Drew vowed, no matter what it took, no matter where Cannon was hiding, he would find that lying son of a bitch and make him tell the truth.

Last chance, he told himself again, rolling over so that he was once more on his stomach, looking down on the cabin. The slender blond was still working in the patch of garden behind it. The little girl was having a tea party under the shade of the oak that spread its branches like sheltering arms over the house.

As Drew watched the child serve an imaginary meal to

her dolls, his stomach growled. Despite his frustration, his mouth moved into a reluctant smile. At least he had been getting three squares in prison, and that was more than he could say since he'd been camped out in these mountains.

Food was whatever he could find or steal without arousing suspicion. Luckily, it was summer, and there were things to eat, *if* you knew what you were doing. And having grown up in the mountains, not so very far from this very location, Drew did.

That was the thing that had made it possible for him to get this far. This close to his goal. He could disappear into this environment, not only because he knew the land, but because he knew the people. He had been one of them, a long time ago, and he could be again, slipping into the never-forgotten cadence of their speech and mimicking their mannerisms with a bred-in-the-bone familiarity.

He had ditched his prison garb, of course, as soon as he'd found something suitable to replace it with. Thankfully, there were still people in these scattered communities who dried their wash on outdoor clotheslines, so Drew had had little trouble finding something that would fit. He had picked up underwear, jeans and a shirt as he'd traveled, careful to steal no more than one item at a time. Maybe no one would notice the theft of a single garment or maybe, he hoped, even if they did, they wouldn't put it together with the escape.

Drew knew that if they did notice their loss, these people might not necessarily report it. They were not only insular, but self-sufficient, preferring to keep their own counsel and to take care of their own problems. They might chalk up the disappearance of a garment to someone having more need of the clothing than they did, and let it go at that.

When Drew had collected everything he'd needed, he had buried the prison-issue, digging a hole in the forest loam with his bare hands. He had covered the discarded clothing carefully, first with a layer of dried pine needles and then with a few rocks.

Thankfully the shoes weren't as dead a giveaway as the clothing that he was a convict. No one who saw him now would necessarily associate him with the wreck and the escape.

And he couldn't do anything about the week's growth of whiskers, but maybe those would even help disguise his identity. There were no pictures of Martin Holcomb with a beard, and it did change his looks. For one thing, it was fairer than the brown of his hair. And in addition to the concealment of the shape of his jaw the beard offered, his skin was beginning to darken from exposure to the Southern sun. Even after only a week, he looked very different than when he'd fled that burning bus.

His eyes still on the woman below, Drew wondered idly about the others. Wondered how many of them were still at large and how widespread the manhunt that had been mounted to round them up. He had put a lot of rugged mountain terrain between him and the accident site. By asking a few discreet questions when he'd gotten near enough to this area to think he might get answers, he had managed to find the Cannon cabin. Now if he could only locate Cannon himself....

The woman straightened, putting both hands on her lower back and leaning back slightly. It didn't matter how toned the muscles were, as hers seemed to be, Drew acknowledged, unconsciously evaluating her figure, the kind of cultivation she was doing was always backbreaking work.

As he watched, she put one hand up to her forehead, shading her eyes as she gauged the position of the sun. Even from here, Drew could see that her fingers were stained with the rich black earth she had been working.

Whatever the sun told her, she bent again, this time not to weed, but to pick a few items from each row of her neat garden. Drew knew from experience that in a few minutes the smell of freshly cooked peas or squash or corn would waft upward to the small overhang where he lay. At the memory, his mouth watered. In response, his lips lifted again, almost a smile.

After two years spent in one of the most notorious prisons in Tennessee, Drew Evans had believed he'd forgotten how to smile. There was something so domestic about the serenity of the scene below, however, that as he had kept watch, he had had that inclination more than once. The lives of the woman and child seemed peaceful and unhurried. As if they had somehow been caught in a time warp that eluded the rest of the world.

Given the chaos of his own life, this simplicity was as appealing as a Rockwell print. And just about as unrelated to his situation, Drew thought, the smile slowly fading.

Where the hell are you, you bastard? His eyes searched the property again. *Wherever you're hiding, it isn't going to do you any good. You're going to tell them you lied, and then you're going to tell them the truth about that night, and about who paid you to finger me. And if you don't...*

Once more, his gaze fastened on the woman, maybe because he had realized subconsciously that she was moving out of the garden and toward the house. She called to the child, and obediently, the little girl began to gather up her dolls, piling them and the toy dishes into an old red wagon. When everything had been loaded, she pulled it behind her to the cabin door, which her mother held open. Together they lifted the wagonload over the threshold, and the child disappeared inside. The woman raised her eyes to scan the mountainside, seeming to look right at the outcropping where Drew was lying.

He resisted the urge to move, to hide from that searching gaze. He knew she couldn't possibly identify his as an alien shape among all these rocks and vegetation. She couldn't possibly see him; still, it appeared she was looking for something. Or someone.

As he watched, however, she stepped back, closing the cabin door behind her. If the pattern of the previous nights he'd kept watch held, she wouldn't come out again until morning.

He could wait until then, Drew decided. He couldn't afford to wait much longer, but he could give it at least one more night and hope Cannon would show up.

Again the question of why the authorities weren't out here brushed through Drew's consciousness. Why hadn't they figured out that this would be the first place he would come? That Tommy Cannon would be the first person he'd be looking for?

They would probably get around to doing that eventually, Drew reasoned. And before they did, he knew he would have to go down there to see if he could find out what was going on. Why wasn't Cannon living here any longer?

Wasn't living here... he thought, repeating the phrase. Examining it. And hoping like hell that the answer wasn't as ominous as the question.

MAGGIE AWOKE with a start, pulled too abruptly from sleep. Nightmare? she wondered, her mouth dry and her breathing uneven. It didn't feel as if she had even been dreaming. There were no images floating in her brain that might explain the terrifying sense of threat that had jerked her awake. Nothing she could remember of a dream that might explain why she was so terrified.

She lay still for a long moment and listened to the familiar darkness. There wasn't a sound that was out of place. Nothing that wasn't known and identifiable. The tick of the clock on the mantel in the den. The soft, regular drip of the leaky faucet in the bathroom. Nothing she didn't hear every night.

She turned onto her side, pushing her pillow into a more comfortable shape under her head. It wasn't until she had closed her eyes, preparing to go back to sleep again, that she realized what was wrong. It wasn't that any sound was out of place. It was rather the absence of some that should have been there. That were always there.

She opened her eyes, slowly this time, and listened again. The summer noises of the night creatures, so familiar they almost went unheard, certainly unacknowledged, had been silenced. Which meant there was something outside in the darkness that was making them wary. Something they considered dangerous.

She pushed the sheet off her legs and sat up on the side of the bed, still listening. Even as she did, she was unlocking the drawer of the bedside table with the key she wore on a chain around her neck. She lifted out the revolver that she kept there, her eyes fastened on the window.

She had drawn the curtains before she went to bed last night. She had done it out of force of habit and not because she had ever imagined anything disturbing the quiet, even tenor of their lives. And, of course, she reassured herself, whatever had caused the night creatures' silence didn't have to represent a threat to her and Laurie.

They lived in an area that was full of wildlife. The presence of a bear or a mountain lion or some other predator would certainly be enough to quiet the less aggressive inhabitants of the small clearing where her cabin was located.

She tiptoed to Laurie's room, the weight of the weapon in her hand comforting. The night-light in the hall provided enough illumination to assure her that whatever was outside hadn't disturbed her daughter's sleep. Laurie's eyes were closed, her breathing deep and regular.

Her primary concern relieved, Maggie slipped back down the hall to the kitchen, where the windows that looked out over her garden were covered only by thin cotton sheers. Thin enough to see through, but there was nothing out there to be seen. Nothing but floating shadows, cast by the high-riding clouds.

Maggie visually checked the lock on the back door, relieved that she had remembered to turn it. Sometimes she didn't, but maybe the bulletins all week about the escaped convicts had made her more cautious than normal.

Not that she was worried about the escapees. Not all the way up here. Not as far away as they were from where that prison transport had wrecked and burned. Those men, the few who had managed to elude capture, would surely be heading in the opposite direction, heading toward civilization.

Still uneasy, however, she made the rounds of the doors and the windows, checking locks and looking out into the yard by lifting the sides of the curtains and peering through the narrow openings she created. When she had completed her circuit and returned to the kitchen, she had seen nothing to explain either her anxiety or the continuing stillness outside.

Some animal, she decided. Nothing to be concerned about. She glanced at the clock on the stove, surprised to find it was almost four. There didn't seem to be much point in trying to go back to sleep. It would be daylight in a little while.

For some reason, however, she hesitated to turn on the kitchen light. With the darkness outside and the sheer fabric of the curtains, whoever was out there would be able to see straight in through the windows. *Whoever was out there?* she repeated that unthinking phrase in disbelief. There was *no* one out there. She had already determined that. Nothing moving but shadows.

Despite her sense of unease, she walked across to the counter and opened the canister that held coffee. The scent of it, rich and pungent, seemed more powerful in the dark. She took a filter from the stack beside the coffeemaker, fitted it into the basket, and added four level scoops of coffee. Then she walked across to the sink, carrying the carafe with her.

Her mind already considering the tasks of the coming day, she glanced up absently, looking out through the windows over the sink. Maybe her eye had been attracted by movement or maybe she only saw that after she looked up. She couldn't be sure, but she was sure of what she had seen.

Someone had been cutting across the back of the clearing, skirting and then quickly disappearing into the trees that marked the beginning of the woods. Someone and not something, she realized in the split second the shape had been visible before it had melted into the dark forest.

Upright. But the size was wrong for a bear. Not enough bulk. And it moved wrong. It moved… With deliberate stealth, she decided, replaying the image in her mind as the inexplicable sense of dread that had driven her from her bed transformed into fear.

Her eyes found the dead bolt, and she was again reassured that it was turned. Locked. Safe.

She thought briefly about calling the sheriff. He probably wouldn't appreciate being awakened at four in the morning. Not for something this vague. After all, whoever was out there hadn't really done anything. Trespassing up here was hardly the crime it was in areas where property lines were more easily distinguished. Hunters crossed her land all the time.

Maggie owned more than a hundred acres, running all the way to the top of the mountain and beyond. The fact that someone might be on her property wasn't all that surprising. The fact that whoever it had been was this close to the cabin was.

She looked at the phone, debating. She didn't like Rafael Dalton. She didn't know anything concrete about the sheriff that could explain her dislike, but nevertheless, it was very real.

Maybe it had been the way his eyes had moved over her body, lingering too long on the neckline of her nightgown that predawn morning when he'd come to tell her about Tommy's death. Or maybe it was the fact that he'd come back too many times to "check" on her. To see if there was anything he could do for her, he had said. The whole time his eyes said something else.

It was foolish, she admitted, considering that there was someone out there in the darkness, way too close to her house, but she didn't want to call Rafe Dalton and get him up here in the middle of the night. And there was no doubt in her mind that he would be the one who would show up. Not one of his deputies, but Dalton himself.

She'd almost rather take her chances with whoever had been skirting the edge of her woods, she decided unreasonably. Her grandmother used to say something about the dangers known. She couldn't remember the exact words, but the sentiment it expressed seemed to fit this situation.

Maybe what she had seen had been some kind of animal after all, she told herself. Maybe with the shadows and the darkness, she had been mistaken in thinking whatever was out there was a person. In any case, she'd be able to tell more in the morning from the tracks that would inevitably have been left in the soft earth of the garden.

And until then… She looked down at the gun she had laid on the counter when she'd begun to fix the coffee. Until then, she would keep this near at hand. What she wouldn't do, she decided, was call Rafe Dalton. Not until she absolutely had to.

No SIGN OF LIFE at all, Drew thought, cursing his stupidity. Now there was no movement. No nothing around the cabin below. And there hadn't been for the past hour or so.

Due to his foray last night, he had been later than usual in reaching his vantage point. By this time on the previous mornings, the little girl had been playing outside and the woman had been going about her daily chores. Feeding the chickens. Working in the garden. Things that took her in and out of the various buildings scattered around the clearing. Not today. It was as if the inhabitants of the cabin had vanished in the night.

Drew's mouth tightened in frustration, furious with his own lack of patience. Something had tipped her off that he'd been nosing around. He had known all along that going down there was a risk, but the ominous sense of time slipping away had outweighed any chance he was taking. He couldn't waste any more days staking out the wrong location.

He had thought that he might find some indication that Cannon was living here. Of course, he'd found nothing that could be considered proof. There was only one vehicle in the shed, a beat-up old pickup, which didn't prove a thing.

He knew Cannon was a mechanic because he had said that in response to the prosecutor's questions. And there had been some tools of the trade in the shed, including an engine hoist. It had been covered with spiderwebs, however, as if it hadn't been used in a while. So maybe—

"Who are you and what are you doing on my land?"

The voice had come from above and behind him. And it was feminine. The implications of that information took a half second longer to form in his stunned brain, but they were what eventually caused a coldness to settle in the pit of his stomach.

His concentration had been directed below, but he had been trained well enough to never lose consciousness of every element of his environment. The approach of whoever this was had to have been soundless or he would certainly have noticed it.

"Turn around," she ordered. "And do it slowly."

Drew hesitated another second or two and then rolled onto his back, carefully raising his upper body by propping himself up on his elbows. His eyes searched the section of rock-strewn woods above him, but he couldn't locate the speaker.

"What are you doing up here?" she asked.

Following the sound of her voice, he finally found her. And the sense that he had made an irreversible error intensified. It was the woman from the cabin below, the one he had assumed was Cannon's wife. She was holding a rifle, pointed straight at him, and she looked as if she knew how to use it. Of course, most people who lived around here had grown up handling guns.

The barrel was resting on top of the rock behind which her body was hidden. He couldn't have chosen a better situation for what she was doing had he been setting up this ambush himself. If he weren't in so much trouble, he might even feel admiration.

"Ma'am," he said politely, emphasizing the Southern drawl, a residue of his childhood.

"Who are you?" she asked again, apparently unimpressed.

A hundred possible explanations chased through his head. It must be obvious from his position that he had been watching her cabin. "I was just passing through" probably wouldn't work. The truth would scare her to death. She'd have the authorities down on him in a heartbeat if he told her he'd just escaped from prison and had come to question her husband.

He had known from the beginning, however, that if Cannon didn't show up pretty quickly, he'd have to confront this woman. He just hadn't intended to be confronting the business end of a Winchester while he did it.

"I'm looking for Tommy Cannon," he said.

There was a reaction. He wasn't close enough to read her eyes, but something in her face had changed.

"What for?" she asked.

"I need to talk to him."

"What about?"

He hesitated, knowing he was treading on dangerous ground. "Something personal. And private. You Cannon's wife?"

This was something he needed to know before he went any further. If she wasn't, he needed to find out if she knew where the family had gone. Then he'd worry about getting himself out of this predicament.

"I was," she said.

The two words stopped the steady rhythm of his heart. He had already wondered about the possibility of divorce, so maybe that's what she meant. Her next sentence destroyed that hope.

"*Now* I'm his widow," she said.

He fought against any revelation of the crushing disappointment. What the hell was he going to do now?

"Why don't you tell me what you wanted with Tommy," she suggested. "What kind of 'private' business do you have with a man who's been dead for more than a year? *And* while you're at it, you can explain what you were doing wandering around outside my house last night."

Truth or consequences, Drew thought, but he wasn't sure any of it mattered anymore. If Cannon was dead, then so was his best hope of clearing his name. Trying to follow the convoluted path back to whoever at the agency had issued the orders to eliminate him would be nearly impossible without a place to start. Tommy Cannon had been that place.

"I was trying to find out if Cannon was still living up here."

"And now you know he doesn't," she said flatly. "You still haven't told me what you wanted to talk to my husband about."

"I don't suppose it much matters," he said.

Moving carefully, he pushed his upper body up until he was sitting. He wished he could get to his feet, but she probably wouldn't stand for that.

"It matters. It might help me decide what to do with you."

"'Do with me'?" he asked cautiously, although he knew what she meant. The last thing he wanted was to be turned over to the authorities. He couldn't decide what he could tell her that might keep that from happening.

"In case you haven't heard, there's been an escape."

"'An escape'?" he repeated.

All he was doing was buying a little time. Trying to keep her talking. Hoping she'd tell him something useful. Or that she would make a mistake. He was still feeling a little shell-shocked at the sudden destruction of the hope that had driven him during the hardships of the last week. One thing he knew with absolute certainty, however. He wasn't going back to prison.

He had made that decision even before he'd left the scene of the accident. Maybe Cannon's death destroyed any chance he had of clearing his name, but that didn't mean he was going to rot in jail for a crime he hadn't committed. Not if he could help it.

"Escape," she said, her voice mocking. "As in convicts. Prisoners."

"I hadn't heard. That's got nothing to do with me, ma'am. I just need to talk to your husband."

"Tommy owe you money? If he did, you've probably been able to figure out by now that I can't pay you."

"No, ma'am, he didn't owe me any money. Just…a favor."

He was hoping that she would let down her guard, so he was doing his best to give the impression that he offered no threat to her or her child. For the first time, he wondered where the little girl was. He knew enough about Cannon's wife to know that she didn't leave her daughter unattended. She left the back door open when the child was in the yard without her, even if she were going to be inside for only a few seconds.

"I think you and I should go down to the house. And then I think I should let Sheriff Dalton know that you're up here looking for Tommy," she said.

"Sheriff Dalton? Why—"

"Let's not play games," she said sharply, cutting off his protest. "I suggest you start telling me the truth," she warned. "Or, if you prefer, you can tell it to the sheriff. It doesn't make any difference to me which of us you talk to, but one way or the other, I promise you, I'm going to hear the truth."

Chapter Two

"Inside," Maggie ordered, careful to keep enough distance between them so that the man she was covering couldn't turn and grab the barrel of the rifle. That would be highly dangerous, of course, but he might just be desperate enough to try it.

It had been obvious her prisoner hadn't wanted to come down the mountain with her. However, she wasn't buying what he'd told her about his reasons for spying on her cabin. And what he had told her, when she got right down to it, wasn't all that much.

So the next step was to do exactly what she'd threatened to do and call Rafe Dalton. She had caught this man spying on her, his tracks clear in the damp earth at the back of the clearing.

Still, there was some part of her that was hesitant to turn him over to the authorities. There was more to this than appeared on the surface. She felt it in her gut. For one thing, no matter what he said, this wasn't the kind of man her late husband associated with. There was about him none of the easy conviviality that Tommy Cannon had carried like a cloak.

This man was hard and cold and dangerous. And if, as she'd always heard, the eyes are the windows of the soul, then the soul had been sucked out of him. All that was left within was anger. And a pain that was almost palpable.

It didn't matter what she felt, Maggie told herself again, following him inside. And it certainly didn't matter what she imagined she saw in this man's eyes. She had no option but to call Rafe Dalton and get him out here. Then, after she had turned over her prisoner, the sheriff could sort the truth out from the fictions he had been telling her.

"Take a seat on the couch over there," she ordered, gesturing with a movement of the barrel of the rifle. "And keep your hands on top of your head."

One too many action movies, she thought, hearing the ridiculous words come out of her mouth. Those had been Tommy's favorite. She had never dreamed, however, as she had sat in a darkened theater watching violence explode across the screen, that she would one day be applying any of the melodramatic lessons she'd learned there.

As the man walked across the room, she opened the kitchen drawer where she had hidden the revolver before she'd taken Laurie to her neighbor's. She located the handgun by feel, laying the rifle down on the counter beside her. Then she shifted the revolver to her right hand and reached for the phone with her left.

She hesitated, knowing she'd have to look down to find the sheriff department's number. It was conveniently on a sticker on the phone, along with the number of the volunteer fire department, but still... It would probably be better to dial 9-1-1, she decided, and let the dispatcher send someone out.

"I really wish you wouldn't do this," the man said softly.

He had reached the other side of the room and had turned around to face her. His hands were on top of his head, but he hadn't sat on the couch as she'd told him to. Maggie wasn't sure whether to make her demand again or simply to punch in the emergency number, getting somebody out here as soon as she could.

There was something about his watchful stillness that unnerved her. It was as if he were waiting. For a chance to overpower her? she wondered.

Not as long as she held the gun, she vowed. She had never shot anyone, but she wasn't about to let this stranger take this gun away from her. She would shoot him first. And she didn't doubt her ability to pull the trigger if he made an unexpected move. She would have no choice.

"You haven't given me any explanation for why you were watching my house," she said out loud.

"What if I did?" he asked.

"Then…" She paused, holding his eyes, trying to read them. "I don't know," she admitted finally, unwilling to make any promises about what she would do until she had heard what he had to say. "I *do* know that if you don't tell me something more believable than what you were spouting up on the ridge, I'm calling the sheriff. He can decide what to do about you."

Even from across the room, she could see the depth of the breath he took. "Your husband's testimony sent me to prison."

Sent me to prison. The soft words were chilling, especially when she remembered the warnings in the bulletins the state authorities had issued after the escape of those convicts. They had said that some of those men—

"And everything he said in court was a lie," he added.

A lie? It took a second for her to understand what he meant. "Tommy lied? In court? Is that what you're saying?"

"Yes, ma'am. And those lies put me in prison for something I didn't do."

"Tommy Cannon had a lot of faults," Maggie said, her voice as low as his, but very sure, "and believe me, I had firsthand experience with most of them. But one thing he wasn't was a liar. He was the most honest man I've ever known."

During the years of their marriage, Tommy had told her things she didn't really need to know, hadn't wanted to know. Whatever this man was up to, he had picked the wrong excuse.

"He lied about me," her prisoner said.

His eyes were steady on her face. There was emotion in them now. She just wasn't sure what the emotion was.

"I think you're going to have to do better than that," Maggie said again.

She glanced down at the phone she still held in her left hand. As she did, he moved. Alerted by that motion, she raised her eyes. She dropped the receiver, the gun she held extended toward him, her left hand moving under her right for support.

"Don't," she warned. "You take another step, and I'll put a bullet into you. I swear to God I will."

She was talking too much. Tommy always made fun of people in the movies who made threats about what they were going to do with a gun. *If you point a weapon at some poor son of a bitch,* her husband had said, *then use the damn thing. If you aren't going to use it, don't point it in the first place.*

"I can't let you phone the sheriff, Mrs. Cannon," the stranger said. "I'm not going back to prison. The only reason I was there in the first place is because of your husband's lies."

"Tommy didn't lie," she said.

She sounded like a child. *Did, too. Did not.* What did it matter? Even if there was a sliver of truth in what he was accusing Tommy of doing, she couldn't let this man go. She didn't have any choice but to call the law. He was their problem. Their responsibility. Not hers.

And besides, she didn't have any idea what he was talking about. The only time she could remember Tommy testifying in court had been about some traffic accident. At least, that's what he had told her. At the time Laurie had been so sick that everything else had seemed unimportant. Whatever any-one told her then had gone in one ear and out the other.

She tried to dredge up the memory of what her husband had said. Someone had died. And Tommy had seen part of what happened. Maybe that's what this was all about.

"The accident? The one Tommy witnessed? Is that what you're talking about."

"There was no accident. A man was murdered. And your husband's testimony put me at the scene. He swore in court he saw me pull the trigger. And it was all a lie."

"Tommy would never—"

"He did," he broke in, his voice determined. Passionate. "Either because he was involved in the murder or because somebody paid him to give that testimony. Those are the only two things that make sense. Believe me, Mrs. Cannon, I've had a lot of time to think about this. Nothing *but* time for the last two years."

The last two years, Maggie thought, counting back. The timing would be right. That was about when Tommy had testified in the accident case. Just about the same time…

She swallowed the sickness that surged like bile into her throat. *Somebody paid him to give that testimony.* The stranger's words beat at her heart. *Somebody paid him…*

She shook her head, denying an evil she couldn't bear to think about. Something she knew she couldn't deal with. *Maybe Tommy couldn't, either,* her conscience whispered. Maybe this would finally explain what had happened after-ward.

The laughing Tommy Cannon she had married five years ago had disappeared after that court case. She had never put those two events together before, but she should have. Tommy had told her that he'd taken out some loans to pay for Laurie's treatment, and that he was under a lot of pres-sure to repay them.

After his death, she had waited for those merciless cred-itors to appear. She had lived in dread for months, trying to think what she could do if they began to hound her for their money, as her husband had implied they were hounding him.

At the same time, she had been trying to figure out how she and Laurie were going to survive up here without any income. Of course, during the weeks before Tommy's death, there hadn't been all that much income. She had attributed that to the fact that he was paying off the loans that had saved Laurie's life.

What if that miraculous money hadn't been a loan at all, but…something else? Something very different. Something no one would ever try to collect. No one but this man.

"You *know* what I'm talking about, don't you, Mrs. Cannon?"

Maggie realized that she had let her attention wander as she'd thought about the past. And she knew better than that. Especially with *him.*

"You know he lied," he suggested. "And you know why."

Maybe deep down in her heart or in the back of her mind, where she had kept it hidden because she couldn't bear to face it, she supposed she had always known Tommy had done something wrong to get that money. And if she *had* known—

He moved again, taking his hands off the top of his head and holding them up, palms facing her, the classic gesture of surrender. "Listen to me, Mrs. Cannon…" he began.

"Don't," she said softly. "I'm warning you. Don't move. Don't talk. I don't have any choice," she said, each word distinct, trying to make him understand. "Sheriff Dalton can figure this all out. It's not my responsibility."

She reached for the phone she had dropped, the gun still extended at arm's length. When she had retrieved the receiver, she added, "You can tell the sheriff about your case. About what you say Tommy did. You can get a lawyer."

"I had a lawyer," he said bitterly. "A hell of a lot of

good it did with your husband telling everyone he saw me kill a man.''

''Tommy wouldn't lie,'' she said again, stubbornly, trying to convince herself. ''Not about something like that. Not about something important.''

As important as Laurie? she thought. Was there *anything* in Tommy Cannon's life that had ever been as important as his daughter. Anything in her own life? Maggie wondered.

''I'm telling you he did. And you *know* he did. I saw it in your eyes. You know he lied, and damn it, you know why. All I'm asking you for is to give me a chance to prove my innocence. I deserve that. So…please, Mrs. Cannon,'' he said, modifying his voice. Making it calm and reasonable. ''Put the phone down. Let me tell you about what really happened.''

He moved again, taking one step nearer as he tried to persuade her.

''Don't,'' she said sharply, almost a note of pleading in the command. She tried to think what she could do if he rushed her. And there was only one option. She couldn't know if he was telling the truth or not. Maybe it was just a coincidence that Tommy had somehow come up with the money they'd needed so soon after that court case. It didn't prove anything.

Blood money, she thought, but even as she did, her mind went back to the images of those days. Reliving them. The somber faces of the doctors. Watching the bills pile up and knowing they would never be able to pay them. Knowing there was no way to get Laurie to the specialist the hospital had told them about, which was their only chance to keep her alive.

They had been so afraid they would lose her. So afraid, Maggie thought, remembering the feel of that terrible fear.

Afraid enough that Tommy was willing to trade Laurie's life for someone else's? For a stranger's? For a man he didn't know and didn't think he would ever know? Had the fear of losing his daughter been enough to cause a good man like Tommy Cannon to do what this man was claiming he had done?

"Why did your husband do it, Mrs. Cannon? What did they promise him?" The stranger took a step toward her, even as he asked those unanswerable questions.

Maggie hesitated, her finger on the trigger. Despite her resolve, she was reluctant to squeeze it. Reluctant to compound whatever injustice her husband might have done to this man.

Maybe Tommy didn't do anything at all, she told herself fiercely. Maybe this man's lying about everything.

There were a hundred ways he could have learned enough about them to concoct this story. Maybe the person Tommy had testified against in the accident case had sent this man here to get revenge. Maybe—

Her captive took another step toward her, his eyes still holding hers.

"Don't," she said again, her voice pleading. "I don't want to have to hurt you."

"Then put the phone down," he said calmly. So persuasively. "You know they won't listen to me. They'll come here with their dogs and their sirens and their shotguns, just looking for an excuse to kill me. You *know* that. You know how this works. Put the phone down, Mrs. Cannon, so we can talk."

She was thinking about it, Maggie realized. There was something compelling, seductive even, about his voice. And his eyes. Something in them that made her *want* to believe what he was saying.

The sign of a good con man, her grandmother would have said. They make you want to believe them. Except if she allowed herself to believe this man…

Blood money. His life for Laurie's. Was that what Tommy had done? Had he traded this man's life for his daughter's?

If she told anyone what she suspected, if she told the

authorities what this man was demanding she tell them, then what would happen? Would the people who had paid Tommy for his testimony come to collect the debt she would then owe them? A debt Tommy had ultimately paid with his own life.

"Sheriff Dalton isn't like that," she said, but the image he had drawn was too accurate. She had seen the kind of manhunt he described portrayed in a few of the movies she and Tommy had watched. Along with images of the casual brutality of prison. The heartless violence that seemed to permeate society today.

Had it already touched their lives—even here? Had Tommy made a deal with people like that to save his daughter's life? A deal with the devil? And what would happen to Laurie if Maggie went against them? If she undid whatever they had done in sending this man—this stranger—to prison?

"I don't have a choice," she said, knowing that she did. And knowing she had made a coward's choice even as she said it.

Whatever deal Tommy had made, it had cost him his life. That was enough payback, she thought, even if what this man said was true. She couldn't endanger Laurie. Not even if it meant that this man…

As she reasoned through her decision, her eyes had again fallen to the phone, preparing to punch in the three-digit number that would give her the emergency system dispatcher. And then, almost before she could bring them back up, almost before she had identified the sound that had attracted her attention, he was there. Right there in front of her, reaching toward the gun. Somehow he had managed to close the distance between them, moving in almost total silence, and now he was just suddenly here.

Too close, she thought, panicked by that realization. *Too close*. She squeezed the trigger automatically, lifelong lessons taking over. The motion of her finger had been made without any conscious direction from her brain, except for its acknowledgment that he was too close.

The sound of the shot reverberated in the small cabin. The stranger's upper body jerked backward as if he had been hit in the chest by a two-by-four. He staggered a couple of steps away from her, and despite the realization that she had just shot a man, Maggie was relieved by the distance that had opened up between them.

His mouth opened, but he didn't say anything. His eyes, stretched wide, dilated with shock, simply held on hers. He raised his right hand, cupping it over a spot high on the left side of his chest as if he thought he could keep the blood inside. And then, like a marionette with cut strings, he crumpled to the floor.

Maggie waited, her breath coming in short gasps through her opened mouth. Breathing as if she had been running. She could hear the panting inhalations as she watched, desperately hoping for the rise and fall of his chest, willing it.

His hand had dropped away when he had fallen, and now she could see the spreading stain on the front of his shirt. She wanted to scream that she hadn't meant for this to happen. She hadn't meant to shoot him. She had told him not to move. If he'd only stayed across the room…

The thoughts ricocheted wildly through her head, but finally one emerged, clearer than the rest. More rational. She had to see if he was alive.

She felt light-headed and disoriented, as if this were happening to someone else. As if she were watching someone act out what had just happened on the screen in that darkened theater where she and Tommy had spent so many hours.

Maybe he isn't hurt too badly, she told herself, but the darkly crimsoned splotch on the pale cloth of his shirt belied that hope. She had to stop the bleeding. She knew that, but no matter what she knew, she couldn't seem to make her feet move.

No choice, she told herself again, repeating it almost savagely this time. She had just shot a man, and she had to see if he were alive. She had to see if she could keep him alive, she amended. Because if she couldn't...

She started to lay the gun down on the counter beside the Winchester, but some instinct for self-preservation took over. She would be too vulnerable without the gun. Without its protection. Vulnerable *if* he were still alive. And that was what she needed to find out, she reminded herself.

Knees trembling, she crossed the distance between them. His eyes were closed. His face was without color, his skin the gray-white of milk that has been skimmed. Colorless except where his recent exposure to the sun had burned a copper tinge across the bridge of his nose and along the high cheekbones. His mouth was open slightly, but she couldn't tell if he was breathing.

Slowly, hardly daring to breathe herself, her gaze found the center of his chest. The strong muscles curved upward on either side of the flat breastbone, and she watched the slow rise and fall of them with a sense of gratitude so strong it made her eyes sting. Then she looked back at his face, focusing on the eyelids, which lay unmoving over his eyes. So transparent it seemed she could see the blood pulsing through the small blue veins that underlay the skin.

Unconscious? Or was he trying to trick her? Too many movies, she thought again, her eyes tracking back to the crimsoned fabric on the left side of his chest.

Stop the bleeding, she told herself, pleased at the logic and coherence of that thought. She hurried over to the kitchen drawer and, laying the gun she was carrying down on the counter, she took out all of the clean dish towels she had stacked there three days ago. Washed in hot water and dried in the dryer because of the rain, they were as sterile as anything she had in the house.

She hurried back to where the man she had shot lay. His eyes were still closed and, despite her fear, she was relieved that he hadn't regained consciousness. She laid the stack of towels on the floor beside him, and then her fingers hovered hesitantly over the first of the buttons on his shirt.

It was only then that she realized she had left the gun in the kitchen. Her eyes lifted quickly to his face. Even his lips seemed paler, a contrast to the wheat-colored whiskers that surrounded them. He was bleeding to death while she worried about whether she needed the gun. And if he died, she would be a murderer. She would have killed a man.

A man who claimed he had done nothing wrong. A man who claimed Tommy had lied to put him in prison. Lied because someone had paid him to. Had someone paid Tommy a lot of money which he had used to save their daughter's life?

Blood money, she thought again, her eyes falling to the spreading stain. *Blood money.* And there was only one way that a debt like that could ever be repaid.

Chapter Three

The voices seemed to come from a great distance. They were low, like the hum of insects on a summer day, the words indistinct. Drew thought they had probably been there a long time, just below the level of consciousness as he had drifted in and out of sleep.

A man and a woman, he decided finally, the conclusion almost an abstraction. It seemed strange to be hearing a woman's voice here. There were no women on this cell block. No female guards. So whose voice? he wondered, but the effort it would take to arrive at an answer seemed beyond him.

He licked his lips, surprised at how painfully dry they were. He thought about opening his eyes, but it was easier just to lie here, letting the voices swirl, unidentified, in the background. Too much effort, he thought again. Too much work to force his eyelids up. Too much…

Except there was someone beside him, he realized. He wasn't sure why he was so certain of that. The sounds of breathing, maybe? Someone was watching him as he slept. And it felt like an invasion. He opened his eyes and realized they hurt, too. A dull, throbbing ache centered behind them.

The ceiling above his head wasn't the familiar plaster of his cell. As it slowly swam into focus, he realized he was looking at logs, cunningly cut and fitted together, their near-black color indicative of age.

He tried to think where he could be, but his headache was becoming more intense by the second. Or maybe he was simply becoming more aware of it, moving out of a fogged world where its pain had been masked by unconsciousness.

And he still had that eerie sense that he was being watched. He turned his head, moving carefully so he wouldn't set off the agony he suspected was waiting for his first unrestrained movement, and found a pair of blue eyes, fringed by nearly white lashes. They widened, even as he watched.

It was the child who held tea parties under the oak. The daughter of the woman...

As the memories bombarded him, he fought the urge to close his eyes again. It would be escape, but not the kind he needed, so he allowed the images to fill his aching head. When he got to the sound of the shot and the memory of the bullet hitting his body, he was suddenly aware of pain in his chest. The injury throbbed with each inhalation, but as long as his breathing was shallow, and instinctively it had been, it was bearable.

He opened his mouth, testing to see if breathing through it would help. When he did, the child's blue eyes widened a little more, and one small finger touched her cupid's bow lips. The signal was unmistakable. He tried to raise his eyes in the direction from which the sound of the voices came. Adults. *A man and a woman,* his brain reminded him.

He couldn't see them, and even the attempt exhausted him. He closed his eyes, wondering what the hell was going on. And was forced to acknowledge that whatever it was, there wasn't a damn thing he could do about it now.

"YOU BE SURE and call me, Maggie, if you see anything suspicious. You hear?"

"You don't think there's any reason that Holcomb would

show up here?'' Maggie asked, interjecting what she hoped was a credible note of nervousness.

"Don't see why he would, but…you can't be too careful. That's why I thought I'd come on by and let you know that one of them had been spotted in these parts."

"And he's from around here?" Maggie probed.

She kept her voice casual, not wanting to make Rafe Dalton suspicious. And he didn't seem to be. He seemed far more interested in the shape of her breasts, clearly delineated by the thin, washed-too-many-times fabric of her shirt.

"Pretty close. Over at Elyton. At least, he lived there for a while. But remember, this may be a false alarm. We always get false sightings any time we put out a bulletin. However, we can't afford to take a chance. We got to check out each and every tip. And with you living all alone up here…" He let the suggestion fade, his eyes tracing the neckline of her shirt.

"Thank you, Sheriff Dalton. I appreciate you letting me know. And I'll keep an eye out, I promise."

"You call me if you see anything suspicious. Even if it don't seem like much of anything, don't you take a chance, Maggie. Not with your little girl up here and all."

"No, I won't," Maggie said.

He held her eyes a fraction of a second too long, the corners of his mouth tilted into a smile. Then he reached up and touched his hat. Despite that implied farewell, however, he didn't move off her front porch. And his eyes didn't release hers. They were very green, Maggie realized, the clearest, coldest green she had ever seen, without even a trace of brown to cloud the intensity of their color.

"You take care now, you hear," he said softly.

Despite the casual words, his tone was intimate. As if they were alone. As if his deputy weren't waiting out in the patrol car, watching everything. Maggie nodded agreement without speaking, unwilling to do anything that might prolong the conversation. She had no idea if he suspected anything. Or if he was, in fact, simply doing what he had claimed—issuing a warning to a widow-woman who lived alone with her little girl.

Finally, Dalton touched his hat again, and then he turned, taking her front steps two at a time. She watched him walk to his car, his stride long and purposeful, the pants of his uniform stretching over the hard muscles in his thighs as he moved.

He crawled behind the wheel, settling himself in the seat. After he said something to his deputy, he glanced up at her again. It seemed she could feel the force of his gaze, even from this distance. She was relieved when he looked over his shoulder to back the car, turning it around and then heading down the dirt road that led off her mountain.

Even when the dust had settled, Maggie still stood on the porch, looking in the direction where the car had disappeared. Laurie's hand slipped into hers, and surprised, she looked down.

"Who was that?" her daughter asked.

"Sheriff Dalton," Maggie said.

"He was awake," Laurie said.

It took a second for the meaning of those out-of-context words to penetrate. If Laurie was right, she realized, and the man she had shot was awake, then the two of them needed to have a conversation, one that was long overdue. Especially in the wake of the sheriff's visit.

No use crying over spilt milk, her grandmother had said. In this case, however, Maggie wasn't sure she was right. She had fought the urge to cry every time she had looked down at the face of the man lying in the same bed she and Tommy had once shared.

Blood money, she thought again, looking down now on her daughter's small towhead, the precise part in her hair running like a pink line between two curling ponytails.

"Why don't you play with your dolls at the kitchen table while I go see about him," she suggested.

"I could play in there," Laurie said.

"Maybe later. Right now, I think it might be better if you stay in the kitchen." Maggie opened the screen door and, her hand on the back of Laurie's head, ushered the child inside.

"Are you afraid of him?" Laurie asked. Her blue eyes, raised to her mother's face, were earnest and a little concerned.

"Afraid of him?" Maggie repeated. She stooped quickly, putting her hands on her daughter's shoulders. "I'm not afraid of him, buttercup, and I don't want you to be. He's very sick. There's no reason to be afraid of that man, Laurie. No reason at all," she said, imbuing her voice with certainty.

"Was the sheriff looking for the sick man?"

Maggie hesitated, trying to think what she could say that would relieve Laurie's anxiety and yet protect the dangerous secret she was keeping. Her daughter didn't come in contact with many people, but a chance word to the wrong person might give away Martin Holcomb's presence here.

Maggie didn't want that to happen, at least not until she could get to the bottom of the accusation Holcomb had made two days ago—that Tommy's lies had sent him to prison and that someone had paid her husband to tell those lies. Maggie wasn't convinced that was the whole story, but there were enough things that fit with what she *did* know that had kept her from calling the authorities as Holcomb lay bleeding on her floor.

"That man doesn't want anyone to know he's staying with us," Maggie said finally. "Not while he's so sick. It's a secret," she said softly, smiling at the little girl.

"Like at Christmas?" Laurie asked.

They had made presents for friends last December. She wouldn't have thought Laurie would remember her admonition not to tell anyone about what they were doing. Apparently the word "secret" had made a bigger impression than she'd realized.

"Just like Christmas," Maggie said, relieved.

"Okay," Laurie said.

Maggie released her hold, watching her daughter run toward the kitchen and the wagon where she kept her favorite toys. Then Maggie stood again, but she didn't move immediately toward the bedroom. She hesitated, not only because she wanted to make sure Laurie was settled, but because she wasn't looking forward to what she was about to face.

What do you say to a man you've put a bullet into? Especially when that man claims to have spent two years in prison as a result of something your husband did. Something Maggie suspected Tommy had really done.

If what Holcomb claimed *was* true, how could she ever make up to him for what he had suffered? Unconsciously, she shook her head, and then rubbed her palms down the side of her thighs, the rough denim of her jeans somehow comforting. She took a deep breath, as if girding for battle, and walked toward the bedroom.

IT WAS THE SAME SENSATION he had had before. That someone was in the room with him. Watching him. Maybe the little girl had come back. Drew listened for the voices, but all he heard was the sound of water dripping somewhere, the distant plop as regular as a heartbeat. He gradually relaxed into its regularity, feeling himself drifting away again, and unwilling to fight the escape from pain unconsciousness offered.

"Mr. Holcomb?"

Without opening his eyes, he tried to place the voice. The identification tugged at the edges of his mind, but he couldn't quite make the connection. And he was almost too tired to try. Instead he turned his head, facing the direction from which the sound had come. At the same time he opened his eyes.

Not the child, he realized. The wide blue eyes were the

same, but the lashes that surrounded them were longer and darker. As was the hair that framed the face. It was as fine, and as softly curling, as the child's, but honey-colored rather than flaxen. It had probably darkened with age, just as his own had.

His eyes considered the face as his mind searched his memory for the name that went with it. The little girl's features were a miniature of these, which were stronger, however, the bone structure more clearly defined, unsoftened by the layer of baby fat. The cupid's bow was the same, the bottom lip full and sensual, and the blue eyes clear and direct.

"Who are you?" he whispered. His voice was strained and alien, and almost too weak to project the words despite the slight distance that separated them.

"My name is Maggie Cannon," she said.

He pulled his gaze away from her eyes and concentrated on her mouth, trying to make sense of the words that came out of it. And gradually he did. Maggie Cannon. Cannon. Tommy Cannon.

Who was dead. The pain of that remembrance was searing. Hot moisture stung the fever-dried eyes. Tommy Cannon was dead, and with him had died any chance Drew might have had to clear his name. Any chance to reclaim his life. He closed his eyes, fighting against the welling tears. He couldn't remember the last time he had cried.

Not when they'd sentenced him. All he had felt then had been fury, a useless anger perhaps, but it had gotten him through those first few terrible weeks after the trial. Right now he couldn't seem to drum up any emotion except a deep sense that it was all over. He had run from that burning wreck with such hope, feeling that he had been given another chance. And now...

"Mr. Holcomb?"

Reluctantly he opened his eyes again, focusing on her

face. It was slightly blurred with the residue of tears, so he blinked, and her features came back into focus.

"Not Holcomb," he said. That was the name the CIA had given him, but it wasn't his.

"But…" She hesitated, a crease between her brows.

"Not Holcomb," he said again. "That's a name they made up. A man they made up."

He wondered who had told her who he was. Maybe it had been on the news. Maybe she had heard the name and made an assumption. He wondered if that meant he was the only one of the escapees still at large.

"Then who are you?" she asked.

"Drew Evans."

Just saying his real name, after all this time, was a relief. Putting some of the nightmare of the past two years behind him. Getting a little bit of his life back. That's what this escape was supposed to be about. Getting his life back.

At least, that's what it *had* been about. Until he'd found out Cannon was dead. The lying son of a bitch was dead, he remembered. Drew closed his eyes again against the harsh reality of that. A reality he didn't want to face.

"Are you all right?" she asked.

He nodded, licking his lips and forcing his eyes open.

"Would you like some water?"

He nodded again, watching as she crossed the room to an old-fashioned dresser where a sweating stonewear pitcher sat on a tray that also held a glass. She poured water into that and brought it back to the bed.

He thought about pushing up on his elbows and taking the glass from her. In truth, the water looked wonderful, a few small pieces of ice floating on the top of it. More trouble than it's worth, he decided finally, slipping into the lethargy that seemed too strong to escape.

He was suddenly aware that she was bending over him because the scent of her body was in his nostrils. No perfume. This was an aroma comprised of soap, clean, warm skin, and freshly laundered clothing.

She put her arm under his head, moving carefully, and then she lifted it just enough to allow him to put his lips over the rim of the glass. The water tasted better than he had anticipated. Crisp and cold and free of chemicals. Spring water, he identified without knowing how he was so certain.

She let him drink his fill. And when he released the rim, she lowered his head just as carefully as she had lifted it. He closed his eyes again, trying to gather what strength remained in his body. Which seemed little enough.

That was the result of blood loss, he supposed. And fever. Maybe not eating much for a few days, nothing other than what he'd found on the mountain, and not even that since he'd been shot. And he had no idea how long that had been.

"How long have I been here?" he asked.

"Two days," she said.

Her voice seemed to come from a great distance. He was slipping into that half world he had occupied during those days.

"We have to talk," she said.

He opened his eyes, looking up into her face. Something had changed, he realized. Something... And then, with a deep sense of surprise, he realized what it was. Realized exactly what he was seeing in those blue eyes.

She believed him. She hadn't before. Not when she'd forced him down to this cabin at gunpoint. Not when she'd been threatening to call the sheriff. And certainly not when she had pulled that trigger.

Something he had said or something Maggie Cannon had learned since then had convinced her Drew was telling the truth. And throughout this entire ordeal—from his arrest until today—she was the first person who had believed him. Slowly, holding her eyes, he nodded again.

Then exhaustion overcame the euphoria and his eyelids fell, dropping like a china doll's. The last thing he saw before he went to sleep was Maggie Cannon's face, lips set and an ineffable sadness in her eyes.

"MR. EVANS?"

He had been dreaming. He couldn't remember all of it—he never could—but the dream had had something to do with his days at the CIA. With the Team. With Griff Cabot's External Security Team. His friends. And he didn't want to be pulled out of that dream. Or away from memories of the days when he had been on the right side of the law.

Except this—this painful awakening—was the reality. The other, remembering men he had worked with for more than ten years, was the dream. Most of those men were now dead or had been dismissed from the agency. Scattered. Their identities destroyed. Just as the team they had all been a part of had been deliberately destroyed. And that had been done by their own government. Betrayed by those they had faithfully served.

"Mr. Evans?" the woman said again. "You need to wake up. I've brought you something to eat."

And he was hungry, Drew realized, salivating a little at the thought of food, remembering the smells emanating from the cabin every night as he had watched it from the ridge above. Smells of Maggie Cannon's cooking.

He opened his eyes and found her leaning over the bed. She smiled at him, but he knew that was reflex. A nervous response to meeting his eyes and to the unfamiliarity of the situation she was in. After all, despite her demonstrated competence with a gun, he doubted Maggie Cannon had ever shot anyone before.

"Think you can eat something?" she asked. The smile had faded but the concern was still in her eyes.

He nodded, still moving carefully, although he had already determined that his head didn't hurt nearly as bad as it had the last time he'd awakened. When the little girl had been in here, he remembered. When there had been voices outside. He'd have to ask her about those, but first he wanted to hear what she had to say. Maybe even get an explanation of why she hadn't called the authorities like she'd threatened.

"Good," she said. "I think it would be better if we put another pillow under you."

She had already slipped her arm behind his shoulders, and now she lifted them, as gently as she had before. Then she stacked another pillow on top of the one he had been lying on and eased him back down. The pillowcase was cool under his skin, and involuntarily he turned his head, rubbing his cheek against the smooth, fragrant cotton.

"I'll change the sheets this afternoon, if you feel up to it. Your fever got pretty high, but thankfully..."

She hesitated, her eyes meeting his. *Thankfully you didn't die.* That may not have been what she was going to say, but her intent was the same. The cause of her thankfulness.

He didn't say anything, not just because the slight exertion had taken all of his strength, but because he figured the quieter he was, the more she would talk. That was human nature, and a trick he had learned from Griff.

"It's just soup," she said. "I thought that might have the best chance of staying down on an empty stomach. And you can drink it out of the mug."

Maybe she expected him to reach up and take the cup. Drew knew, however, that even if he managed to hold on to it long enough to get any of the soup down, his hands would shake. And he wasn't eager to demonstrate exactly how weak he was. His life was in Maggie Cannon's small, capable hands right now, but he didn't think announcing that to anyone, even to her, was a good idea.

After a moment she bent as she had before and put the rim of the cup against his mouth. Again, he could smell her. The scent of her skin, warm and moist from the unremitting heat. A hint of soap. The pleasantly floral fragrance of her hair, or rather of whatever shampoo she had used to wash it. This time there was another aroma mingled with those. Something he hadn't smelled in a long time. Maggie Cannon had been baking bread, and the scent of yeast clung to her clothes.

She tipped the cup, and the liquid it contained, warm and rich with meat juices, entered his mouth. It was neither too hot nor too cold. He had been as thirsty as he was hungry, Drew realized, gulping the soup as if he were a starving man.

She let him rest a couple of times, never seeming to hurry him or to be impatient with the necessarily slow process of feeding him, until there was nothing left in the mug.

"More?" she asked.

"Not now," he said, his voice sounding rusty from disuse.

"While you're awake, I need to take a look at…that," she said. She tilted her chin at the place on his chest, and almost unwillingly, Drew looked down. He wasn't wearing anything, at least from the waist up, and there was a neat white X of tape over a gauze pad that lay just below his collarbone.

As soon as he saw it, pain lanced through him. Not real pain, but the memory of her doing something brutal to the wound that lay under that bloodstained pad. She had tied his hands to the headboard of the iron bed and then dug out the bullet she'd put into him. Drew had only a clouded recollection of that, but still, he knew she had done it. And that it had hurt like hell.

"You dug the bullet out," he said.

It wasn't a question, and it brought her eyes back to his. She had put the mug on the bedside table, beside a cellophane-wrapped square of gauze and a small tube of what looked like ointment. Antibiotics, he guessed.

"You weren't real pleased about that," she said, a hint of amusement in her voice.

"I wanted to kill you," he said.

He knew as soon as the words were out of his mouth that they were a mistake, but when she had been digging around in his damaged flesh for the bullet she had put into him, he had really felt that way. If he could have gotten his hands free, in his delirium and anger and agony, he might have hurt her.

"I didn't really mean that," he said.

Her eyes were on his face, but he couldn't read what she was thinking. Maybe regret that she hadn't let him die?

"That's why I tied you down," she said.

And then, without another word, and without changing the bandage on his chest, she picked up the mug that had contained the soup and walked out of the room.

Frustrated with his own stupidity, Drew took a deep breath—or at least half of one. The resulting pain seared along a thousand nerve endings, burning all the way down into the fingers of his left hand. He grimaced, but allowed no sound to escape. He had no idea how many people were in the house.

Just the woman and the little girl? He couldn't know that, and he had definitely heard a man's voice earlier. This morning? Or yesterday?

He shook his head in frustration. He was as weak as a newborn kitten, the object of a multistate manhunt, and doing a damn fine job of alienating the only person who had shown any inclination to help him during the last two years.

Who was also the person who had shot him, he reminded himself. And the widow of the man whose lies had put him in prison. All he had to do now was to figure out what he was going to do about any of that.

Except, he thought, feeling exhaustion wash over him in an unremitting wave, he wasn't going to do anything right now. Now he would sleep. Just for a little while. And then, after he'd rested a bit, he'd work on figuring out where the hell he went from here.

Chapter Four

It was night. That was the first thing Drew realized when he woke again. The second was that his head didn't hurt. The third, and the most critical, was that he badly needed a bathroom.

Apparently dehydration and fever had taken care of this necessity before. Or maybe that had been Maggie Cannon, he acknowledged. There was something troubling about the thought. About the intimacy of that between them. Between strangers.

He lay in the darkness a few minutes, listening to the now-familiar noises of the cabin. The dripping water. The distant clock. The hum of the summer insects outside. Listening and willing himself back to sleep. Until he realized that even if he did drift off, he would have this same problem in the morning. He might as well get it over with while neither set of blue eyes was around to watch.

The water drip would act as a locator beacon, so all he had to do was get himself up and to the bathroom without passing out. He should be strong enough to manage that, he thought. After all, he had eaten something yesterday. Two meals, actually. First the soup and then scrambled eggs and oatmeal for supper, which Maggie had fed him with the same patience she'd exhibited at lunch.

Maggie? he questioned. When the hell had Tommy Cannon's wife become "Maggie"? She was Cannon's wife, and that's all she was. Other than the person who had put a bullet into him and had then changed her mind and dug it out. *After* she'd tied him down like a steer about to be branded. Saving his life in the process, he acknowledged, for which he should be grateful.

It was as if the capacity for gratitude or any of the other emotions that make one human had been torn out of him. That had happened when everything he had believed in his entire life had failed him. Not only failed him, he amended bitterly, but betrayed him. The agency. The justice system. His friends.

Last chance, he thought again, repeating the words that had brought him this far. By rights he should still be in prison. By rights, he should be *dead.* And he wasn't. So maybe...

He moved his legs first, slowly inching them over to the edge of the bed and then resting, letting the left dangle off the side. At some point in the process he realized he was nude. Again, the thought of Maggie Cannon caring for him like this, even while he was unconscious, caused a stirring in his gut. A strange and uncomfortable reaction.

God knew, he was no prude. And no stranger to intimacy. Except lately, he admitted, his lips moving into a twisted smile.

Only delaying the inevitable, he thought, and as he did, he moved, his right hand flattened against the mattress to force his body upright. The pain was like a blowtorch directed at his upper chest, but he managed to get himself into a sitting position without fainting.

And finally, after a little maneuvering, he was sitting on the edge of the bed. He was hunched over like an old man, automatically trying to protect the damaged muscles and nerves. He held his left arm across his body as if that might prevent some internal organ from falling out. Which was what it had felt like when he sat up.

As he waited for the pain to subside, he resisted the urge to close his eyes against it, afraid that if he did, he'd pass out. He focused instead on the dim light coming from outside the bedroom. The door to his room had been left open, probably so Maggie could hear him if he called her.

Mrs. Cannon, he corrected, annoyed with the stubbornness of his subconscious. The woman who had shot him was not Maggie. He couldn't afford to let her become that. Not to him.

Thinking about her as Maggie, as a person, wasn't something he could deal with right now. He had more than enough to handle without getting emotionally involved with Tommy Cannon's wife.

Widow, his brain reminded him. *Tommy Cannon's widow. And that's a hell of a big difference.*

He pushed up off the mattress, doing it in slow, creaking stages, his knees trembling with the effort it took to stand. His upper body was still bent forward. He knew instinctively that if he straightened, he would set off the agony again.

He raised his right hand and put his palm on the wall. Leaning against it, he rested a moment and then took a step. Right foot. He found that he could manage the pain. Or rather, he could endure it. He moved his hand, sliding it along the wall a few inches, and then he pulled his left foot even with the right. That motion was not so good, but he could do this, he decided. As long as vertigo didn't close in.

He took another step, still using the support of the wall. And then another, shuffling along like an escapee from some nursing home. But he was making progress, he realized when he looked up to gauge the distance to the light.

He was in the doorway now. And looking to his left, he could see the small, dim bulb of a night-light that had been pushed into a socket near the baseboard. He prayed that the open door beside it was the bathroom. Because if it wasn't…

A few more steps, he told himself, negotiating carefully through the door and into the hall. For some reason, how-

ever, he couldn't seem to make that left arm release its protective position around his body. Just as he couldn't force
himself to straighten because he knew what would happen
if he did.

He took a couple of lurching steps without the support of
his hand on the wall, and then felt the blackness closing in
around him. He leaned against the wall, breathing through
his mouth, fighting his own weakness.

If he fainted, a couple of embarrassing things would happen, neither of which would be pleasant for anyone involved. So just keep shuffling, he told himself. He started
again. Right foot. Then drag the left foot forward.

He wouldn't have believed that moving his left leg could
impact on the damaged muscles in his chest, but it did. The
pain was nothing like that when he'd pushed up off the bed,
but the dull ache from the injury was constant now, and he
almost hated to take that next breath because he knew how
much it would hurt.

He made it to the door beside the night-light, and found
he'd been right. It was the bathroom. Small enough that only
a couple of steps would take him to his goal, gleaming white
and so damn inviting.

When he had accomplished those two steps, he finally
gave himself permission to close his eyes, wondering if this
relief should count as one of life's ultimate pleasures. Right
now, it would certainly rank high on his list. No doubt about
it.

"You should have called me," Maggie Cannon said.

He turned his head, physically unable to do anything else.
She was standing in the doorway. Her eyes, midnight-blue
in the darkness and carefully impersonal, were locked on
his.

"I've been doing this on my own for quite a while now,"
Drew said.

Her mouth moved, but whatever that reaction had been—
amusement maybe—it was quickly controlled. She was

wearing a gray nightshirt, made like a long T-shirt, with a University of Tennessee logo in orange on the front. Its hem hit about midthigh, and in the murky light, her legs were long and slim and pale. As well-shaped as they had appeared to be under her jeans.

He pulled his gaze away from them, turning his attention back to the task at hand, which frankly seemed never-ending. Embarrassingly so. "Go back to bed," he ordered, his voice harsher than he'd intended.

For a few seconds she didn't answer, and then she said, "I don't want Laurie to wake up and find you in here. Or passed out in the hall."

He looked to his right, focusing again on her face. "Laurie? Your daughter?"

"You remember her?"

He nodded, thinking about the little girl who had been beside him the first time he'd awakened. Laurie. Nice name. It fit. Just like Maggie fit her mother.

"I'll use a towel," he said.

"A towel?"

"Around my waist," he explained. "I'm all right. You can go back to bed."

"Look—" she began, and then stopped because he had. Finally.

Moving carefully, right hand on the wall, he deliberately turned to face her. Full frontal nudity was what they called it in the movies. Of course, in the movies it was designed to titillate. This wasn't, and they both knew it.

This was more like a challenge. A form of intimidation. If she was determined to hang around and watch him navigate his way back to bed, something he wasn't real eager to have any witness to, then she might as well figure out what she was in for. He thought that when she had, she'd turn tail and run.

She didn't. She held his eyes for a second or two, and then she lowered her gaze, allowing it to move down his body without the least sign of haste or embarrassment. And then to move back up, just as slowly. By the time she made it back to his eyes, hers deliberately unimpressed, he was struggling not to grin.

Apparently Maggie Cannon wasn't easily intimidated. Of course, he should have known that a woman who had the balls to put a slug in him wasn't going to back down because he wasn't wearing pants. Without releasing her eyes, he reached out with his right hand and pulled a towel off the rack beside the toilet. Now what? he thought as soon as he had it in his hand.

Gut-check time. He forced his left arm away from his body, something he had thought only minutes before that he couldn't possibly do, as his right carried the towel behind his back. He somehow reached around far enough for the fingers on his left hand to make contact with the terry cloth. He felt a sense of accomplishment way out of proportion to that achievement as he pulled the towel around his waist, overlapping the ends in front.

When he was decently covered, he looked back up. Maggie Cannon hadn't moved. "Show's over," he said.

He put his right hand on the towel rack and took a step toward her. And then another. And a third. With each one, he expected her to retreat. To move out of the doorway. To do something. She didn't. She stood her ground until they were face-to-face.

And he could smell her again. He had never before in his life been this conscious of how a woman smelled. Maybe it was the heat. The close confines of the cabin. The fact that she didn't use perfume.

Or maybe he was just too damn conscious that she was a woman. And it had been way too long since he'd come into contact with one of those. *Way too long.*

He paused, but not because he needed to rest. He just couldn't seem to make his feet carry him past her. He didn't want to. He wanted to stay right here in the pleasant dim light of the bathroom and drink in the sight and the smell of Maggie Cannon.

Her eyes hadn't left his face. They didn't reflect fear or anxiety. They looked a little... He searched for the word, and realized that they reflected exactly what he was feeling. Off balance. As if she, too, had been caught off guard by the emotions that suddenly seemed to arc between them.

What was going on in *his* head, and moving way too fast into his aching body, probably had a lot to do with the two years he'd spent behind bars. Even as he acknowledged that, he realized that it might very well have been almost as long a sexual drought for her, as well.

Her husband was dead. And her isolation, way up here on this mountain, didn't lend itself to a wealth of social— or sexual—opportunities. If that were true, however, it wasn't a good thing. Not in this situation.

He needed Maggie Cannon. He needed her help to prove he wasn't a murderer. He needed her help to trace back along that trail of betrayal that had led to his arrest and her husband's testimony. What he sure as hell didn't need was emotional involvement. Not with her. Not with anybody or anything that might get in the way of clearing his name.

First priority. Because if he didn't accomplish that, then somebody else would eventually put a bullet into him, and next time he wouldn't walk away. Not anywhere except back to prison.

"Let me help you," she said.

He held her eyes as his head moved once, a single negation. "I can make it," he said, knowing that was bravado. Or stupidity. His legs were trembling and the place on his chest had become a deep burn, the pain gnawing all the way down to the bone. This was what he had always imagined napalm might feel like. He took another step, but she still didn't move.

"I've been thinking about what you suggested," she said,

glancing down the hallway toward the door to the other bedroom. When she looked back at him, her eyes were harder.

"What I suggested?" he questioned.

"About Tommy."

"About his lies?" he asked, the bitterness clear.

She nodded. And then, when he didn't say anything, she swallowed, the movement of the muscles down the long, slender column of her throat visible even in the dimness.

"You believe me?" he asked, a jolt of emotion inside at the renewed realization that she did.

"He got a lot of money. Just about that time. The time you said he gave the testimony. He told me the money was a loan, but…"

"You didn't believe *him*."

"I did then. At least…"

She hesitated, and he sensed her reluctance to finish whatever confession she had begun. It didn't matter, of course. Not to him. What mattered was that this might mean she would help him. And even if she wouldn't, it explained why she hadn't called the law on him.

"I wondered why someone was willing to just give us the money," she continued softly. "We didn't have any credit. Not enough income to justify the kind of money we needed to borrow. And then, all of a sudden, Tommy just…had it. I thought maybe he had done something wrong to get it, but I put the idea out of my mind. I made myself stop thinking about it because I guess if I had really known that's what he had done…"

The words had come slower and slower until finally they trailed away, but Drew knew he needed to hear this. After all, by remaining silent about her husband's windfall, Maggie had played a part in whatever had been done to him.

"And if you *had* known?" he asked.

The silence stretched. It lasted long enough that he was aware again of all the nighttime noises he had listened to as he'd lain in bed.

"I don't know," she said finally. Her eyes met his, open and unflinching. "I don't know what I would have done. And maybe that makes me as guilty as Tommy," she said.

His eyes narrowed, trying to imagine what the hell she meant. Before he had reached any conclusion, however, she turned and disappeared into the darkness of the hallway, leaving him alone in the small bathroom.

More alone than he had ever felt in his life.

"MY MAMA'S FIXING breakfast."

The words had come as soon as he'd opened his eyes. She was right beside the bed, leaning against the mattress, with her chin resting on her crossed forearms. Just looking at him.

Remembering last night, he glanced down at his body, thankfully covered below the waist by the sheet. Exposing himself to a woman who had already been caring for him for days, a woman who must have known what to expect when she came into the bathroom last night, was a very different proposition from this.

"You hungry?" Laurie asked, shifting her weight from one foot to the other, so that the bed moved slightly.

He was, he discovered. For the first time since he'd been here, the aroma of coffee wafting from the kitchen smelled good. He nodded, and the little girl nodded back.

This morning her hair had been divided down the middle, and each half had been plaited into short, fat braids. It should have looked ridiculous, but instead it looked just like a little girl's hair should look.

"Laurie?"

Maggie Cannon's voice came from the kitchen. It was raised to carry above the music blaring from an oldies radio station. Even from a distance, the sound of that single word evoked the same response her presence had last night. A subtle shifting of the muscles in his stomach. A small ache. Woman ache.

"I gotta go," Laurie said. "I'm not supposed to be in here," she confided in a whisper. Again she put her finger to her lips, urging him to a conspiratorial silence, and then she turned and ran out of his room on small and dirty bare feet.

Drew realized he was smiling. He hadn't had much experience with kids, not of any age, and certainly not any this young. And then, smile fading, he reminded himself that he didn't want to become any more involved with Tommy Cannon's daughter than he did with his wife. Find out what Maggie knew about why her husband had lied—and there was no doubt after last night that she knew something—and then get the hell out of here before the law honed in on his location.

He thought again about the man's voice he'd heard. Could that have been somebody looking for him? Was that why the kid had told him to keep quiet? Or had that distant conversation had nothing to do with him at all?

Just as he reached the conclusion that he ought to have asked those questions long before now, Maggie Cannon appeared in the doorway, carrying a tray. Her sun-streaked hair had been pulled behind her ears, revealing high cheekbones and the delicate shape of her jaw.

Today she was wearing a sleeveless navy top and khaki shorts, exposing about the same length of leg that had been exposed last night. Her skin was flawlessly tanned, smoothly brown. She looked strong and healthy, despite her slimness. And about a hundred years younger than he felt.

Getting shot played hell with your self-image, Drew decided.

"You want this now?" she asked.

As opposed to when? he wondered. She held the tray and his eyes, waiting for his decision. Maybe she wondered if he needed to make a return trip to the john. Thankfully, he didn't. He'd face that when he had to. And he didn't plan on clearing his schedule about that, or about anything else, with Mrs. Cannon.

"Now," he said.

She hesitated a second longer before she walked over to the bed. "You need some help sitting up?" she asked.

In answer, he cautiously pushed himself up onto his elbows, sliding back against the pillows. It wasn't a procedure he wanted to repeat anytime soon, and he leaned back in relief when it was over, letting the pain fade before he tried to speak.

She put the tray down on his lap before he had reached that point. There were eggs again. Toast, butter and jelly. And coffee. He couldn't help breathing in the fragrance of the latter. He shouldn't have. He controlled the grimace that resulting twinge had prompted, keeping his eyes on the food.

"You're very welcome," she said.

By the time he'd lifted his eyes, she had turned and started across the room. He played with a couple of phrases in his mind that expressed belated gratitude and then decided to let it alone. He didn't owe Maggie Cannon anything. She's the one who had put him in this damn bed. And her husband was the one who had put him in prison. To hell with her expecting manners.

Letting his anger build, he stabbed the fork into the eggs and raised a mouthful. They were still hot, very fresh, and probably the best scrambled eggs he'd ever eaten, he realized as he chewed the first bite. By the time he'd finished them and the coffee, he couldn't even drum up enough righteous indignation to be irritated that she hadn't returned for the tray.

He turned his eyes toward the windows, concentrated on the rock and roll coming from the kitchen radio, and forced himself to relax. Despite the urgency of his situation, he knew rationally that he had to give his body a chance to heal. He could pick Maggie Cannon's brain in the meantime, but there wasn't any use getting antsy because he was laid up. It was going to take him a few days to get his strength back and trying to rush the process would only delay it.

"All done?" Maggie asked from the doorway.

"It was delicious. Thank you, Mrs. Cannon."

She cocked her head, mockingly, as if waiting for the other shoe to drop. And then she walked across and lifted the tray off his lap. "I really need to look under that," she said. "The bandage," she added unnecessarily, and a telltale flush moved into her neck, clearly visible despite the tan.

She hadn't blushed last night. Maybe that had been because of the quiet, almost intimate feel of the darkness. Or the situation. Sexual innuendo was a little more embarrassing in the full light of day.

Drew opened his mouth, and before he could get a word out, they both froze. The knock at the front door had been peremptory and impatient, as was the man's voice that accompanied it. "Miz Cannon? Maggie? You in there?"

Chapter Five

Maggie's gaze flew to his, holding there a heartbeat. She put the tray back down on his lap, wiping her hands on the sides of her shorts as she hurried to the door of the bedroom and disappeared through it.

It seemed a lifetime until he heard her call a greeting to whoever had knocked. As she moved toward the front of the house, her voice became less distinct, until once again he could hear the hum of the conversation, none of the words distinguishable.

Same person who had been here before? he wondered, and realized he still hadn't asked her who that had been. And whoever it was, he represented danger. Not only to Drew, but to Maggie, as well, he realized belatedly, since she was now guilty of harboring a fugitive. He wasn't sure what the penalty for that was in Tennessee, but he knew it wouldn't be light.

She could always claim he had forced her to let him stay here. Of course, given the fact that he was lying nude in her bed with a breakfast tray she'd fixed across his lap, that didn't sound too credible to him. It probably wouldn't to whoever came looking for him, either.

Drew lifted the tray, moving it carefully to the other side of the double bed. He pushed the sheet off, easing over to the edge of the mattress. From the sound of their voices, he didn't believe Maggie and the man had come inside. Maybe they were on the front porch with the door standing open. Hopefully, she could keep whoever it was out there, at least until Drew could make it out the back and into the woods.

He looked around the room, searching for something to put on. He wasn't sure he could manage the jeans he'd been wearing, even if he could find them. And he couldn't.

But he didn't relish trying to make it up the mountain without any protection from insects and vegetation. Maybe there was something of her husband's in the closet.

He found what he was looking for in the very back. A few men's clothes, pushed behind the dresses hanging there. Still being careful to make no noise, he slipped a pair of navy cotton work pants off a hanger. He held them out in front of him, and then, leaning back against the wall, he lifted one leg and then the other to step into them, grimacing against the pain.

After he'd rested a few seconds, he pulled the pants up to his waist, zipping them and fastening the button. They were too short and tight, but Cannon had been a smaller man than he was.

He reached back into the closet and pulled out one of the cotton knit shirts, dark like the pants. It was going to hurt like hell to get it on over his head, but he needed to cover the bandage. Maybe that would keep them from shooting first and asking questions later.

As he struggled to get the shirt on, he was straining to hear the voices. To keep them located. They didn't seem to be getting any closer, and he was relieved. Just keep him outside, he urged. Whatever you do, don't let him come in the house.

He bent as much as he could and pulled the clothes hanging in the closet to one side, searching the floor for a pair of men's shoes. There weren't any, and he knew he wouldn't get ten feet on that rough, mountain terrain barefooted. Maybe Maggie had put the shoes he'd been wearing under the edge of the bed, he thought. A lot of people in this part of the country did that.

Drew made his way back across the room, his chest burning again. He put his hand flat on the bedside table, preparing to ease his body down to try to take a look under the bed. As he touched the table, he had a flash of memory, like an image from a half-forgotten dream. There was a gun in the drawer of the table he had his hand on.

He didn't know exactly how he knew that. Maybe he had seen Maggie put it away during the days he had lain here, drifting in and out of consciousness. Whatever the explanation for the image, he knew with absolute certainty there was a gun in there.

He pulled on the handle of the drawer, but it wouldn't open. He should have known Maggie wouldn't leave a gun in an unsecured location with her daughter around. He pulled again, harder this time, giving the drawer a couple of strong jerks and making enough noise that he stopped and listened once more to the voices.

Nothing had changed. Apparently they couldn't hear the noise he was making, which sounded loud enough to him to wake the dead. Maybe they thought it was the little girl playing. In any case, he didn't have much choice. If he was going to make a run for it, he needed that gun.

Drew pulled again, applying every ounce of strength he could muster. The drawer flew out, the slender piece of metal that had formed its lock broken. The contents spilled with a heart-stopping clatter, items dropping out and rolling noisily over the heart-pine floor.

He froze, breathing suspended, and listened. His heart was pounding so loudly that for a few seconds he couldn't hear anything at all—beyond the roar of blood through his ears. And then slowly the two voices, their tones unchanged, floated back to where he was standing, a cold sweat covering his body.

He remembered to breathe. The gun had slid to the back

of the drawer, which was dangling from his fingers. He couldn't decide if their trembling was caused by fear or weakness.

He picked up the gun, hefting its solid weight in his left hand, feeling infinitely better with it there. Then he laid the drawer soundlessly on the bed. He left the rest of the junk that had spilled out of it scattered on the floor as he stepped over it and headed for the doorway.

Laurie Cannon was standing there, watching him. She smiled at him, and then her eyes moved away from his, looking down the hall. Looking at Maggie's visitor? he wondered. Was he coming?

Drew calculated the distance between him and the little girl and knew with a surge of despair that in the shape he was in, he couldn't get there fast enough to prevent her from taking off, maybe running to tell her mother that he was up and dressed. She liked to report on his progress.

Her gaze came back to his, and he lifted one finger to his lips, laying it across them. He shook his head. Her eyes widened, but he couldn't know whether she understood or not.

And then, without a word, she did exactly what he had been praying she wouldn't. She turned and disappeared, bare feet slapping on the wooden floor. Running in the same direction in which her mother had disappeared a few minutes earlier.

He could hear the excitement in her voice as she called. "Mama! Mama! Guess what, Mama!"

As LAURIE CAME RUNNING through the front door, Maggie put out her hand to stop the little girl's forward progress, pulling her against her side. "In a minute, Laurie," she said calmly, trying to defuse the child's excitement.

Maggie wasn't sure what her daughter was in such a rush to tell her, but if it had anything at all to do with the man in her bedroom, now *wasn't* the time, not with Rafe Dalton watching them both with that paternalistic smile on his face.

"But, Mama—"

"Mind your manners," Maggie interrupted, softening the command by rubbing Laurie's back. "Adults are talking."

Laurie's eyes studied her face, which was deliberately arranged in a far sterner expression than she usually used in dealing with her daughter. There was a lot at stake, however. Not only for Drew Evans, but for the two of them, as well.

"What's got you all excited, missy?" the sheriff said. He bent, balancing on the balls of his feet, so that he was at eye level with the little girl. He was still smiling.

Maggie held her breath as Laurie turned her head to look at him. Then her daughter glanced up again, meeting her eyes. Maggie didn't smile, her face still set in the same serious expression, hoping that Laurie would remember either her manners or their discussion about secrets. With her hand still on Laurie's back, she could feel the breath the child took before she looked once more at the face of the man stooping in front of her.

"Laurie, isn't it?" Rafe said.

The little girl nodded.

"I thought so. Brought you something," Rafe added, reaching into his shirt pocket and pulling out a two-cent sucker. He held it out, the sunlight catching the clear cellophane that covered the red circle of hard candy.

"What do you say?" Maggie prompted. Maybe if Laurie had the lollipop in her mouth, she'd be less prone to blurt out something incriminating.

"Thank you," Laurie whispered.

"Take it," Maggie urged, eager to get this over with. Eager to get the child's mouth occupied. So very eager to get Laurie inside and the sheriff back in his car and off her property.

"Is he a stranger?" Laurie asked.

There was a second of shocked silence. Maggie was examining the question to see if it made reference to the stranger she was sheltering. The escaped convict stranger. She didn't relax until Rafe laughed.

"Good girl. You keep right on being careful about strangers. Will you promise me that, Laurie? Promise me you won't take candy from a *real* stranger. And I'm not, you know. I'm an old friend of your mama's. Since she's standing right here with us, you don't have to worry about taking this."

"You're a friend of my mama's?" Laurie asked.

Rafe's clear green eyes lifted, seeking Maggie's. "That's right," he said. "Your mama and I go back a long ways. Isn't that right, Maggie?"

She hesitated before she answered, not liking the intimacy of his claim. Of course, what did it matter what he said? There was no one but Laurie to hear it. And the tone in which that statement had been made would go right over Laurie's head.

"Mama's got another friend who's—"

"It's all right, buttercup," Maggie said, resisting the urge to put her palm over Laurie's mouth. She hoped she had spoken loudly and quickly enough that Rafe hadn't heard much of that. "You can have the candy."

She reached for the sucker herself, taking it out of the sheriff's hand and tearing the wrapper off and holding it out to her daughter. "Take it and run on back inside," she instructed. "I need to talk to the sheriff a little while in private."

"Okay," Laurie said.

She plopped the sucker into her mouth, eyed the sheriff again, and then slipped inside through the open door. Maggie stepped into the house and pulled the front door closed.

"I don't want her frightened by talk of the escapees," she said by way of explanation, not moving from her place at the door.

Rafe Dalton's lips pursed, but he nodded agreement. "I

don't blame you. I've been worried about the two of you all alone up here since I came up the other day. Just had to stop by this morning and make sure everything's okay.''

"We're fine.''

"You're being careful now, aren't you?''

"Of course. I can't imagine why someone like this Holcomb would show up here. That doesn't make a lot of sense to me.''

She could tell by something in his eyes that Rafe Dalton knew why this particular escapee might pay a visit to Tommy Cannon's cabin. She wasn't sure why he hadn't bothered to explain it to her. Maybe just to keep from scaring her to death.

"Crazy people do crazy things.''

"You think he's crazy?''

"I think anybody that takes another person's life is crazy. Don't you?''

"I guess,'' Maggie said.

"You keeping your gun handy?''

She nodded.

"And you got my number?''

On his last visit Dalton had given her his home phone number in case she needed him at night. It would keep her from having to go through the dispatcher to get help, he'd said. After all, his place was closer to hers than the deputies in town would be.

It had all sounded perfectly logical when he'd offered it. Kind, even. Maggie knew she never would have used that number, even if she weren't hiding a convicted murderer in her bedroom.

"I've got it,'' she said.

"I could send somebody up to check on y'all every couple of hours. We patrol this part of the county fairly regular. No trouble at all to give the units orders to come up here and take a look around when they make their rounds.''

"Thank you, Sheriff Dalton, but I don't think that's necessary. I promise I'll call if I see anything suspicious."

"Rafe," he corrected. "Like I told your little girl, you and me go back a long ways."

They had gone to high school together. Of course, everybody within a forty mile radius had gone to school together. It didn't make you friends. Actually, Maggie couldn't remember much about Rafe Dalton from school. He'd been Rafael then, his family as dirt poor as hers had been. As most of the county kids had been, she supposed.

"Rafe," she said obediently.

Too conscious of the danger Laurie represented, too conscious that she was harboring an escaped convict, she would have called him anything she thought would get him off her front porch and back into his patrol car.

"What'd she mean?" he asked.

Her heart stopped, a coldness settling where it normally beat. "Mean?" she repeated like an idiot, buying time, trying to remember exactly what Laurie had said.

"About your friend."

About your friend. Maggie couldn't think of one single lie to tell him. The community was so small she couldn't make up a fictional boyfriend. Dalton knew everybody in the county and almost everybody in the surrounding ones.

"Who knows?" she said. "You know kids."

"You got a special friend, Maggie? Since Tommy died?"

She hesitated a fraction of a second too long before she got the words out. "No. Nobody special."

He nodded, holding her eyes again. "Good. I was getting a little worried there," he said with a slow smile. "Always did think you were the prettiest woman in these parts. Tommy just got there first, I guess. Always regretted that."

Maggie knew she should say something. Something gracious. Charming. Something that would at least keep him from being suspicious. But for the life of her, she could not bring herself to flirt with Rafe Dalton.

"I have to check on Laurie," she said. She put her hand on the knob of the door behind her.

"Didn't mean to make you nervous, Maggie. You got no call to go running off," he said, smiling at her. "I'm not rushing you. I just wanted you to know that when you're ready…" He paused, and his eyes considered her throat, flushed with embarrassment. Then they drifted lower. He was still smiling after he lifted his gaze back to her face. "When you're ready to start seeing someone, I'm tossing my hat into the ring."

Her throat felt tight, but she forced the words out of it, "I don't think I'm quite ready for that."

"Like I said, I'm not rushing you. I'm a patient man. I just didn't want to make the same mistake I made before and let somebody else move in while I was working up my nerve to tell you I'm interested."

She nodded, holding his eyes. "I need to check on Laurie," she said again.

"I'll see you soon," Rafe said. "And if you notice a patrol car up here, don't mind it. I'll feel better having somebody look in on you periodically. Just to be on the safe side."

Be gracious, she told herself again. Gracious and suitably grateful. "Thank you, Sheriff Dalton. I appreciate that."

"Rafe," he corrected, touching long fingers to his hat.

She opened the door behind her and stepped through. When she closed it, she leaned against its solid barrier in relief. She took a deep breath as she listened to his footsteps cross the porch and then move down the wooden steps. She waited until the car engine kicked to life, and he began turning the vehicle in the yard, preparing to head back down the dirt road.

She turned her head. And looked straight into the cold hazel eyes of Drew Evans. He was holding her revolver in his right hand, holding it as if he knew how to use it. His back was pressed against the wall, the window between them. He would have been able to watch everything going on out on the porch.

"Where's Laurie?" she asked.

She didn't much like the fact that he was waving a gun around her daughter, but given the circumstances, she supposed she couldn't blame him. He had warned her he didn't intend to let them take him back to prison.

"In the kitchen," he said, his gaze following the sheriff's car, which was moving down the slope now. "What'd he want?"

As the sound of the motor faded in the distance, he stepped away from the wall. He was wearing Tommy's clothes, Maggie realized. The garments were too short for him, and they should have looked ridiculous, she supposed. They didn't, but they did bring back memories. Memories she didn't welcome.

"He was just checking on us. It seems there's a dangerous convict on the loose," she said.

She realized that she was more bothered by the sheriff's visit now than while she'd been talking to him. She had been too busy then struggling to keep her wits about her and not to betray what was going on. With Dalton gone, the adrenaline rush was over and reaction had set in.

She was trembling. The danger of what she was doing had been forcibly brought home to her by having the law on her front porch and the man they were looking for just a few feet away. What would have happened if Rafe had insisted on coming inside? Would Drew have shot him? If so, Laurie could have been hurt.

"Something going on between the two of you?" Drew Evans asked, pulling her mind out of that fearful spiral of what-ifs.

"Something going on? What does that mean?"

"It seemed like he was hitting on you."

She wasn't sure whether she was more embarrassed by Rafe's inept flirting or by the fact that Drew had overheard it. She couldn't quite figure out why that would bother her, however, so she let the question go, turning to look at him.

"I can't do anything about what he's *trying* to do, but I can promise you, there's nothing between us."

"He suspect I'm here?"

Did he? She replayed the scene on the front porch, thinking about Dalton's demeanor. Was he suspicious? It hadn't felt that way. It had felt a little slimy, she admitted, but there hadn't been anything that made her think he knew what was going on. Not even Laurie's remark seemed to have given him a clue.

"No," she said. "He wouldn't have left if he had."

Drew nodded, finally lowering the gun.

"I'd like to have that, please," she said, holding out her hand. "I don't like guns around Laurie."

He hesitated a couple of seconds and then laid the revolver in her outstretched palm.

"Thank you," she said, realizing that she had been holding her breath in anticipation of his refusal.

"That's too small," he said, hunching his left shoulder as if it hurt. It probably did. "Not enough stopping power."

"If it had any *more* stopping power, Mr. Evans, you'd be dead. Be grateful you weren't around to advise about size when this was bought." She held his eyes, and then, carrying the gun she'd shot him with, she walked out of the room.

Chapter Six

"We have to talk," Drew said when she brought his lunch.

His foray to see what was going on out front had taken its toll. He had spent the remainder of the morning in bed, impatient with both his weakness and his inability to decide what to do next. He hated to admit how much he had been counting on being able to force Cannon to recant his testimony, but he didn't have much else. Nothing other than his belief that Maggie knew why her husband had lied. That didn't mean, of course, that she necessarily knew anything that could help him clear his name.

"About what?" she asked, setting the tray across his lap after he'd pushed himself upright against the pillows.

The effort required to do that took what little strength he had managed to rebuild since he'd returned to bed. He waited a moment before he answered, afraid that weakness would be revealed in his voice. "About why your husband lied."

"You got the reason for *that* right on the first guess," she said. "Somebody paid him."

"Paid him to tell lies about a man he didn't know."

"Apparently." Her face was tight.

"You better understand this now," Drew said harshly. "I'm not going back. I didn't do what they said I did. What your husband testified I did," he added bitterly. "I was framed, and I'm not doing any more time for a crime I didn't commit.''

"What you do is nothing to me," Maggie said. "As long as you do it off my property. But I won't stand for you putting my daughter in danger like you did this morning. You aren't going to play cops and robbers in this house.''

She had already begun to turn away when he reached out and grabbed her wrist. His sudden movement upset the tray. The glass teetered and then toppled, spilling iced tea all over the bed. The tray itself slid off the side of his lap, and the sandwich fell off and onto the sheet that covered his lower body.

Maggie jerked her arm, trying to pull it away. Drew refused to release it, a little surprised at the strength in his fingers, fueled by his anger, of course. "Then explain to me why you didn't tell the sheriff I was here," he challenged.

She held his eyes a long moment. "What Tommy did was wrong. I don't deny that.'' She hesitated, taking a breath. "But I can't undo it. I'm not sure I would if I could. And I feel bad that I shot you. That's going to make it easier for them to catch you, and I really do hope you get away. I'll hide you until you get your strength back, but that's *all* I can do. Don't go counting on me doing you any more favors.''

"You know that what your husband did was wrong, but you won't help me undo it?''

"Not at the risk of losing Laurie. If I help you, and they find out, they could take her away from me.''

She was probably right, Drew thought. Aiding and abetting an escaped murderer was a felony. She could go to jail for it, and if anyone wanted to push it hard enough, she probably could lose custody of her daughter.

"At least tell me what he got in exchange," he demanded. "What exactly was his thirty pieces of silver, Mrs. Cannon? How much did it take to buy your husband's rotten, lying soul?''

Her eyes went cold. When she pulled her arm this time, he let her go. She didn't look back before she disappeared through the door. Drew closed his eyes, breathing through his mouth, angry that he'd let his bitterness explode. He couldn't lose control like that. Right now, his life depended on Maggie Cannon's goodwill.

And being dependent on anybody frustrated him almost as much as not being able to take some action. Any action. He pushed the tray violently away. And then, recognizing that his options had narrowed even more with Maggie's declaration, he picked up the sandwich. It was soggy from the spilled tea. He brought it to his mouth and forced himself to take a bite, although whatever hunger he might have felt had dissipated during their exchange.

Until you can get your strength back, she had said. Getting his strength back couldn't happen soon enough to suit him, and to do that, he needed to eat. He took another bite, trying to put things into some kind of perspective. Trying to plan.

Maggie Cannon was right. She didn't owe him anything. It wasn't her fault he was in this fix. His own stupidity had put him in this bed because, despite his experience, he had misjudged her from the beginning. There weren't many people, especially not many women, who would have pulled that trigger. It had been the right thing to do in the situation, but looking into her eyes, he hadn't believed she'd have the guts to do it.

He should have. It took guts to do what she did every day of her life. Struggling to raise a kid by herself. Living way up here all alone. And from what that redneck sheriff had implied, her being alone wasn't from a lack of offers.

Maybe she hadn't accepted any of those because she had really loved her husband, Drew thought, chewing the ruined sandwich stoically. Maybe she was still mourning Tommy Cannon.

And what the hell do you care? he mocked himself. Even

as he asked it, he was aware on some level that he *did* care. The thought that she had loved that lying bastard enough to still be grieving bothered him. Just as listening to the sheriff had bothered him.

He took a deep breath, putting the half-eaten sandwich back on the plate. He had already acknowledged that if there was one thing he didn't need, it was an involvement with Maggie Cannon. And that was still true.

Get his strength back. Find out everything she knew about what her husband had done. And then get the hell out of here before Sheriff Whatever-His-Name-Was came courting again.

"NOT TOO BAD," Maggie said that night, touching the swollen area around the bullet hole. "Still inflamed, but I think it's better today than it was yesterday."

He didn't respond, his eyes locked on the ceiling. He had counted logs while she'd soaked off the bandage and examined the wound. When she had applied the salve he'd noticed earlier, her fingers had been as gentle as they were now.

And he could smell her again. She hadn't been baking today. She had spent a couple of hours out in the garden while he'd napped, drifting in and out of a lazy half sleep, occasionally waking with a start, heart racing, expecting to hear patrol cars pulling the rise up to the Cannon cabin.

A faint scent of earth and vegetation clung to Maggie tonight. Along with that subtle, so-damned-evocative scent of woman. He took another breath, savoring it.

"That hurt?" she asked in response, her eyes lifting to his.

He shook his head. He didn't want to talk to her. He didn't want her to talk to him. He just wanted to feel her hands moving against his skin. Nothing sexual on her part, he knew, but the sensation of those slim, cool fingers against the heat of his aching shoulder was something he wanted to enjoy in silence.

He wanted no reminders of their situation. He wanted the freedom to imagine she was someone else. Something else. Not a widow still grieving for her dead bastard of a husband.

Or maybe even more than that he wanted freedom to imagine he was someone else. Not a fugitive on the run, with half the law enforcement officers in the state on his tail.

He wanted to be just a man in a small, dark bedroom with a woman. The scent of her body around them. The evening shadows lengthening so that there was something intimate and mysterious about the narrow cone of light cast by the bedside lamp. It illuminated only half her face, highlighting the texture of her skin. Emphasizing the length of her lashes and the frown of concentration that had formed between her brows as she worked.

Someone else. Another time. Another place. Another chance.

"There," she said, the corners of her mouth inching up in satisfaction as she surveyed her handiwork. "I think that should do it for a day or two."

Drew looked down at the patch of white bandage, stark against the darkness of his skin. "Thanks," he said, looking straight into her eyes for the first time tonight.

"You're welcome."

She broke the contact between them by turning away and putting the scissors she'd used to cut the two strips of tape on the table.

"I need you to do something for me," he said.

Her gaze came back to his face, eyes slightly widened. She didn't ask what he meant. She didn't ask anything. She simply held his eyes.

"Find out everything you can about the man who was murdered. You can do that at the public library. Check the microfiche for the newspapers around the date of the murder and the trial—"

She had begun shaking her head long before he'd stopped, but her eyes weren't cold as they had been when she'd refused him this afternoon. "I can't do that," she said. "I told you."

"You're Tommy Cannon's widow. You have a right to be interested in a trial that—"

"Being his widow doesn't explain why two years *after* that trial's all over I'd suddenly be interested in the man who was murdered. And besides, I wouldn't know how to start looking for those articles. I'd have to ask them for help. The people at the library. Someone might start wondering why I was all of a sudden so interested. It might get back to whoever paid Tommy. I can't chance that. I told you this morning."

He locked his eyes on the ceiling above his head again, his mouth tightening to keep the harsh words from coming out. And when he did open it, his anger was hidden behind the calm rationality of his tone. "Your husband died shortly after he testified. If I were you, I'd want to know if there was any connection between those two events."

"You aren't me," she said. "And my husband's death wasn't connected to the trial."

"Exactly how *did* your husband die, Mrs. Cannon?"

There was a long silence, and he waited through it.

"His car went off the road and down into a ravine."

"Just a routine traffic accident," he said mockingly.

"Tommy was drunk, if that's what you're getting at."

It made sense, he thought. That was always a good excuse for anything they wanted to do. Nobody questioned another drunk driver making a fatal error. "Was your husband a big drinker?"

Another silence, more tense than the first. He looked at her then. Even in the lamplight, her face looked pinched and strained. It was obvious she didn't want to talk about this.

No other way, he told himself. *Last chance.*

"Not…a big drinker. Not until after he testified," she admitted.

"Not until he got up on that stand and lied. Not until he sent a man to jail for a crime he knew he didn't commit. *That's* when he started drinking? Is that what you're saying?"

"I thought it was the money. I thought he was worried about the money."

"About repaying a loan?"

She nodded.

"But now you know he didn't borrow any money, so something else must have been bothering him."

"Whatever made Tommy drink too much that night, the bottom line is he's dead. He paid for whatever wrong he did. He can't help you, Mr. Evans. And neither can I."

"Can't or won't?"

"I'm not going to start asking questions that might make the people who paid Tommy nervous."

He let the silence build a moment before he broke it. "You ever wonder if that accident was really an accident?"

He watched her eyes dilate, the dark pupils slowly expanding. "No," she whispered.

"Tommy was the only one who knew what they'd done. He knew I hadn't killed that guy. Maybe they decided to eliminate any risk that your husband might slip up one day and tell someone. Maybe they saw him start drinking. Maybe they got worried that one night in a drunken fit of guilt he'd tell you what he'd done. You or someone else."

"It was an accident," she said softly.

"These people are good at arranging that kind of accident."

"'These people'?"

He hadn't intended to tell her who he thought had set him up. He didn't want to put her into any danger with the agency.

"What people?" she demanded when he didn't answer.

"People who wanted to get me out of the way."

"Who are they?"

"Enemies," he hedged. *The U.S. government. CIA.*

"I don't need to make your enemies mine," she said. "And if you're implying they killed Tommy because he knew too much, that isn't much of an inducement for getting me to help you."

"It can't put you in any danger to read the newspaper accounts of the murder and the trial." He couldn't see how it would. Not if she were careful. It wouldn't matter if she had to ask for help. Not if she approached the library staff in the right way, with the right story. He had thought about all that before he'd broached the subject.

He needed legs, at least for a little while. He needed somebody who could legitimately ask those questions. No matter how much he needed those things, however, he would never knowingly endanger her.

"We don't go poking sticks into hornet nests around here," she said. "We know what will happen."

"The people who paid for your husband's testimony aren't interested in you. And they won't be, not even if by some remote chance they did find out you're asking questions. They'll think it's natural for the widow to want all the particulars of what happened to her husband. They won't care about you doing that. All they care about is me."

"How can you know that for sure?"

"Because I know *them.*"

She held his eyes again, trying to read them. He kept them full of conviction.

"You said Martin Holcomb was a name they made up. A *man* they made up."

He remembered telling her that and wished now that he hadn't. It was all too hard to explain. He knew how incredible the truth would sound. "At one time I was in on some pretty sensitive government stuff. When I got out of that business, they didn't want anyone to be able to trace me back to them.''

"The government?"

He nodded.

"And some of the enemies you made working in this sensitive government stuff framed you for a murder?"

From her tone it was obvious how little of that she was buying. He wondered if she'd buy it if he told her that he really believed the government agency he'd worked for had done the framing. That they had created a new identity for him and then set out to destroy the man they had created.

"It looks that way," he said.

Why complicate things any more than they were? After all, he needed her cooperation. More than that, he desperately needed her help in clearing himself. He'd get nowhere if he started with the agency itself. The only way to do this was to start with the framing and to follow its trail back to whoever at the CIA had left the bread crumbs. "Your husband was just a tool. Somebody they used to get me."

"They were willing to pay for using him," she said bitterly.

"What happened to the money?" he asked. It was obvious that whatever Cannon had been paid, none of it was left now.

"It saved my daughter's life," Maggie said.

"Saved her life?" Drew repeated, not sure if she were being literal. Given the poverty in these mountains, he supposed the expression might be figurative.

"Laurie had a brain tumor." Somehow, the horror of that was still in her voice.

"Cancer?" Drew asked, picturing the towheaded little girl who had seemed so fascinated with his recovery.

"No. But it was as life-threatening because of its aggressive growth. We had insurance, but the only treatment that would give her a chance, a kind of gamma knife surgery, was considered experimental for the location of Laurie's tumor. They wouldn't pay for it. We were fighting it, but it was taking too long. What Tommy did…'' Her voice faded, maybe remembering exactly what Tommy had done to save his daughter's life. And at what cost.

"He used the money to pay for that surgery,'' Drew said, understanding for the first time why Tommy Cannon had been so willing to lie.

"To save Laurie's life. And it did. And I'm not going to put that into jeopardy again. Not for you. Not for anybody. I'll take care of you until you recover enough to leave, but I can't change what Tommy did, Mr. Evans. Not even if it was wrong. Tommy made his choice. He saved his daughter's life by sacrificing yours.'' Her voice had softened on the last. She looked down at her hands before she looked back up, straight into his eyes. "You can stay here until you're strong enough to go, but I'm not asking anybody any questions. Not about what happened to you. Or what happened to Tommy. He's dead. It's over. And nothing I can do will bring him back.''

MAGGIE LET THE CURTAIN fall over the window again and turned to look at the bed she'd crawled out of a few minutes ago. Laurie was still sleeping as soundly as only the innocent can sleep, the same deep, seemingly dreamless sleep that had eluded her. But then, Maggie was no longer one of the innocent.

Despite what she'd told Drew Evans this afternoon, she wasn't nearly as comfortable with her refusal to help him as she'd pretended. Somewhere inside she knew that she owed him. After all, the money Tommy had taken for sending him to prison had kept Laurie alive. In some twisted way, it seemed as if she owed Drew Evans for saving her daughter's life. She knew that was illogical, but still, the feeling was there whenever she thought of the man sleeping in the next room.

Tommy had sent him to prison, and she had shot him.

And then she had refused to even consider doing anything to help him undo the injustice that had been done to him. It was no wonder she couldn't sleep. And there really wasn't much point in pretending she was going to, she decided. There were things she could be doing. Things more profitable than standing here staring out into the darkness.

She debated getting dressed, but that might disturb Laurie, whose bed she'd been sharing since Drew had been sleeping in hers. Come daylight, she'd sneak back in here and put on her clothes. She crossed the room and eased the door open, glancing back at the small mound in the bed to be sure the little girl was still asleep. Then she stepped out into the hall and closed the bedroom door soundlessly behind her.

The door to the other bedroom was closed, as well. She resisted the urge to open it to check on her patient. His temperature had been down almost to normal tonight, so there wasn't any need to disturb him. Need? she questioned as she headed toward the kitchen. Was that what that urge had been? Just a normal, everyday need to verify his continuing recovery?

She shook her head at her attempt at self-deception. She knew why she wanted to open that door, and it had nothing to do with any kind of concern for his health.

She flicked on the kitchen light. Drew Evans was standing beside the open pantry door with a pillowcase in one hand and half a loaf of bread in the other. He looked up when the light came on, blinking against the sudden glare.

He was wearing the jeans and the shirt he'd had on the first day. She had washed them, working hard to get the bloodstain out of the material. Then she had put them in the bureau drawer in the room where he was sleeping. Apparently he'd found them on his own, since she'd forgotten to tell him they were there.

"What are you doing?" she asked. For a moment she really didn't know, but by the time the words were out of her mouth, she had put it all together. He was leaving.

"I'll send you the money for this as soon as I can. And for what you've fed me since I've been here."

"You want to *pay* me for the food you're stealing? Is that what you're saying?" she said, fighting a sense of disappointment she didn't understand. She didn't care what he took. He was welcome to whatever she had. And she knew she should be relieved just to get him out of the house.

From the very beginning Drew Evans had represented nothing but danger to her and Laurie. All she had to do was remember that scene this morning—yesterday morning, she amended. Him waving that gun around and Rafe Dalton standing not three feet away, with her in between them. Let him go, she told herself. Just get him out of the house. And good riddance.

Maggie knew that's what she should be feeling. For some reason it wasn't. This felt like…desertion. He had been planning on leaving without telling her. Walking out in the middle of the night, taking whatever of hers he could fit into a pillowcase. Whatever he could steal and put in *her* pillowcase.

And suddenly she was furious. Furious with him. Furious with herself for caring what he did. For caring if he left.

Good riddance, she said again, but there was no conviction beneath the bitterness. Maybe because his face was, despite the beard, so thin, still gray and haggard in the too-bright glare of the fluorescent lighting. Fever, deprivation, and blood loss. Disappointment that Tommy was dead and she had refused to help him.

She *couldn't* help him, she told herself again. She couldn't put Laurie in danger. If she did, that would invalidate the sacrifice Tommy had made. *And that makes no more sense than thinking I owe Drew Evans something.* There was no logic behind the feeling he'd had a hand in saving Laurie's life. No sense.

In the long silence that had fallen after her accusation, he turned and put the bread back on the shelf. He took a couple of steps across the room and laid the pillowcase on the table.

There wasn't much in it, Maggie realized, watching the cloth collapse, only a couple of small bulges to indicate it contained anything at all. He hadn't taken much. Of course, she didn't have all that much to steal.

"I'm sorry," he said.

"Where are you going?"

"I don't know, but you're right. You don't owe me anything. And every minute I'm here, I'm putting you into danger."

Her own words, and in his mouth they sounded hollow. She wanted to take them back. To say something different. To be heroic. To be willing to do the right thing. She wanted to see this man get the justice he claimed Tommy had deprived him of.

In the midst of that regret, the image of Laurie was in her mind's eye, as clear as the image of Drew Evans, who was standing right before her. Tommy had made this same terrible choice, and he had chosen his daughter. Could she do any less?

So she nodded permission for him to leave, her gaze never leaving his face. There was something in Drew's eyes tonight that she had never seen there before. She had seen him angry and hostile. In pain. And even pleading. What she was seeing now was none of those.

This was defeat. An inward acknowledgment, if not an open one, that when he left, he had nowhere to go. That there was nothing for him to do but keep running until they ran him down and either killed him or took him back to prison. And somehow she knew with frightening clarity which of those he would prefer.

"Thanks for what you've done," he said. "For taking care of me. For not calling the sheriff. For not telling him I'm here."

She nodded again. ''Are you sure you're strong enough to—''

''I'm sure,'' he interrupted, cutting off her concern.

Everything about him said that was a lie. His posture, the damaged shoulder still hunched forward. The color of his skin. And that soulless defeat in his eyes.

What he felt was *nothing* to her, she told herself. It was him or her daughter. The choice was simple.

''Take the food,'' she said. She walked across the room and picked up the pillowcase, peering inside. There was nothing in it but a couple of cans of Vienna sausage that had been in her pantry since before Tommy died. He had chosen those because they had pop tops, she realized. Something he could open.

She walked past him to the pantry. She put the loaf of bread back in the sack and then considered the rest of the contents. Most of what was there were staples. She took out a half-empty jar of peanut butter and dropped it into the bag.

There wasn't much else here that he could use, she decided. Maybe in the refrigerator, she thought, closing the pantry door. She had some fruit and cheese. She laid the sack on the table and had started toward the fridge when his hand stopped her.

It closed around her wrist, almost in the exact place as he had gripped her earlier today. Except this time he hadn't touched her in anger. She didn't know why she was so certain of that because his grip wasn't loose.

She looked down on the long, brown fingers wrapped around her wrist. The bones in her arm looked like a child's compared to the thick virility of his. She didn't resist when he used a slight pressure against her wrist to bring her closer.

She didn't know what he intended, but suddenly she knew she wanted his fingers against her skin. His hand around her arm. And when he pulled her against him, she knew that she wanted this, too. Her knees went weak with the sensation of his body pressed intimately along the length of hers.

She hadn't known how much she had missed this. She hadn't admitted, not even to herself, how lonely she had been. How hungry. Hungry for a man's touch.

He held her a minute, giving her time to protest, she supposed. Enough time to push him away. Time to step back, out of his embrace. She didn't think she could have done that if her life had depended on it. She wanted him to hold her. She wanted to lay her head on his shoulder and close her eyes. Just to let someone else be strong and in control for a change. Just for a little while, she thought, trying to justify the feelings that were moving deep and so strong within the lower part of her body.

She wanted his arms around her. She wanted him. And somewhere inside, pushed into the darkest recesses of her soul, was the knowledge that she had wanted this almost from the first.

He leaned back, and she lifted her head, looking up into his face. His eyes were shadowed and very dark, despite the too bright light overhead. His mouth was unsmiling. He looked down into her eyes for a long time, and then his head began to lower.

Slowly, moving as if in a trance, she rose on tiptoe until their faces were almost touching. So close that when his mouth opened, she could feel the warmth of his breath against her lips. Last chance to say no, she thought. He would let her go if she moved. That promise had been inherent in everything he had done. It would be her decision. Her choice.

And she made it almost without being conscious that she had. Her mouth opened, and her head turned slightly, an automatic alignment. Her body stretched upward the fraction of a millimeter it would take to bring her lips against his.

With that movement, it was as if the floodgates opened. Permission granted. His head tilted, his mouth fitting over hers as though he had been starving for the touch and the taste and the feel of it. Maybe he had. Maybe for him, too, these feelings had lain just below the surface of everything they had said. Everything they had done and thought. Beneath everything.

His hands found her shoulders and, using them, he pulled her upward, straining to bring them closer. His tongue ravaged, plundered, no longer asking but simply taking. The intensity grew as the kiss went on and on. When their mouths broke apart, it was only momentary. A brief release that gave way immediately to a new melding. Another heated exploration.

Now not only were her knees weak, her entire body trembled with need. With desire. And she knew exactly how he would make love to her, she realized. It would be like his kiss. He would be in charge, and she would be swept along in the sheer unconscious power of what he was doing.

And that was not the kind of woman she was. It was not who she wanted to be. Maggie put her hand on his chest, the tips of her fingers almost on his shoulder, and pushed away from him as far as his arms would let her.

She hadn't meant to hurt him, but she saw the grimace before she heard the small gasp. He stepped back, the gesture protective, hunching his shoulder again. His hand caught the one of hers that had pushed too hard against his wound. He took her fingers away from his chest, holding them in his.

"I didn't mean to do that," she said softly. "I just think we should…" *Should just stop?* Is that what she wanted? Did she want him to stop kissing her? Did she really want him to leave? "I think we should slow down," she said instead.

He nodded, his breathing as ragged as hers. She was relieved to realize that. And it excited her. She liked to think that as dominated as she had just felt, she had affected him that much, as well.

"I can't think," she whispered.

He nodded again, and then he leaned forward, putting his

forehead against hers. His breathing was still sawing in and out. "I know," he said.

Maybe it was the harshness of his breathing. Or maybe it was that her mind was on something very different. When she finally heard it, the car pulling up the incline in front of the cabin was much too close. And she knew in that instant she should have been aware of the noise long before she had been. She took one step away from him, and her hand swept the light switch, the one by the back door, plunging the kitchen into darkness.

"What is it?" he asked.

"Car," she whispered, her throat constricted with fear.

"Could they have seen the lights?"

"I don't know. I don't think so." She didn't. Not with the summer foliage, thick and green around the cabin.

Together they listened in the darkness. Drew was still standing near enough that she could hear him breathing. She closed her eyes, concentrating on the sounds at the front of the house and not on his closeness. A car door closed, the noise distant and muffled, probably a deliberate attempt at quietness. She knew by the whisper of fabric that the man beside her had moved.

"If they knock on the door, you'll have to answer it," he whispered.

"I know."

"Give it a minute. Pretend you were asleep."

She nodded, unsure he could see her. She tried to imagine who could be out here in the middle of the night. Then she remembered Rafe's promise to send the deputies when they made their regular patrols of this section of the county. Maybe…

They waited a long time in the darkness, but there was no knock. No steps crossing the wooden porch out front. They would have been able to hear them there, even from back here. Even if whoever this was was trying not to make noise.

As she thought that, Maggie heard the sound she'd been waiting for. Footsteps. Not out front, however, but coming around the side of the house. Coming toward the back.

She reached out and her fingers closed around the hard warmth of Drew's forearm. She began to back across the room, pulling him with her. She was barefoot, her steps soundless. His weren't, but that was a chance she had to take. The kitchen curtains were so sheer that she couldn't risk someone looking in and seeing their shapes in the center of the room.

She wasn't sure how much anyone outside could see, but the moonlight was bright enough that with the light off and her eyes now adjusted to the darkness, she could see out into the backyard. The tomato stakes stood like shadowed sentinels, marking the beginning of her garden.

When she reached the pantry door, she pressed her back against it, moving as far into the shadows as she could get. Drew stood beside her, his entire attention directed toward the windows. It was only now that she realized he had her revolver. He held it pointed at the back door, his waiting stillness so profound it was almost frightening, his concentration palpable.

She looked back at the windows and realized someone was moving out there. Between the house and the garden. She could plot their progress by watching the dark shape move in front of the line of tomato stakes.

They were coming toward the back door. Coming closer to where the two of them were hiding. Drew reached over and pushed her behind him, leaning back against her. His body was tense, every muscle tight. Both hands on the gun, holding it out in front of him, he simply waited. She didn't dare to breathe, and then into the silence came the unmistakable sound of someone trying the knob of the back door.

Chapter Seven

The door didn't open, of course. Checking the locks was something Maggie had gotten far more careful about since the night she had seen someone in her garden. Since she had seen Drew Evans in her garden, she amended.

Whoever was out there tonight didn't try the door again. And after a moment there were more footsteps. From where she was standing, she couldn't determine in which direction they were moving, but at least she knew it was away from the door, and she finally remembered to breathe.

Just as she did, Drew stepped forward. She grabbed for him, her fingers digging into the top of his back. He didn't stop, but pulled away from her hand by lowering his shoulder until her fingers slipped off it. He tiptoed across the room until he was standing beside the kitchen window, his back against the wall, just as when he'd looked out the window at the front of the house this morning.

He stood without moving for a long time. She waited in the darkness, watching him and listening as intently as he seemed to be. If this was the sheriff's patrol, then the stillness of the house should reassure them.

Just as long as they hadn't seen the kitchen light go off in response to the sound of the car. And turning that light off had probably been stupid, Maggie admitted. She wasn't up to something like this. Lying and hiding. Cloak-anddaggering. She had gotten through that interview with Rafe Dalton yesterday morning, but she wasn't sure she could ever do anything like that again. She had never been a good liar. The more times she had to lie to people, the more likely she was to make a mistake.

She realized suddenly that she couldn't hear the footsteps any longer. She didn't know if that was cause for relief or worry. After a moment Drew began to slide down the wall, one hand flattened against it for support as he eased down.

Then, on his hands and knees, still holding the revolver, he crawled under the windows. Then he stood, careful to keep his body to one side of the exposing glass. Surveying the yard from a different angle, she realized. Obviously trying to determine where their unidentified visitor had gone.

She could see Drew's face, revealed by the moonlight, the shape of the bones too prominent beneath the skin. Every atom of his being seemed focused on whatever was going on outside.

Suddenly he turned away from the window, looking toward the front of the house. He listened for a moment, but whatever had attracted his attention wasn't audible from where she was standing.

Then he moved, more quickly than a man with a bullet hole in his chest should be able to move, heading toward the front of the house. Startled, she hesitated only a second or two before she followed him. When she was halfway across the room, she realized what had precipitated his move.

The car they had heard earlier was leaving, its motor fading away down the slope even as she arrived at the front windows. Drew was looking out, no longer concerned about keeping out of sight.

"The sheriff was going to send the patrols up here," she whispered. "I told him I didn't want him to, but apparently—"

She stopped, recognizing that she was talking too much. Relief maybe. Aftermath of her fear. Nerves.

Drew Evans didn't seem to be listening. He was still looking out the window. "No bar lights," he said.

"Bar lights?" She had a mental image of the garish neon signs on the nearest dive that had a liquor license. Bar lights?

"No lights on the top of the car. It wasn't a county car."

He was talking about that bar of flashing red-and-white lights on top of a patrol car, Maggie realized. She didn't think she'd ever heard the term, but it made sense.

"It could have been Sheriff Dalton himself. In his personal car, I mean. Off duty or something," she said. She couldn't imagine who could have been up here in the middle of the night if it hadn't been someone from the sheriff's department. She didn't get all that many visitors even in the daylight.

Drew turned his head. His eyes searched her face a moment. "Were you supposed to leave the back door open for him?"

It took a second for what he had said to register. "What's *that* supposed to mean?" Maggie asked angrily. "You think I was setting you up? You think I told Dalton you were here?"

"I think the sheriff is a whole lot more interested in *you* than he is in me, Mrs. Cannon." Drew lowered the gun, as if he had just remembered he was holding it.

Maggie didn't even bother to deny what he had said. There was no doubt that Rafe Dalton had been making a play for her. As much as she despised his flirting, she would rather have the sheriff interested in her than in her houseguest.

"Which should be to your advantage, don't you think?" she said with an edge of sarcasm.

"You would think so, wouldn't you?" he said softly. His tone had changed. She couldn't identify what was different about it, but something was. He had leaned tiredly against the wall, closing his eyes, the revolver hanging loosely from his hand.

"What's wrong?" she asked.

He opened his eyes and looked at her again, but he didn't answer. Finally he pushed away from the wall and slowly began walking toward the kitchen. Moving as if it were an effort.

It was only then, danger past, that she remembered. He had kissed her. And he was leaving.

She took one more look out the front windows. There was nothing there now. Nothing but moonlight and shadows. She shivered, and then, knowing she didn't have any other option but to let him go without saying goodbye, she followed him.

DREW DIDN'T TURN the light on in the kitchen. He had found the first time he'd been in here that there was enough moonlight to see what he needed to see. As much as he hated to take anything from Maggie, he knew he should take the few provisions in that pillowcase. He would send her money for them. *If* he got away. And he was pragmatic enough to know how unlikely that was.

Maybe if he'd had some resources. Any resources. Money. The kind of ID the agency could have supplied at a moment's notice. Or even a friend he could count on.

After all, he knew all the tricks of changing identity, of melting invisibly into a new location. He had done that when he'd moved back to Tennessee. And he knew he had done it right.

That was the main reason he had believed the agency must have had a hand in his arrest and conviction. It wouldn't have surprised him to discover that someone outside the agency was out to get him. He had made some enemies outside the CIA during his days with the External Security Team. What he didn't believe was that anyone other than the CIA would have been able to find him.

Since someone had, his former employer, who had more

information on him than anyone else, had almost certainly been doing the tracing. The tracing *and* the eliminating. Now if he could just figure out why they had decided this late in the game that he represented a danger—

"You can take the gun, too," Maggie said.

He resisted the urge to turn and look at her. She was wearing another nightshirt, this one even shorter than the first, the material thin enough with repeated washing that the pebbled tips of her nipples were clearly visible beneath the cotton knit.

He didn't need another look at them, he decided. And he had intended to take the weapon all along. It and enough food to keep him alive.

"If I can, I'll send you money to pay for it," he said, sticking the revolver in his waistband. He winced against the now-familiar pain that jolted through his chest whenever he moved his left arm. "And I'll pay for the supplies I take," he added.

"I don't want your money."

He didn't bother to argue, since he knew how unlikely it was that he would ever be able to send her anything. Just as unlikely as the possibility that he'd ever see her again.

He took a breath, for some reason remembering Dalton's eyes this morning. She would probably end up married to someone like that in a couple of years. She had done it once before, and Drew had seen enough to know Maggie wasn't making it financially. She would want better for her daughter. Everybody did. No matter how much she had loved Tommy Cannon, Maggie would eventually succumb to somebody's offer, for that reason if for no other.

And there were probably other reasons she'd succumb, he thought, remembering the feel of her body pressed tightly against his. She had seemed as hungry as he had been for that physical contact. Despite the way she had responded to him, however, the offer she succumbed to wouldn't be his. Because, as a man on the run, he had nothing *to* offer her.

"I wish I had something else to give you," she said.

He turned at that, examining her face in the moonlight. Her eyes were as wide and dark as they had been in the bathroom that night. She didn't mean what he was thinking, and he knew that, but he was thinking it anyway. "It's okay," he said.

"Cheese," she said, walking over to the refrigerator and opening the door.

As she stood in front of it, the light from inside silhouetted the shape of her body through the thin fabric. *Just what I need,* Drew thought, unable to pull his gaze away.

"And there's a couple of apples. And I think…" Her voice faded as she bent to open the drawer at the bottom. The back of the nightshirt rose until he could see the edge of the white panties she wore under it.

He did turn his head then, closing his eyes as a wave of desire so strong it was physically painful swept through him, burning its hot, aching way though nerve and muscle. Setting his blood on fire, pushing it through his body like a torrent until his groin felt engorged enough to explode. He needed to get the hell out of here, Drew thought savagely. Just get out before he did something he'd regret. Something *she'd* regret.

"It's okay," he said. "There's plenty here." He picked up the pillowcase and began carrying it toward the back door.

"Don't forget these."

He stopped in response to that command. He knew it was a mistake, but he couldn't seem to force his trembling fingers to open the door so he could disappear through it into the night.

"Here," she said.

He half turned and realized she was right beside him. She took the makeshift sack from his hand and dropped a package of cheese and some fruit into it. Then she knotted the top of the pillowcase, about halfway down, and handed it back to him.

"I know you don't understand—" she began.

"I understand," he said, cutting off whatever explanations she wanted to make. He didn't need to hear them. He *did* understand. He had no right to ask for her help. She didn't owe him anything. She hadn't done anything wrong. Even if Tommy Cannon had, she wasn't responsible for her husband's actions.

And Drew had decided she was right about the other, as well. There was a remote possibility someone might notice if she started asking too many questions. It was better not to get her involved in whatever was going on. Better for her, he amended. Not necessarily better for him.

If he got away from here without being spotted, he'd have to chance using a library somewhere to get information about the man he was supposed to have killed. It was a place to start, anyway.

"Be careful," she whispered.

Just like she was sending him off for the weekend. Some kind of pleasure trip. *Be careful. Have a good time.* He almost smiled at the absurdity of it. Of course, everything about this had been absurd, from his arrest to his escape. As if some giant hand were directing him, a pawn in a game he could never win. One step forward and two back. Do not collect two hundred dollars, even if you somehow manage to stumble past Go.

He put his hand on the knob of the door. He hadn't time to turn it before her arms slid around his waist. She leaned into his back, the softness of her breasts flattening against the muscle as she laid her cheek on his shoulder blade.

He closed his eyes, fighting the sheer raw need that surged through his body. Every instinct told him to turn the knob and get the hell out. *Just turn the knob and step through the door and don't ever look back.*

She didn't need the complication he represented in her life, and he sure as hell didn't need her in his. There should be only one thing on his mind right now. Figuring out a way to get out of this mess. A way to clear his name. A way to prove he hadn't had anything to do with the murder for which he'd been framed.

Except what was on his mind right now had nothing to do with escape and a whole lot to do with the feel of her body in close proximity to his. A whole lot to do with those two long years that lay between now and the last time he'd been with a woman.

Too long ago. Way the hell too long ago to walk away from what he thought she was offering. Except maybe she wasn't. Maybe he was all screwed up about the signals she was sending. Maybe his needs were getting everything all mixed up.

"What the hell do you think you're doing?" he asked harshly.

He felt her stiffen. After a second or two her joined hands released their hold on one another, and she stepped back, putting enough distance between them that he could no longer feel the warmth of her body or the taut, hard nubs of her breasts rubbing against him as he breathed.

"Maybe you ought not to go tonight," she said. "They might have left somebody out there watching the cabin. They could be up there in the woods, just watching, and we'd never know."

"I don't think there was but one person in that car."

"You can't know that for sure," she argued.

He couldn't. And he had thought all along that the authorities would stake out Tommy Cannon's place, figuring he'd show up out here eventually. They wouldn't do that in daylight. They would come at night, set it up when there was less chance of him seeing them. Less chance of anybody seeing them.

Almost without his volition, his hand lifted away from the

knob. Think, he demanded, willing the constriction in his jeans to shrink, the pain to fade. To let him think. Just to let him get out of this alive.

"I can't leave in the daylight," he said. The implication was clear. As well as the warning. *If I don't leave now, then I'm going to spend another twenty-four hours in your house. And you need to understand what that means before you push it.*

"I can check it out tomorrow," she said. "I'll check the ridge behind us. Up where you were. There are couple of other places they could set up. Somebody who knows the area…"

She paused, her voice fading so that only the slow drip of the faucet and the tock of the mantel clock could be heard.

"And then tomorrow I can do what you said. About the newspapers, I mean." The words were very low, but there was no doubt about what she had just said.

She was offering to do what he'd ask her to. And now he had to decide if he were willing to let her. He turned around and found her eyes on his face.

"You were right before," he warned. "Someone might notice."

"I know there's always that possibility, but…you could tell me how to find the stuff. The microfilm or whatever."

"Microfiche," he corrected automatically, still trying to decide if he could let her take the risk.

Of course, there was nobody else going out of their way to help him out. There hadn't been all along, and that had been one of the most painful realizations that had come out of all this. Despite his years with the agency, despite the friendships he thought he had formed, not one of those men had stepped forward to help him. And they *must* have known. After all, not much went on that those men didn't know about.

Maggie Cannon was the first person in more than two years who had believed him. Believed *in* him. The first who had offered help. Which meant he didn't have enough other offers that he could afford to turn this one down.

"I'd be grateful," he said truthfully. "But only if you're sure..." He waited until she nodded, trying to contain his elation. And his relief. "I can walk you through the library stuff here. You'll probably have to ask some things once you get there, location of the machines for example, but I can prepare you enough that they won't have to know what you're researching. Once they show you where to begin, you can take it from there."

She nodded again.

"And what happened tonight..." he went on, choosing his words carefully. "What happened tonight shouldn't happen again. Not...while this is going on."

She didn't say anything, but her eyes searched his, maybe looking for the answer to the obvious question she didn't ask. And he didn't try to explain. Even if she didn't understand why nothing else could happen between them, he did. Until he got to the bottom of what had been done to him, there was no room in his life for any kind of emotion except the drive and determination that would be necessary to clear his name. And despite the hard reality of his physical needs, Maggie Cannon wasn't the kind of woman who could be used and then discarded.

That was the kind of thing the Rafe Daltons of this world might enjoy. The man Drew Evans had once been would not. And Maggie Cannon was the only person in two years who had treated him as if he were still that man. For her, he would be.

WHEN DREW WOKE, sunlight flooded the bedroom and the cabin was empty. He could tell that even lying in bed. It felt empty. No voices. No radio. No sounds of Laurie playing.

Maybe they were outside. Or maybe Maggie had already gone to do what she had promised him she'd do last night. Would she have taken the kid with her? he wondered. He

lay without moving a few minutes longer, evaluating the
soreness in his shoulder and chest by lifting and turning it
a little. Maybe it was some better, but it still hurt like hell
whenever he moved.

He thought there might even be some nerve damage. Not
that he could do a whole lot about it if there was. All he
could do was try to let it heal. Get his strength back. And
of course, lying here all morning wasn't going to accomplish
that. He worked his aching body around until he was sitting
on the edge of the bed. Then he sat there a minute, letting
the pain subside.

He'd tried to do too much yesterday. He could feel every
one of the hours he'd spent out of bed in the trembling
weakness of his legs when he pushed up off the mattress.
He put his hand on the wall again, wondering how he had
thought he was going to make a run for it last night. He
would probably have passed out at the bottom of the first
ridge he'd tried to climb, easy pickings for Fearless Dalton
and his boys.

Of course, the sheriff hadn't been the only thing he'd been
running away from last night. He began to make that slow
journey across the room and down the hall, still using his
hand on the wall for support. He was glad Maggie wasn't
around to watch him. Glad he didn't have to pretend he was
more on the mend than he was. Glad he didn't have to look
at that pitiful excuse for a nightshirt she had worn.

His lips quirked in memory. Nightclothes like that were
a pretty good indication there hadn't been a man in Maggie's
life in a while. Or maybe she was like his mother, saving
the fancy negligees his dad gave her in her bureau. When
she had died, two years after his dad, Drew had gone home
to clean out and sell the house. He had found those night-
gowns in her drawer, most of them with the tags still on
them.

He had run his hand over the silky fabrics, picturing his
mom's work-worn fingers carefully folding them in tissue

paper and laying them there. She had planned to wear them "someday." That's what she always said on Christmas morning when she unfastened the department-store-wrapped-packages his dad had slipped under the tree a few days before. *Someday,* she'd say, her eyes shining. *It's too nice for every day.* And then she had never worn them. Instead, she had folded them and carefully put them away. Someday had never come.

And why the hell was he thinking about that? he wondered as he entered the bathroom. When he was through with a long, hot shower and had brushed his teeth with the new toothbrush Maggie had laid out a couple of days ago, his eyes considered the guy in the mirror.

The untrimmed, two-week-old beard made him look like a stranger. A hungover stranger, he thought, examining the red-rimmed eyes and the grayish tone of his skin. He wondered that Maggie had let him kiss her last night.

He fingered the whiskers, thinking how much better he'd feel if they were gone. The thought he'd had before, that they were a pretty good disguise, entered his mind, but it didn't have much impact. Just because he felt like death warmed over didn't mean he had to look like it, too.

He opened the medicine cabinet and lying there on the shelf, as if waiting for him, was an electric razor. He picked it up, hefting the weight of it in his hand. It was a big sucker, heavy and old fashioned. His thumb caressed the switch. It probably wouldn't start, he thought. Not if it had been lying here since Tommy Cannon died. He applied pressure and the resulting buzz filled the small room.

He flicked it off and just stood there a moment, the razor in his hand. Stupid, he thought. *Maybe, maybe not,* the analytical part of his brain argued. As far as the authorities knew, he was still wandering around in the wilderness. Still hiding. Maybe the bulletins they'd issued lately had taken that into account. Maybe for several days now they'd already been showing some artist's conception of Martin Holcomb with a beard. Since Maggie didn't have a television, he had no way of knowing.

Besides, a few whiskers weren't going to keep someone like Rafe Dalton from shooting first and asking questions later. With the beard gone, he'd look a little less disreputable than he did now. And maybe a little less suspicious.

He was almost through when, even over the noise the razor was making, he heard the door slam. He shut it off and listened. He could hear Maggie's voice. And the child's. Cabinets opening and closing. Nothing else.

After a minute he turned the razor back on and finished the shave, even trimming his sideburns. When he cut it off again, he laid the razor back on the shelf where he'd found it, fingering his now-naked chin and reevaluating the man in the mirror.

At least he looked familiar. And less villainous. He turned his head a little, still evaluating. Out of the corner of his eye, he saw Maggie standing in the doorway, watching him. He looked at her and saw her eyes widen before she looked down quickly and then back up.

"What do you think?" he asked. "Less 'escaped murderer'?"

She nodded, her eyes examining his face. Her lips tightened, but she didn't make any other comment until, the silence stretching uncomfortably after his question, she said, "I took a look around outside. I didn't see anything that looked suspicious. If they are staking out the house, they're doing it from a distance."

That would mean equipment. At least binoculars. Which was always possible. "You look at the tracks outside?" he asked.

"I only found one set, but the ground's pretty hard."

He nodded. "And the other?"

"You didn't tell me you could print that stuff out. The librarian showed me how. I've got it in the kitchen."

"Anything interesting?" he asked.

"I'm not sure what you were hoping for, but... Yeah, I think there may be," she said.

He didn't know what he'd been hoping for, either, but he had to admit that sounded promising. Like the shave, it was something minor, something that probably didn't amount to a hill of beans as far as his situation was concerned. But for the first time since Maggie had told him her husband was dead, there was a surge of anticipation in his stomach. Maybe, just maybe, he thought, things were beginning to look up again.

Chapter Eight

Sitting at the kitchen table, Drew read through the copies of the clippings Maggie had found. She kept refilling his coffee cup as she cooked lunch. Even as he tried to concentrate on the information the newspapers had carried about the investigation of the murder and the trial, he was aware of her. Too damn aware.

Laurie was working a puzzle on the coffee table in the front room. The whole situation, incredibly domestic, was a little surreal after the past two years. Actually, Drew couldn't remember anything like this scene since his own childhood.

"What do you think?" Maggie asked. She was standing beside his chair, looking down at the photocopied sheets.

Drew tried to think of something positive to tell her. In reality, he didn't believe there *was* much that was positive. Or helpful. At least not here. According to the papers, the man he had supposedly murdered had been a pillar of the community. An outstanding citizen, husband and father. Maggie had even copied the guy's obituary, which listed his church and civic offices.

"I don't think there's much here that I didn't already know from the trial," Drew said truthfully, fighting his frustration.

Maybe when he felt stronger physically, he would feel

more optimistic that there was going to be something useful out there to find. Something that would clear him. All he felt now was tired. As if he were swimming in quicksand and going nowhere.

Maggie put the dish towel she'd been holding down on the table and fingered through the pages. He didn't have any idea what she was searching for, but she pulled out the obituary and another of the early reports about the murder, arranging the two of them in front of him. "What was he doing there?" she asked.

Drew shrugged, scanning the article and ignoring the obituary. Despite the fact that he hadn't had anything to do with the guy's death, reading about the wife and three kids he had left behind wasn't pleasant. Of course, not much he'd read in those clippings could be called pleasant.

"Probably what everyone else was doing," he said. "Having a drink. Doing a little socializing."

"At one o'clock in the morning?"

Drew shook his head, not getting whatever point Maggie was trying to make. "That's not all that late. Not for Saturday night. I doubt he's the first good ole boy to whoop it up while the wife and kids wait at home." He looked up at her again, but her eyes were still on the two papers she'd pulled out.

After a moment she turned to face him, lips slightly pursed. "Maybe," she said, "but somehow it just doesn't ring true to me."

"Because he's married? I wish I had a nickel for every married guy who went out on the occasional Saturday-night tear."

"Not that. Not *just* that he's married. Look at this." She ran her finger along a line in the obituary, and Drew dutifully read the words she was pointing to.

"So? The guy was an elder of the Mt. Nebo Living Church of the Word," Drew said, with an edge of sarcasm in his voice. "That's like being married, Maggie. I wish I had a nickel for every good Southern Baptist who's out getting juiced on Saturday night. Put all those nickels together and—''

''It's not Baptist.''

''Okay, Methodist, Episcopalian, Catholic, whatever... You name it, they've all got their share of people who bend the rules. In church singing hymns on Sunday morning, even if they've been at the Wagon Wheel on Saturday night.''

That was the name of the roadhouse where, according to Tommy Cannon, he had put a couple of .44-caliber slugs into Charles ''Charlie'' Brundridge. Drew had never been there in his life, but he'd lived in the South long enough, before and after the years he'd spent with the CIA, to have an idea what the place was like.

''Mt. Nebo is Pentecostal,'' Maggie said, as if that should mean something. ''He wouldn't have been there.''

She picked up the dish towel and walked back to the stove. Drew half turned in his chair, watching her, momentarily distracted from thinking about Charlie Brundridge's death by the way her faded jeans fit over her hips and thighs.

''You can't know that for sure,'' he said.

He hated to have to deny the significance of whatever she thought the guy's religion meant, but he couldn't believe that there was any denomination free of hypocrites. It wasn't a big deal that the victim had been a churchgoer out having a drink or two. Plenty of them did, even in the more fundamentalist Southern sects that totally forbade the use of alcohol.

Maggie turned around, the wooden spoon she'd been using to stir whatever was in the steaming boiler still in her hand. She held his eyes a minute, without speaking. And then she shook her head, as if she'd made up her mind about something.

''*That* guy wouldn't have been having a Saturday night toot. I'm as sure as you can be about anybody. Besides, it wasn't Saturday night. It was Sunday morning. And that means it was the Sabbath. He wouldn't have been there.''

It wasn't the kind of evidence that would have made an impact in any court, and Drew wasn't sure it had any validity in what he was trying to do, either. After all, Brundridge hadn't been breaking any law. He had every right to be in a roadhouse on a Saturday night. Sunday morning, Drew amended, forced, despite his doubts, to think about what Maggie had said.

No witness had put Brundridge inside that bar. Just in the parking lot. Maybe everybody had made the assumption that he was coming out of or going into the Wagon Wheel, just as Drew had, but nobody had testified at the trial that they had seen Brundridge inside.

Actually, the only person who'd done much testifying at all was Tommy Cannon. Along with a couple of sheriff's deputies who had answered the call. And the coroner, who had given what meager forensics evidence had been presented. That had been simple enough that even the papers had gotten it right.

One bullet, which had nicked an artery as it had exploded through the center of Brundridge's chest, and another in the back of his head, execution style. According to Cannon, Drew had fired that last shot after his victim was down, probably already in the process of dying from the first.

The coroner's testimony hadn't disputed the scenario. Neither did the patrons of the Wagon Wheel who had heard the two shots and rushed out in time to see a pickup speed away. And a corpse on the asphalt. And Tommy Cannon.

"Did your husband go there a lot?" Drew asked.

If Cannon hadn't been a drinker before he testified, which was what Maggie had implied, then what was *he* doing there that night? Of course, nobody at the trial had put Tommy inside that bar, either. According to his testimony, he had driven up just in time to witness Drew shoot Brundridge and then peel rubber.

"To the Wagon Wheel?" Maggie asked. "I don't think so."

"He was just out having himself a little *toot* that particular night?" Drew probed, using Maggie's word.

For some inexplicable reason he wanted to know more about Tommy Cannon. More about his and Maggie's relationship. It bothered him on a level deeper than the intellectual. Even deeper than having a legitimate need to know his enemy. More primitive than that. And his mind kept revisiting the issue the way the tongue pokes at an aching tooth, knowing it's going to hurt.

"I don't know what he was doing," Maggie said. "I was at the hospital with Laurie. Maybe he stopped by for a drink on his way home. I don't even remember that particular night. I didn't know until I read those clippings which night this happened."

"He never told you any of it."

"He told me he had to testify about an accident. I thought he meant a car wreck, but… Even when he mentioned the trial, I didn't ask for details. I had too much else to worry about."

"Does it make sense that your husband would witness a murder and not tell you about it?"

"Maybe. At the time. We were both pretty strung out. Exhausted. Worried about Laurie. Our relationship…" She hesitated, and Drew waited through the pause. "We didn't have the best relationship right then. We were going through a rough patch in our marriage. Too many stresses, I guess."

She turned back to the stove, stirred the pot again, and then she cut off the burner. She arranged the three bowls she'd taken out of the cabinet around the boiler and began dipping out soup with a metal ladle and spooning it into them.

"Laurie, you need to go wash your hands," she called. She glanced into the living room, and then her eyes skated over Drew's face before she went back to serving up the soup.

"But he was still living here?"

"As far as I know," she said.

"What does that mean?"

Her hand hesitated, leaving the ladle resting against the rim of the boiler as she turned to look at him. "I don't know where he was living. I don't know what he was doing. I know that sounds awful, but it's the truth. I was sleeping on the floor of Laurie's hospital room. I couldn't make the drive back and forth. It was too far, and we didn't have money for gas. Or for a motel. But Tommy was still living here, as far as I know."

"He didn't come to the hospital?"

"When he could. He had started working two jobs to help with the expenses. And he had really irregular hours. He was trying to get in as many as they'd let him work at both places. I never knew where he was or when he was going to be home. I'd call, but a lot of times he wouldn't pick up. He was grabbing sleep when he could. I was always afraid I was going to wake him up, so I never let it ring for long."

"Wake who up?" Laurie asked.

Drew turned and found her standing beside the table. Her eyes were on the copies of the clippings. Despite the fact that there wasn't any danger of her being able to read them, he began to gather those up and stack them into a neat pile. As soon as he had, Maggie set one of the bowls of soup in front of the place beside Drew's, near the chair where Laurie was standing.

She took the papers he was holding before she said to her daughter, "It's still hot. Be careful."

Laurie climbed into the chair as Maggie turned back to the stove. When she returned, Maggie no longer had the papers. She put a bowl of soup in front of Drew and the other at the place across from his, in front of the chair she took.

"I'll say the blessing," Laurie announced importantly. "Bow your heads."

Drew's eyes met Maggie's. She held them a moment before she lowered her head, closing her eyes. Laurie started praying before Drew had time to follow suit. He couldn't remember the last time he had said grace over a meal. Or had listened to anyone else say it, for that matter.

"Amen," Maggie repeated when the little girl finished. She picked up the paper towel beside her plate and put it in her lap. Laurie stuffed a corner of hers into the neck of her T-shirt.

"Wake who up?" she asked again.

"Nobody. We were talking about something that happened a long time ago," Maggie said. She spooned up a bite of soup, and as she raised it to her mouth, her eyes met Drew's again.

"You were talking about my daddy," Laurie said. "I heard you say his name. I heard you say Tommy."

They both turned to look at the little girl, but she was carefully lifting a spoonful of soup close enough to her pursed lips to blow on it. Maggie's mouth tightened briefly before her eyes came back to Drew's. She shook her head slightly.

Topic forbidden. Which was okay with him. He wanted to read the clippings again and think about everything that had been said at the trial. He'd had two years to remember the testimony, but he had concentrated on Tommy Cannon's. He had believed that getting Cannon to recant would be the key to clearing his name.

After all, that testimony was what had put him behind bars. That's what he had been planning to attack. He still was, only now he was going to have to go about it from a different angle. And he didn't have much to go on. Or much time to get it done.

DREW HAD SPENT most of the long afternoon lying on Maggie's bed. He had lain there, with the drapes pulled and his eyes closed, reliving the few days of his trial in his head. Listening again to the testimony.

He had been surprised at the speed of everything. From his arrest to his conviction had taken less than two months. However, this was a small rural county with a very low population density. It would have had a less crowded criminal court docket than most of the rest of the country. And despite his lawyer's efforts, the trial itself had lasted less than three days. Given Cannon's eyewitness account, the jury had deliberated less than thirty minutes. Slam-bam-thank-you-ma'am justice, and the cell doors had closed behind him for the next thirty years.

During those two months, Drew had written to several of the agents he'd worked with. A couple of those letters had come back marked Address Unknown. He had expected that, given what the agency had been doing to the members of External Security Team. The others had simply gone unanswered, so that Drew had never been sure they had reached their intended recipients.

Since he had truly believed that the agency must have had a hand in framing him, he didn't try to go through official channels to seek help. After all, as far as the CIA was concerned, Drew Evans was dead. They had deliberately and permanently cut all ties with the man he had once been.

And even if he had wanted to appeal to them, there wasn't anyone there to listen to or to respond to his plea for help. Griff Cabot, the man Drew had worked for for more than ten years, had been killed in a terrorist attack. The men Cabot had trained were scattered, their identities destroyed, just as Drew's had been. By the agency's design, there was no way to find them, even if he hadn't been operating out of the Cooper County jail at the time.

''I've been thinking,'' Maggie said.

She was standing in the doorway to the hall when he opened his eyes. Only then did he realize how late it was.

It was almost twilight, and with the curtains pulled, the room was heavily shadowed. "About what?" he asked.

He propped up on his elbow to look at her, but the resultant discomfort made him push the pillows into a pile behind his shoulders instead. He leaned against them gratefully. His eyes, their focus hidden by the darkness, examined Maggie's body, highlighted from behind by the light coming from the kitchen.

"Why Brundridge? Did they pick him at random?"

"Maybe he was just in the wrong place—"

"At the wrong time," she finished for him. "Except that's what I was trying to tell you. He wouldn't have been in that place. So his murder wasn't random. It couldn't have been."

"Maggie—"

"No, listen. I've really thought about this. I reread all that stuff, and it doesn't make sense. It doesn't add up."

Drew didn't know what to say. She had been convinced there was something strange about Brundridge being at the Wagon Wheel since she'd read that obituary. Drew was too cynical, however, to buy into what she was getting at.

"He was there, Maggie. There's no denying that."

"What would you do if you saw someone get shot?" she asked.

Drew laughed, the sound short and bitter, thinking about how many times in the course of his job he had seen that. "You're probably asking the wrong person that question."

"Okay, what would *I* do?" she said. "Someone like me."

"I don't know, Maggie," he said, holding on to his patience because he knew she was trying to help. Which was more than anyone else had, he reminded himself. "What would you do?"

"I'd try to help them. Feel for a pulse. Give mouth to mouth, maybe. I'd do *something*."

She probably would, Drew admitted.

"Most people would," she said, her voice full of conviction. "I think Tommy would have. I can't prove it, but...I think he would have.'' She stopped, as if that was supposed to mean something to him. As if he were supposed to understand.

"Maybe he did,'' Drew conceded. The "So what?'' was unspoken.

"There was no blood on his clothes. I never washed anything of Tommy's that had blood on it.''

Drew shook his head, moving it slowly back and forth and expelling a long sigh because this was so ridiculous. What the hell could it possibly matter that Cannon hadn't gotten any blood on his clothes? "Maybe he washed them himself,'' he said. "You said you were staying at the hospital.''

"He never washed,'' Maggie said. "Not once in all the time we were married. Tommy never put a piece of clothing in the washing machine in all the time he lived in this house. I doubt he even knew how to turn it on.''

She's trying to help, he reminded himself. "Then maybe he didn't get any blood on them. Maybe he was careful. People *are* careful about touching blood nowadays.''

Maggie nodded as if she had already thought of that. "The first bullet nicked an artery on its way out of his chest. That's what the coroner testified to. Wouldn't something like that bleed. I mean, wouldn't there be a lot of blood?''

She was too earnest not to at least give her the courtesy of hearing her out. In Drew's experience—and he'd had more of that than he cared to admit—either of those wounds would have produced a lot of blood. Or rather both would, especially as closely spaced as the testimony indicated they were time-wise.

"Maybe,'' he admitted.

"Then…I want you to come look at something,'' she said, an edge of excitement in her voice that up until now had been determined, but coolly logical. She turned, started through the doorway, and then looked back to make sure he was following.

More than anyone else has tried to do. Reluctantly, Drew levered his body off the bed and got to his feet. Every time he did that, the process was a little easier, but he still felt as if his recovery could be measured in millimeters.

As he walked down the hall, he wondered what Maggie wanted to show him. Surely not some bloody clothes she'd found. Something that had been hidden away for the last two years.

When he got to the kitchen, however, the clippings were spread out over the table again. Of course, Maggie had said she had read them all one more time. She picked two of the copied sheets up and held them out to him.

Drew looked into her eyes, his still narrowed as they made the adjustment to the strong, almost painful fluorescent glare. Maggie's were clear and wide and excited. Anticipating, just as her voice had been. She really believed she had found something that would help him, and in spite of his doubts, in spite of his natural cynicism, Drew was touched.

He looked down, as much to hide that surge of emotion as to examine whatever she had handed him. Two pictures, he realized, both from the newspaper. One was of a body, covered by a small tarp or a cloth of some kind. It was hard to tell exactly what it was from the photograph. The other was the traditional crime scene chalk outline marking where the body had lain. That one had obviously been taken the next morning, because there was a lot of light in the picture, while the first, the one of the shrouded body, was grainy and dark.

He hadn't seen the original press coverage of the crime, of course. He hadn't known anything about the murder at the Wagon Wheel until after the cops had picked him up, supposedly based on Cannon's description of his truck and part of his license plate number. Drew couldn't remember any pictures, certainly not these, being shown in court.

He looked at them for several minutes, even scanning the accompanying text, trying to find whatever it was that Maggie thought was significant. Finally he looked up again. Maggie's eyes were still on his face. "So?" he asked.

"So where's the blood?"

This was what she had been talking about in the bedroom. The lack of blood on Tommy's clothing. He looked back down at the pictures, and it hit him, just as it must have hit her.

There was no blood visible under or around the body. The cloth didn't cover enough of the ground around it to preclude the pool of blood that should have been there from being visible. And there was virtually none within the chalk outline.

Without looking up, he carried that clipping over to the center of the room, directly under the overhead light. The pavement on which the chalk marks had been made was mottled because of the composition of the asphalt, but there wasn't the big dark stain that either of those injuries should have left.

Even if the body had been moved, he thought. Even if someone had turned Charlie Brundridge over and tried to administer CPR. If you have a big exit hole in the chest with a nicked artery and a wound that blew out the back of his head, then there should have been bleeding from both.

"He wasn't killed there," he said, speaking the realization aloud as he made it. "Son of a bitch," he breathed, "they killed him somewhere else and brought his body to the Wagon Wheel."

Chapter Nine

Drew was again sitting at the kitchen table, this time making lists. Maybe they were worthless, but he was writing down everything he thought might bear checking out as he went back through the information about Charlie Brundridge. And he was reading all of it more carefully now than he had the first time.

He knew the fact that the man had been killed somewhere else and then brought to the Wagon Wheel might not turn out to be significant. However, it was possible this could be the key that had been missing since he had learned Tommy Cannon was dead. Maybe he had found another way to work back to whoever had been sent down here to set him up.

Someone had brought Brundridge's body to the Wagon Wheel. Maybe that someone had been Tommy Cannon, working alone. And if so, Drew supposed this would turn out to be another dead end. He knew from experience, however, that moving a dead body isn't all that easy for one person. He also knew from seeing him at the trial that Cannon wasn't a big man. He stood well under Drew's own six feet, with a slender, wiry build. Which argued that he had to have had help getting Brundridge from wherever he'd been killed to that parking lot where the cops had found his body. And if Drew could find the man or the men who had helped him—

"I think she's finally asleep," Maggie said.

Drew looked up in surprise. He had been so engrossed in what he was doing, it seemed as if Maggie and Laurie had been gone only a few minutes. Obviously, from the way Maggie had worded that, it had been much longer. And when he looked down, he realized the list he had been compiling now covered an entire sheet of the yellow legal pad Maggie had given him before she had gone to put her daughter to bed.

"Take a look at this," he invited, pushing the pad toward her. After all, Maggie knew far more about this county than he did. Maybe she could give him information about some of the notations he'd made.

She walked over to the table, and he watched as she read down the list, that small frown of concentration he'd noticed before forming between her brows. "Know anything about any of those?" he asked after he'd waited a decent interval.

"I know they were all mentioned in those articles. Some of them I had heard of before. Some I hadn't."

"Start with the ones you know."

"Donald Raster," she said.

"The coroner."

"And the owner of Raster Funeral Parlor."

"Are you saying the county coroner is a mortician?"

She nodded, her eyes still on the sheet, apparently unaware of the significance of that information. The coroner was not even a doctor, Drew thought, which probably wasn't too unusual for a rural area. And he was certainly not a forensics expert.

"Emmitt Grimes," Maggie said. "He graduated with Tommy. Two years ahead of me." Grimes was one of the deputies who had answered the call to the Wagon Wheel that night.

"How about the other deputy? Thompson. You know him?"

She shook her head. "I don't think so. When I first read

the clippings, I recognized Emmitt's name right away. And I tried to place the other guy. I tried to remember if I'd ever even heard his name, but...I don't think so.''

"Does that mean he's not from around here?''

"He may have lived outside the county when he was growing up. The county line is also the school district boundary. They've built a new high school on the other side of the county now, but back then, we all went to one school. Everybody who lived here attended Cooper County High School.''

"Go on," he prompted, and her eyes fell to the list again.

"And I've heard of this company," she said, putting her finger on an item on the list, "but for the life of me, I can't remember where or what it was about.''

There was only one company on the list. Edgemont Disposal. Which was where Charlie Brundridge had worked as a systems engineer. Whatever the hell that meant. Computers maybe? Drew wondered, knowing that was something else he'd need to check.

"Maybe in the papers? Radio?" he suggested.

"Maybe," she said. "There's an Edgemont community not too far from Jefferson. Maybe that's why it sounds familiar.''

"Is that where this company is located?''

"I don't know.''

"You have a phone book?''

She nodded, her eyes still on the notepad. Finally she looked up and met his. For a fraction of a second some memory of what had happened between them last night was in their depths. Then the long lashes lowered again, hiding whatever he'd seen.

Had she been remembering that kiss? Drew wondered. He had been. Almost all day, in spite of his probably unjustified excitement about having a new avenue to get at what had been done to him and to find whoever had done it.

He wondered if Maggie remembered he had been planning to leave tonight. And then he wondered if she still wanted him to. It seemed to him that what Maggie had discovered this afternoon changed everything. Last night he had given up hope. She had refused to help him, and his efforts to clear himself of the murder had seemed to be at a dead end. All that was left was to run. Now, however...

"You want me to look up their address?" she asked.

When he raised his head, he realized she was looking at him again. Whatever had made him think she might have been remembering last night, however, had been wiped from her eyes, which were clear and open. Nothing hidden.

"Please," he said.

She nodded, her eyes releasing his to fall to his list, and when she spoke again, it didn't seem to relate to the company they been discussing or to anything else he had written down.

"Why would Tommy say he saw you kill that man?"

"You told me why. Somebody paid him to say it."

"I know, but why you? If they were just looking for a scapegoat for Brundridge's murder, why didn't they just tell him to say he saw a man? That he couldn't identify him. Too dark. Too far away. Too something. Why have him lie about you?"

"Because they were *after* me," he said.

"Your enemies," she said, an edge of skepticism in the word.

"My enemies," he agreed, ignoring it.

"Why?"

A legitimate question, he supposed, since he'd never told her about his background. The habit of not talking about what the Team had done had been too deeply ingrained, despite all that had happened to him since he'd left the agency.

"I knew things they didn't want made public."

"Who is *they?* You said people you'd made angry when you worked for the government. Drug dealers? The Mafia?"

When he had told her that, Drew had still been operating within the parameters Griff had established. The External Security Team never talked about what they did. He had continued to abide by those rules, despite the fact that the man who had issued them was dead. And despite the fact that the agency he had worked for had set out to destroy him.

"The government," Drew said.

"*Our* government?" Maggie asked. "But…you said you worked for the government."

"I did. I spent ten years with the CIA."

"And they're the ones you think are after you?" Again, her skepticism was clear. "They're the ones who framed you? To keep you from talking about what you'd done for them?"

"Do you think they tell the truth about everything they do?"

"I don't know. I never much cared whether they did or not, but… It seems to me that if they didn't want to risk you talking about what you knew, they'd just kill you. I mean, if they're going to kill somebody, why not kill you?"

"I don't understand."

"You think somebody killed Brundridge and then brought his body to the Wagon Wheel to frame you. You suggested they might have killed Tommy to keep him from talking about that murder. Why didn't they just kill you instead?"

Another legitimate question. One that hadn't really crossed Drew's mind. He understood how they thought, that weird, convoluted mind-set that controlled all of them. All the bureaucrats in the security agencies.

If they killed Drew, someone might ask why. There might be a local cop who would really work to figure it out. And if that honest cop looked hard enough, he might find out something about Drew's past. Something the agency didn't want known. Something they thought they'd hidden by changing his identity.

If they made Drew Evans a murderer, however, then anything he ever said would be discredited. He could proclaim his innocence, he could reveal what he had done for the CIA, and no one would ever believe him.

And after all, the Charlie Brundridges of the world were much easier to kill than the Drew Evanses would have been. The agency knew that. They were the ones who had trained him and had then given him lots of experience in staying alive.

"If they discredit me, there's no danger of anyone ever believing anything I say. And I don't think they would have found it as easy to kill me as Brundridge. They knew that."

Maggie didn't say anything for a moment. "So they kill another man to get at you? Maybe two other men."

"It's complicated," Drew said evasively, thinking about the conflicting loyalties within the agency.

The CIA had wanted to shut down the External Security Team that Griff had worked so hard to protect. And, Drew believed, they had also wanted to rid themselves of Griff's men. That much had been clear as soon as Cabot was killed. Suddenly his agents were very much persona non grata. However, Drew had believed then that CIA just wanted to stand down the Team.

The External Security agents knew too much. They had done too much that fell outside the careful international boundaries congress had created for intelligence missions after the Kennedy assassination. Those legislated boundaries, however, hadn't changed the harsh reality of the modern world. There were still madmen in positions of power. Men who threatened the security of the United States. Who threatened the security of the world.

And taking care of them had been the job of the External Security Team. Like Griff Cabot, Drew had believed what they were doing was necessary. The CIA was afraid, however, that exactly what the Team's purpose had been might one day be revealed to the American people. So someone had decided it was not enough to destroy the unit that had carried out those missions. They wanted to destroy the agents themselves.

"Maybe what happened here didn't have anything to do with you," Maggie said. "Maybe you were just…a victim."

Drew had thought about that possibility, of course. After all, he had been living in Tennessee under his agency-created identity. According to it, he had no family. No ties. And no background. He would have been the perfect scape-goat.

And if he were anyone other than who he was, Drew might have considered the possibility that he had simply been chosen at random to bear the blame for Brundridge's murder. However, he had found the coincidence of someone picking a former member of a very specialized and clandestine black ops anti-terrorist unit to frame for a local murder was just a little too hard to swallow.

"You think whoever killed Charlie Brundridge just picked my name out of a hat, Maggie? They needed someone to take the fall for that murder, so they just happened on me?"

"Why not? I mean…it's possible, isn't it?"

"Not very likely, I'm afraid. And too big a coincidence for me to buy."

"*One* of you was chosen at random," she said. "Either they were after Brundridge and chose you to take the blame, or they were out to frame you and chose him as the means to do it. I think the fact that they moved his body makes it more likely that *he's* the one who wasn't a random victim."

It *was* logical. And it was enough to make Drew stop and think. Because she was right, of course. Unless the agency was after both of them, then one of them almost had to have been picked at random. And if they hadn't been targeting Brundridge, then why not just shoot anybody coming in or out of the Wagon Wheel? Why shoot someone somewhere else and bring his body there?

"Maybe they killed him where they could be sure there were no witnesses," he suggested.

"And then they brought him to the Wagon Wheel and unloaded his body at the very place where they wouldn't kill him for fear someone might see them? It would take less time to shoot somebody else than it would to drag Brundridge's body out of a truck and arrange that scene."

That was something else he hadn't considered, Drew realized. That truck that he'd supposedly driven away in, the one Cannon had described to the cops, the one whose taillights a couple of the bar patrons said they'd seen disappearing in the distance, must have been driven by whoever had helped unload the body. And even after all this time, there might still be enough blood in the bed of it to prove it had carried Brundridge's body. All it took these days was a microscopic dot hidden under some piece of equipment or a strip of metal.

The problem with that was only Cannon had claimed to see the truck clearly enough to describe it. And he hadn't been describing the truck that had really been there, of course. He had talked about Drew's pickup, that information no doubt provided to Tommy by whoever had set this all up.

"We have to find out who was driving the truck that brought the body to the Wagon Wheel," he said. "And in order to do that, we need to know where Brundridge really was when he was killed."

MAGGIE COULDN'T QUITE remember why she had agreed to this. And by the time her knock was finally answered, she was perfectly willing to back out. Danger signals were going off in her head like lights flashing at a railroad crossing.

Two days ago she had refused to ask any questions at all about the murder trial Tommy had testified in. Today she was out knocking on doors, prepared to ask the hardest questions she had ever asked in her life. And the only thing that had changed—

The door opened an inch or two and a child, who appeared to be only a little older than Laurie, peered out through the crack. At first Maggie wasn't sure whether the child was a boy or a girl. The red hair was close-cropped and the porcelain skin was literally covered with freckles, so close together they seemed to lie one on top of the other. Brown eyes examined Maggie's face without a trace of shyness.

Girl, Maggie decided as her own eyes moved down the child's thin figure. She was clad in a worn print dress that was at least two sizes too large. There was a smear of dirt on one of the freckled cheeks, and when the little girl dragged a grimy knuckle under her nose, it was obvious how that had gotten there.

"Is your mother home?" Maggie asked, resisting the urge to find a tissue and order her to blow.

"Mama," the child called without turning her head toward the room behind her. Her eyes never left Maggie's face. Apparently the Brundridge household didn't get that many visitors.

Maggie took a deep breath and tried not to look over her shoulder. All the way up here she had felt as if someone were watching her. Following her. Since the Brundridge house was almost as isolated as her own, however, and since she had nervously kept a lookout in her rearview mirror as she had driven those twisting mountain roads, she knew there was no chance of that.

She also knew that feeling wasn't based on reason. It was more of the cold-finger-along-the-spine kind of conviction. Cloak-and-dagger wasn't her thing, she acknowledged again, wondering why she was here. And then she answered her own question. She was here because if Drew Evans was ever going to clear himself, someone had to ask these questions. He couldn't, and that left only her.

Besides her growing attraction, an emotion that she couldn't explain away, not even to herself, by blaming her loneliness, she felt as if she owed Drew something. She was more than willing to pay that debt as long as she could do it without endangering Laurie. And like yesterday, when she had looked up those articles in the library, she couldn't see how this visit could hurt her daughter. No one would ever know she had been here.

The door suddenly opened a little wider, and Maggie's eyes lifted from the brown ones of the child to nearly identical ones belonging to the mother. There was no doubt that she was. The freckles were the same, spread with an equally generous hand across big, rawboned features. Her hair was threaded with gray, but its hue retained enough copper to also claim that maternity.

"What is it?" she said. There was nothing of the much-vaunted Southern hospitality in her tone.

"Mrs. Brundridge?"

The brown eyes considered Maggie warily, before the woman nodded. "I told you people on the phone I don't have that money. I'll get it to you. I always pay my bills. There wasn't no call for anyone to come up here dunning me in front of my children."

"I'm not here about a bill, Mrs. Brundridge. I'd like to talk to you," Maggie said.

"What about?" The wariness had increased.

"About your husband's murder."

The black pupils widened slightly, and then the eyes around them grew cold. "I got nothing to say about that," Charlie Brundridge's widow said.

The door had already started to close when Maggie stopped it. "I know he wasn't at the Wagon Wheel that night. I know your husband wouldn't have gone to that place."

Slowly the gap widened again. The brown eyes considered her with the same intensity her daughter's had displayed.

"May I come in?" Maggie asked, pressing her advantage. She was still surprised, however, when the door swung inward, inviting her inside.

"I TOLD THE SHERIFF," Nell Brundridge said emphatically. "They didn't listen to me, but I told them again and again that Charlie would never have gone to a place like that. Not unless he was called to give his Christian witness to somebody there."

"Do you think he was? That night, I mean."

"I *know* he wasn't. I know exactly where Charlie was that night. Just where he told me he'd be when he left here."

Maggie fought the surge of vindication, concentrating on listening instead. "Where was that, Mrs. Brundridge?"

"He was meeting with somebody at our church," Nell said, inclining her head at the same time her brow arched. As if to say, "Now wasn't that worth waiting for?"

"Do you know who he was meeting?" Maggie asked carefully, holding her breath as she waited for the answer.

Nell Brundridge shook her head, regretfully, Maggie thought. "I've tried to figure that out. Spent nearly two years trying to remember anything Charlie might have said that would give me a clue, but truth be told, he was mighty close-mouthed about that meeting. And he wasn't a man who liked to keep his mouth shut."

"What did he like to talk about?" Maggie asked, not really sure what else to ask. Drew would probably have known exactly how to draw information out of Brundridge's widow, but Maggie found herself at a loss.

"The Lord mostly," Nell said. "His tomatoes. His kids. The state of the country. The state of the world. You name it, Charlie would talk about it."

"Was he telling somebody about the Lord that night? Counseling somebody, you think?"

"If he was, he wouldn't have told me. Not the person's name, I mean. Whatever the sin, it was between the sinner and the Lord. Charlie always said he just helped run interference for the Almighty."

Maggie answered the remembering smile, and more of the wariness seeped out of the brown eyes.

"You want some tea?" Nell Brundridge asked unexpectedly.

Maggie didn't, but to refuse would seem rude. "Ice" tea was a summer staple. Drinking a glass with a guest was ritual, and well aware of that, Maggie nodded.

"Come on into the kitchen," Nell invited.

The kitchen was at least ten degrees hotter than the small front room had been. An older girl, her hair more brown than copper, was canning tomatoes on a gas stove. From the jars standing on the counter, all neatly identified with paper labels plastered on the side, she had been at the task for several hours. The sweat trickled down the teenager's throat and gathered in a semicircle under the armholes of her cotton dress.

"My daughter Geraldine," Nell said.

"Hi," Maggie said.

The girl turned her head, acknowledging her greeting with a shy smile.

"Go fix us some tea," Nell ordered, taking over the ladle.

She made quick work of the remaining tomatoes, spooning them into the sterile jars without losing a drop down the side. Maggie wondered how many quarts of tomatoes and beans and peas Nell Brundridge had put up in her lifetime.

When she finished, Nell dried her hands on the towel hanging across the handle of the oven door. She walked over to the square wooden table in the center of the room and indicated with her eyes that Maggie should sit opposite her. As soon as she had, Geraldine set a glass of iced tea in front of her, the sides moist from condensation.

Maggie waited until the girl had walked back over to the

stove before she asked, her voice carefully lowered, "Mrs. Brundridge, do you have any idea why someone would kill your husband and then take his body over to the Wagon Wheel?"

Nell's gaze quickly examined the back of her daughter's head, which was centered by a pale blue scrunchie securing a loosely gathered ponytail. When Nell turned back, her eyes examined Maggie's face a moment before she spoke.

"To throw suspicion on somebody else. On somebody who didn't do the killing. And it must have worked, since they got away with saying Charlie was at that beer joint that night."

"I think it did work, but only because they bought themselves a witness who would testify in court that he saw that man kill your husband."

Maggie had already told Nell about her connection to Tommy when she had introduced herself. It had been a spur of the moment decision, based on her reading of the woman now sitting across the table from her and also because she thought Mrs. Brundridge might remember Tommy's name and make the connection on her own. Maggie was afraid that not confessing her very personal interest in this case might foster distrust. She had softened the confession a little by trying to explain why Tommy had done what he had done. She didn't know if it could be explained, but she had seen no condemnation in the brown eyes.

"Your man," Nell said, nodding. "But he didn't see Charlie. Not there, he didn't. Not on a Sunday morning."

"What time did you expect your husband home that night?"

"When I saw him. A man who loved to talk like that couldn't be expected at any certain time, but he would have been home before the Sabbath."

"And you really have no idea who he was meeting?"

Nell shook her head. "He took the church keys off that

ring over there, and he said, 'Be back in a little while, old woman.' Those were the last words he ever said to me.''

It was obvious that she had told the story before. It was her last memory of her husband, and she had never forgotten any of the details. Maggie only wished there were more of them.

''Who called you to tell you that he was…?''

''Who called to tell me Charlie was dead?'' Nell repeated, not avoiding the word Maggie couldn't bring herself to say. ''Sheriff Dalton come up here hisself. I always appreciated that.''

Maggie nodded, thinking about Rafe Dalton in the role of compassionate news bearer. His name hadn't been mentioned in the articles she's copied, not until later on in the investigation.

Maggie would have figured that one of the two deputies who had been called to the Wagon Wheel would have notified Mrs. Brundridge, but maybe Dalton was just going out of his way to do a nice thing. The more she had thought about the night someone had turned the handle on her own back door, the more Maggie had come to believe it must have been the sheriff, checking that everything was all right, just as he'd promised he would.

''And you have no idea who your husband was meeting or what the meeting was about?'' Maggie asked again.

Nell didn't say anything for a long time, her eyes studying Maggie's face. ''I think it was about something they were trying to do out at Edgemont.''

The company Brundridge worked for, Maggie remembered. Edgemont Disposal.

''Charlie had been upset about it,'' Nell went on. ''I heard him talking to somebody on the phone a couple of days before. When he knew I was listening, he clammed up.''

''Why wouldn't he want you to hear?'' Maggie asked.

''I think he was afraid,'' Nell said. ''I think someone or

something had scared Charlie. Made him afraid to talk. And *not* talking wouldn't have been easy for him, I'll tell you.''

"Did you tell the sheriff about that phone call?"

"I told him Charlie wouldn't have been at the Wagon Wheel. I told him he'd gone to meet somebody at the church and that I thought that meeting had to do with what was going on at Edgemont. He wrote all that down in his notebook.''

None of that had been in the papers, however. And from what Drew had told her, Maggie didn't think it had come out at the trial, either. "Did they ask you to testify about that conversation at the trial, Nell?"

"They never asked me nothing else. Nobody ever talked to me about that night except Sheriff Dalton. And I never told anybody else what I'm telling you. I was always afraid that whoever killed Charlie…''

The brown eyes held on Maggie's for a long heartbeat and then they moved, as if nervous about that prolonged scrutiny, to the jars standing on the stove.

"Take some tomatoes home with you. They'll make good soup come winter,'' Nell Brundridge offered. When she looked back at Maggie, her lips were tight and her eyes were suspiciously moist.

"I'm so sorry my husband lied about what happened that night. That he lied about Charlie. I know you probably can't understand—''

"I got kids,'' Nell interrupted. "I know how you feel about your own flesh and blood. And if it hadn't been your husband, then it would have been somebody else. Whatever Charlie was worried about, they didn't want anybody else to discover it. Maybe they knew how much that man liked to talk,'' she said, her smile a bit tremulous. "It's been awfully quiet around here with Charlie gone. That's what I hate the most. The awful quietness.''

Maggie nodded, reaching out to put her own hand over

the work-roughened ones that lay clasped together on top of the scarred table. And when she walked back out to her pickup, she was carrying two quarts of Nell Brundridge's canned tomatoes.

Chapter Ten

Maggie almost made it home. She probably would have if she had been able to resist the temptation to drive out to Edgemont Disposal. She had looked up the address for Drew last night, and as she'd copied it out of the phone book onto his yellow pad, she had been picturing the location in her mind.

And she found it easily enough. Of course, growing up here meant she was familiar with almost all the landmarks and the small communities that were scattered through the mountains.

There was a guard at the gate of the facility, talking through the open window of his shed to someone sitting inside a pickup parked in front of it. Maggie hadn't turned into the short drive that led to the site. She had stayed on the main road, driving slowly by the entrance.

She couldn't see much of the landfill itself because of the thickness of the summer foliage along the fence that separated it from the highway. Maybe in winter what she imagined to be mountains of garbage might be visible from the road. Now, however, the place looked as green and lushly inviting as did the rest of the landscape. It was situated in a narrow valley that ran between two rugged ridges, neither of which was occupied.

She had to go more than half a mile past the entrance to

the landfill before she found a place to turn around and re-trace her route. The guard had watched her drive by this time, no convenient customer to distract him. Maggie hadn't slowed, but there was very little traffic on the road. Most of the way home she worried about whether the guard had no-ticed her. And she admitted that attempting to check out Edgemont Disposal on her own probably hadn't been the smartest move she'd ever made.

After a while, however, she managed to put that concern out of her mind. She was eager to get back to the cabin and share what she had learned with Drew. Almost as eager to see how he and Laurie had gotten along while she'd been gone. She would never have admitted to him that she had doubts about his ability as a baby-sitter, but her lips tilted at the thought of him and Laurie playing together.

It was then she saw the flashing lights behind her. Bar lights, Drew had called them. Indecisive about what she should do, Maggie drove on a mile or so after she became aware of the sheriff's car following her. Her eyes moved back and forth between it and the twisting road ahead. Then whoever was driving the vehicle tapped the siren, and it would have been difficult to pretend she hadn't heard it.

Maggie couldn't see the driver clearly enough to identify him, but she could tell there was only one person in the patrol car. Long before she pulled the pickup off the shoul-der of the road and rolled down her window, she knew in her heart who would crawl out of the cruiser that had stopped right behind her.

She watched in the mirror as Rafe Dalton crossed the distance between the two cars. He put both hands over the bottom of her opened window, leaning down and into it a little, until they were eye-to-eye.

"Was I speeding?" she asked.

His smile widened, green eyes holding hers. "I get a lot of that," he said. "Guess I can blame it on the lights and the uniform. And no, you weren't speeding, Maggie. I just thought I'd say hello.''

''You scared me,'' she said. ''You know I don't have the money to pay a ticket.''

Maybe that would explain the uneasiness she was afraid her face or her voice would reveal. She wasn't sure why she was so nervous. Because she had felt the guard's eyes following her car as she drove by the entrance to Edgemont?

She shouldn't have gone there. ''Getting too big for your britches,'' her grandmother would have said. Too full of herself, maybe, after her success with Nell Brundridge.

''I'd never give you a ticket, Maggie,'' Rafe said. ''Not even if you *were* speeding. You ought to know that.''

''That's good,'' she said. Her smile felt stiff.

''Where you been?'' Rafe asked.

Maggie hesitated too long before she answered, and she knew she had. She couldn't decide, however, whether to lie to him. If someone had told Rafe Dalton they'd seen her at either place she had visited today, and then she lied to him about being there, that would make him suspicious. After all, she had no legitimate reason to be driving by Edgemont Disposal or to be visiting Nell Brundridge, no matter what Drew had said about her rights as Tommy's widow.

The knowledge that she had done those things might lead the sheriff to wonder, just as she had feared from the beginning, why she was asking questions about Charlie Brundridge's murder at this late date. Or they could make him believe she knew something about Drew. About Martin Holcomb, she amended.

''I had to get some things,'' she said finally.

''Shopping?''

His gaze focused on the seat beside her. There was nothing there except two quarts of Nell Brundridge's tomatoes, with Geraldine's neatly lettered labels plastered on their sides. Maggie thought the writing would be too small for Rafe to read, but it must be obvious she hadn't been doing much shopping. Rafe's eyes then examined the empty bed of the truck through the glass of the back window before they came back to meet hers.

Stupid, she told herself, feeling her heart begin to race. She was probably blushing, and with her skin, he'd be able to see that telltale flush. More grounds for suspicion.

"You headed home?" he asked.

She nodded, her eyes releasing his to focus on her hands, which had a death grip on the wheel. She forced them to relax.

"You think any about what I said?"

She turned back to face him, uncertain how to respond.

"About me tossing my hat into the ring?" he explained.

"I remember," she said.

"Still not ready to entertain gentlemen callers?" he asked, his voice softly teasing.

There was nothing in his eyes except that same teasing, but the fact that Maggie was already "entertaining a gentleman" seemed too much of a coincidence.

"Not yet," she said.

"You be sure and let me know when you are. You hear me, Maggie?" he said. The amusement in his eyes had been replaced by a sexual intensity, which made her almost as uneasy as his earlier question about where she had been.

"I will," she promised.

"Okay," he said. He straightened up out of her window, patting the bottom of it with his palms a couple of times as if in dismissal or benediction. "That's all I'm asking. I'll be looking forward to hearing from you."

She turned toward the front, her right hand reaching automatically for the gearshift. Rafe stepped back, giving her room to maneuver out onto the narrow road. Before she drove off, however, she looked back at him and asked, "Did you send somebody up to check on my place the other night?"

His face revealed nothing except a brief confusion. "A deputy, you mean? Patrol?"

"Anybody," Maggie said.

Dalton's mouth pursed as if puzzled, and then he shook his head. "I can if you want me to," he offered. "I thought you didn't."

"I don't," she said quickly. "I just…I thought I heard a car up there a couple of nights ago. It made me a little skittish. I guess I was hoping it was you."

There was a small silence, and that unfortunate choice of words seem to echo through it.

"That *almost* sounded like an invitation, Maggie."

Again, there was a sexual edge to the comment. And once more she was at a loss as to how to reply.

"Have they caught that guy?" she asked instead. "The convict?"

"Holcomb? Not that I'm aware of. But I don't think he's anywhere around here, if that's what's worrying you. I don't think he ever was, if you want to know the truth. I think somebody's imagination got the better of them."

"That's good to hear."

"You and Laurie sleep tight. And don't you worry. No-body's gonna bother you up there. I promise you that."

She nodded again, and this time she put the car in gear, pulling carefully out onto the road. Her hands didn't start to shake until she had driven far enough that she could no longer see the patrol car in her rearview mirror. And even though she kept looking behind her the rest of the way home, it didn't show up there again.

"WHEN'S MAMA GONNA be home?" Laurie asked for the fourth or fifth time.

Since Drew had been wondering the same thing for the last hour or so, he wasn't annoyed by the childish repetition. Laurie's questions did add to the anxiety he'd felt since Maggie had driven away, however. He should never have let her go, he thought. He couldn't do this any longer. He couldn't use Maggie, even if she were willing to let him.

Just by being here, he was putting her and Laurie into danger. And he wasn't going to do that any longer, he had decided. When Maggie got back, he'd repack that pillowcase, sticking the articles she'd copied into it, and then, as soon as it was dark, he'd head out on his own. Tommy Cannon was dead and Drew was fairly mobile again. There was no reason for him to stay here. At least not any that had a bearing on proving his innocence.

"Pretty soon," he said aloud, trying to keep the anxiety out of his voice. "How about another cookie?"

He wasn't sure what the legal limit on cookies before dinner might be, but he had been relieved when he'd found them in a canister on the counter. He had been doling them out periodically ever since. They and the coloring books Maggie had laid out before she'd left had kept Laurie occupied. Actually, Laurie had seemed perfectly content with the situation until Drew had started checking the windows every few minutes.

But there was no way it should have taken Maggie this long to do what she'd planned. Not even if Brundridge's widow had been eager to talk to a stranger about her husband's death. And knowing mountain people as he did, Drew didn't believe that would be the case.

"You want to color some with me?" Laurie asked.

"Looks like you're doing pretty well on your own."

She really was, he thought, as he walked over to the table to look down on the purple kitten she was putting the finishing touches to. Other than its color, the picture was neat, most of the marks remaining within the lines. Staying in the lines a lot better than he had with his own life, Drew acknowledged.

"I hear a car coming," Laurie announced without looking up from the tail of the cat she was working on.

"That's probably your mom," Drew said, starting toward

the windows at the front of the house. Luckily, he was looking through them as he walked, eager for that first glimpse of the beat-up old pickup. And as soon as the car and its distinctive bar of lights topped the rise, he knew it wasn't Maggie. Apparently the county sheriff had come courting again.

Drew ran back to the kitchen, feeling each jolting step in the half-healed wound on his chest. The doors were all locked, he assured himself. He had even checked them a couple of times after Maggie left. Which meant Dalton wouldn't be coming into the house, not unless he broke in. Drew wouldn't put it past the guy to take a look in through Maggie's windows, however.

"Come on," he said to Laurie.

She looked up from her picture, but she didn't move. Drew didn't have time to talk her into cooperating. He lifted her out of the chair by wrapping one arm around her body, beneath her armpits. He held her against his chest as he began to back toward the hallway. He took one last look toward the front of the house. Two men were getting out of the patrol car. From this distance, he couldn't identify either of them, but they were definitely wearing uniforms.

"Where we going?" Laurie asked.

Damn good question, Drew thought, examining his options and discarding almost all of them. "We're going to play hide-and-seek," he said finally, stepping backward into the hallway.

As he did, he took a final survey of the kitchen, checking for any telltale evidence that he'd been here. Laurie's crayons and coloring books were scattered over the table, along with his empty coffee mug. There was nothing there that Maggie couldn't have left exactly where it was when she had taken her daughter and gone out to run an errand.

"You ever play hide-and-seek, Laurie?" Drew whispered, working on keeping his voice calm and reassuring as he hurried with her down the hall toward Maggie's bedroom.

"Uh-huh," she said.

"Then you know the most important part of the game is to keep very quiet. You can't even whisper. You understand?"

"Are we hiding from my mama?"

"Shh," he cautioned, opening the closet door in Maggie's room. He pulled aside the hanging clothes with one hand and bent to put the little girl down, the movement sending an agonizing pull through the damaged muscles of his chest. He ignored the pain, stooping on his haunches in front of her. He put his hands on Laurie's shoulders, turning her so that she was looking at him.

"Not a sound. Promise me, Laurie."

The little girl nodded, putting one finger over her lips.

"I want you to sit in this corner and be so quiet nobody can find you. And if you do, you'll win the game. Just...don't move. Don't talk. Don't do anything. Be quiet as a mouse. And your mama will come get you as soon as she gets home." He smiled at her, but he knew from her eyes she wasn't buying any of this.

"I want my mama," she said, her voice very soft. Drew wondered if that quietness portended the beginning of tears and then panicked screams, neither of which he could afford.

"Your mama will come get you. You just have to be quiet until she does. Can you do that for your mama, Laurie?"

A pounding sounded on the door at the front of the house. Drew resisted the urge just to shut the closet and lock the little girl inside. He wanted her protected. He also wanted the comforting feel of the revolver that was resting in his pocket in the palm of his hand.

"You hide, too," Laurie said. "You wait for mama in here with me."

"I can't, sweetheart," Drew whispered.

"Don't leave me," she begged, tears beginning to well in the blue eyes.

The last thing Drew wanted to do was to put Laurie in

the path of a bullet meant for him. The closet had been the safest place he could think of to hide her. He had planned to turn the key, and then whatever happened, at least Laurie wouldn't be running around the house while it was going on.

Of course, it was always possible that when Maggie didn't answer the front door, the sheriff and his deputy would go away. The pickup was gone, so they should assume she was out running errands and that she had Laurie with her. They *should* assume that, he told himself again.

The knock sounded once more. "Miz Cannon?" someone called. Drew didn't recognize the voice, but he hadn't heard Dalton's all that clearly that day. He couldn't say if this was the same one.

"I'm scared," Laurie said, clinging to his neck.

"There's nothing to be afraid of." Drew wished he believed that. "I'll be right here until your mama gets home."

"You hide, too," Laurie said again. "You come hide in here with me. Please don't leave me."

All his last chance had come down to, Drew thought bitterly. Being the bad guy. Hiding from every knock on the door. Still a fugitive. As long as he stayed here, he would be doing that. And he would be putting Laurie and Maggie in danger.

The front door opened. The sound was distinct, even from this distance. Without another word, Drew picked Laurie up again and stepped inside the closet with her in his arms, pulling the door closed behind them with the same motion.

"I HAD A FEW ERRANDS to run," Maggie said. "I haven't been gone more than a couple of hours or so. There certainly wasn't anybody up here when I left."

"You understand we have to check these reports out, Miz Cannon. It's our job."

The deputies had been standing on the porch, knocking on her door, when she'd pulled into the yard. A cold sickness had settled in her stomach when she had seen the uniforms. It had gotten worse when she realized they had already unholstered their guns.

That's what had driven her out of the pickup to confront them, despite her shaking knees. They'd explained all about the anonymous tip they'd received. Somebody suspicious had been lurking around her property, they said, and with the recent escape, they were obligated to check out all such information.

Maggie had known they were lying, almost from the first word. There was no one up here on her mountain to see anyone "suspicious" hanging around. Besides, there was something very telling about the way their eyes evaded contact with hers.

She didn't want to let them into the house, and she had delayed doing it as long as she could. She supposed she could have made them go back and get a search warrant, but she had judged from their attitude that they weren't going to leave until they'd had their look around. She could only hope that she had kept them out long enough for Drew to get out the back and be halfway up her mountain.

Her main concern now was Laurie, and as she led them across the living room and into the kitchen, her eyes went first to the crayons and the coloring books on the kitchen table. She had to fight her every instinct not to look at the back door.

"Your daughter didn't go with you, Miz Cannon?"

"She's playing at a neighbor's house," Maggie lied.

The one who had asked nodded, his eyes examining the room. "And you haven't seen anybody wandering around outside your place? Not just today, but anytime in the last week or so."

"No, I haven't," Maggie said.

The other deputy walked over to the window above the sink, the one that looked out on her garden and the woods behind it. Her own gaze followed his across the backyard, but there was nothing out there. She took a small, careful breath in relief.

Drew was a professional, she told herself. He said he had spent ten years with the CIA. He wasn't going to let himself be caught like a rat in a trap. He was gone, hiding somewhere in those thick woods. The only question in her mind was whether he had taken Laurie with him. And if not, where her daughter was.

"You remember me, Maggie?" the deputy who had been examining the yard through the window asked.

She pulled her eyes away from the edge of the forest to consider his features. When she had, she realized he hadn't really changed all that much. His neck and his face were fuller than they had been in high school, matching the belly that was beginning to hang over his utility belt, and his hairline had already started to recede. His eyes were exactly the same, however. Small and dark, almost porcine.

"Emmitt Grimes," she said softly, her chest tightening.

"I was really sorry to hear about Tommy. He was a good friend."

Maggie nodded, afraid to trust her voice.

"You don't mind if we take a look around," he said. It wasn't really a question. He walked over to the door and put his hand on the knob. "Check out the rest of the house," Grimes ordered the other deputy. "Just to be on the safe side," he said reassuringly, those words addressed to Maggie.

She was mentally reviewing the three remaining rooms of the cabin as she had left them this morning. There should be nothing in the bathroom that would make them suspicious—nothing she could remember, anyway. However, she had left that tube of antibiotic salve on the bedside table in her bedroom, along with a couple of unopened packages of gauze squares. And her nightgown was stuffed under a pillow in Laurie's bedroom. If they were smart enough to put two and two together…

"Why didn't Sheriff Dalton know about this anonymous tip you got?" Maggie asked, scrambling for something that might keep them out of those bedrooms.

"Ma'am?" the other deputy asked, looking puzzled.

"I just saw the sheriff not fifteen minutes ago. On my way home. He didn't mention anything about somebody calling in information about a stranger on my land. I'm just wondering why he didn't know about it."

"Maybe it came in after he'd left the station," Grimes said. "I'm not really sure about the timing on that." His eyes moved to meet his partner's. At least the other deputy hadn't left the kitchen yet to take that look around the rest of the house.

"He told me to call him if anything happened," Maggie said.

There was a small silence. Then Grimes's hand released the doorknob. "Like what?" he asked.

"He thought one of those escaped convicts might show up out here," Maggie said, praying she wasn't making a mistake by introducing Drew into this conversation.

Grimes cocked his head. "Is that a fact?"

"Maybe we should call Rafe and let him know what you heard," Maggie said. "He'll probably want to come out here himself. Maybe even notify the state that some stranger was seen on my property." She walked across to the counter toward the phone.

"I don't think that'll be necessary," Emmitt Grimes said. "We'll take a look around, and if we see anything suspicious, we'll let him know. We have to file a report on what we find, anyway."

Maggie looked at the phone, trying to decide how far she could push this. Trying to weigh whether it would be better to direct their interest outside, where they might find some evidence of Drew's flight, or to let them search the house, where they were almost certain to see things that would sound an alarm.

When she didn't reach for the phone, Grimes's eyes left hers to return to his partner. He tilted his head toward the hallway, a silent repetition of his original order.

"I think somebody may have been out back a couple of nights ago," Maggie said. Her words stopped the partner and brought Grimes's attention back to her in a hurry.

"You just told us you hadn't seen anybody. Which is it, Maggie? Somebody been hanging around or not?"

"I thought it was Sheriff Dalton," she said.

"Why would Rafe be out here in the middle of the night?"

She hadn't said "in the middle of the night," and she couldn't decide if the fact that he had was significant or just a natural assumption on Emmitt's part. "He told me he'd have the patrol units check things out up here periodically. I thought that's what he was doing."

"When did he tell you that?"

"When he came up here to tell me about Holcomb."

Something shifted in Emmitt Grimes's eyes. They held hers a long minute before they again moved to his partner's.

The other deputy said, "The sheriff tell you Holcomb might show up here?"

"He thought it was a possibility."

"Because Tommy testified against him?"

Dalton hadn't mentioned that. Maggie hadn't known it until Drew had told her. Apparently everyone in Cooper County had known what was going on, but no one had thought to warn her that a convicted murderer might come visiting her and her daughter.

"It makes sense that he would, doesn't it?" she asked.

"Looking for revenge, you mean?"

Because he was framed for a murder he didn't commit. And because Tommy Cannon had been in on the framing.

"That's a possibility," she said.

"Maybe," Emmitt Grimes said, and Maggie could read nothing from the single word.

"So I'd like you all to take a look around outside," she said. "There may be some tracks or something."

"Did you look, Maggie?"

"Of course," she said. "But…y'all would know more about what to look for than I do."

"Did you see this person, Miz Cannon?" the other deputy asked, but he didn't look at her. He was still looking at Grimes, a question in his eyes.

"No," she said, feeling the tension build in the room and not quite sure what she had started. "I thought I heard something. By the time I got out of bed and in here to the window…" She shrugged.

"Could have been nothing," Grimes suggested. "An animal or something."

"I know, but I thought as long as you're here…" She walked over to the back door and realized the night latch was still on. She felt a sharp sense of panic with that discovery. Drew couldn't have gone out this door. And if he hadn't…

Hoping they couldn't see how much her hand was trembling, she turned latch and then the knob and stepped out into the backyard. She held the door open, inviting them to join her. Again Grimes's eyes shifted to his partner, but they both followed her. Knees weak, Maggie tried not to let her relief show.

The two of them walked around the back of her place for a few minutes, eyes on the ground. Occasionally, Grimes would look up into the woods, but neither of them seemed inclined to investigate up there. Actually, they weren't doing much investigating here, Maggie realized after the farce they were enacting had continued for a few minutes.

"Maybe along the garden," she suggested. "Where the soil is softer. Maybe there'll be some tracks there."

On top of her words came squawks from the radio in their patrol car out front. They had left the windows down, and although the words weren't clear enough for Maggie to decipher, they must have meant something to the two deputies.

Again Grimes tilted his head, this time toward the patrol car. The other deputy walked around the side of the house and back to where they had parked. Maggie followed, her eyes on the ground along the edge of the garden as if she were looking for the evidence they obviously didn't care about finding.

When she had gone far enough that she could see the car and her pickup, she watched the deputy open the cruiser door and sit in the passenger seat. As he listened, Maggie could still hear the voice on the radio, the message was too garbled for Maggie to make heads or tails of it. She prayed the deputies were being called to another assignment. Something that would constitute enough of an emergency to get them off her property.

After a few minutes the deputy got out of the car and began walking back toward where she was standing. Only with his approach did she realize Grimes had moved up beside her.

"Got a call," the other deputy said, pitching his voice to cover the distance. "Rafe says to let this one go."

Maggie turned to look at Emmitt Grimes and found his eyes were already on her face. His lips inched upward a little at the corners, a tight, sarcastic little smile.

"Then I guess we'll be on our way, Maggie. You call us if you hear anything else you want us to check out."

"Thanks," she said, unable to believe that they were really going to leave, almost as unexpectedly as they had arrived.

Grimes nodded, and then he walked toward the patrol car. To reach it, he had to pass by Maggie's truck. Again sickness stirred in her gut at the thought of those two quart jars of home-canned tomatoes sitting on her front seat, with the word Brundridge neatly lettered below TOMATOES and the date.

Why had she taken them? she thought angrily. The image of Nell's work-worn hands lying on that scarred wooden table reminded her of the reason.

Of course, that didn't explain why she hadn't thrown them out of the pickup along one of the roads she'd driven to get back home. Instead, she had brought them back with her. She might as well have worn a placard saying, "I've been sticking my nose into something very dangerous."

Grimes seemed to hesitate as he approached the truck. He didn't do anything as obvious as open the door or look into the window. His steps did slow, however. Enough for him to read the labels? Maggie had no idea.

She didn't breathe until he had walked on by and crawled into the patrol car. The two deputies didn't say a word to each other and they didn't look at her again. They backed out around her truck and headed down the mountain. After a few seconds Maggie heard the wail of a siren. And she stood in the yard listening until it faded away into the distance.

Chapter Eleven

"Drew?"

He could hear Maggie's voice, but he resisted the urge to answer. Resisted the urge to reveal their hiding place until he could be sure she was out there alone and that those clowns weren't using her as bait.

"Laurie?"

There was a note of panic in that call, and Drew had to fight every instinct to open the door and assure her that they were all right.

"That's Mama," Laurie whispered, her mouth almost against his ear. "That's my mama."

"I know," Drew whispered back, squeezing her tighter against his chest.

He listened to Maggie's footsteps head down the hall to Laurie's room. And there was no doubt they were Maggie's footsteps. She was alone. There was no one else moving out there. On these old wooden floors Drew believed he would have been able to tell if there had been anyone else.

He reached out and found the knob, cautiously pushing open the closet door. He tried to set Laurie on her feet, but she refused to release her hold on his neck.

"You have to stay here, sweetheart," he whispered.

She didn't argue, but she didn't let him go, either. If anything, her grip seemed to tighten. Considering his own adrenaline rush, he supposed he couldn't blame the little girl for being afraid. He straightened and, still holding Laurie in his arms, eased soundlessly out of the closet.

As he crossed the room on tiptoe, he could hear Maggie moving in the other bedroom. And nothing else. There was not another sound in the cabin.

He was acting like a fool. They would never have been able to force Maggie to call out his name if they had still been here. No matter how she felt about him, she would never have put Laurie at risk by doing that.

"Maggie," he called softly.

The noise from the other bedroom ceased, and after a few seconds, Maggie appeared in its doorway, looking down the hall at him. He was holding the revolver in his left hand, and his crooked right arm supported Laurie's bottom. Her arms were still wrapped tightly around his neck.

He hadn't realized how frightened Maggie had been until her eyes filled with tears. She still didn't say anything, however. She just stood there looking down the hallway at the two of them.

"It's okay," he said. "We're both okay."

She nodded, a tear escaping to track down her cheek.

"Maggie?" he questioned, his voice very soft.

Her stillness and the tears were scaring him now. Maybe he had been wrong. Maybe the deputies—

"Mommy's crying," Laurie said.

"I think I did something really stupid," Maggie said.

Drew nodded, still studying her face. "Whatever it was—"

And finally Maggie moved. She ran down the hall, throwing her arms around both of them and burying her face against Laurie's legs. The little girl turned Drew's neck loose and wrapped her arms around Maggie's head. Laughing a little through her tears, Maggie lifted her face for her daughter's kiss and then she looked up into his eyes.

Without any conscious decision, Drew lowered his head

and placed his lips over hers. The kiss was gentle, prompted by relief and compassion for the terror he had put her through rather than by the heated passion that had arced between them two nights ago.

Her lips met his eagerly, answering every movement of his mouth. He could taste the salt of her tears, and he felt the shuddering breath she took before she finally pulled away from him to look back up into his eyes.

"I'm so sorry," she whispered.

"It's okay," he said again. "Whatever happened, it's okay. We'll deal with it."

She nodded again. Then she stepped back, reaching for Laurie. The child lunged into her arms and laid her head against her mother's shoulder, wrapping her legs around Maggie's waist.

"What did they want?" Drew asked.

"They said they got an anonymous tip that there was someone suspicious hanging around up here."

"You think someone could have seen me?"

Drew tried to imagine how that would be possible. He hadn't been out of the house since Maggie had shot him. If anyone had seen him while he'd been staking out the cabin, surely they wouldn't have waited this long to call the sheriff.

"I think they were lying. I think they just wanted an excuse to come up here and look around."

"Dalton?"

Maggie shook her head. Her hand had cupped the back of Laurie's head, soothing the little girl's hair, but her eyes, locked on his, were hard and cold.

"It was the other two. The ones who answered the call to the Wagon Wheel the night Brundridge was killed."

"Grimes and Thompson," Drew said, his voice flat.

The identification was almost anticlimatic. After all, if the deputies had been any good at their job, they would have realized, just as Maggie had, that Brundridge's body had been moved from wherever he had been killed to the roadhouse. They would have known as soon as they looked at it that the crime scene was staged.

Since they hadn't said that in court, it suggested one of two things. Either they weren't very much in the way of criminal investigators, which was always possible, or they had been in on whatever had been done from the beginning.

Given what Maggie had told him about their high school friendship, Grimes could even have been the link that had led from the murder to Tommy. Maybe Grimes had remembered he had an old friend who needed some quick cash. Maybe he even knew Cannon well enough to know that Tommy would do anything to get the money to save Laurie's life.

Remembering the feel of those soft arms around his own neck, Drew was even beginning to understand Cannon's willingness to lie about a man he didn't know. Even if he understood that lie would send an innocent man to prison.

"I think they saw me," Maggie said. "Someone saw me."

Drew's eyes narrowed, questioning. "Saw you where?"

"After I talked to Nell Brundridge, I… Oh, God, Drew, I can't believe how stupid I was."

He waited, knowing that whatever she had done, it probably wouldn't have made that much difference. The longer he stayed, the more chance there was that someone would come looking for him at Maggie's. He had expected the law to be poking around up here from the first day he'd approached the cabin.

"I drove by Edgemont. Nell Brundridge told me that Charlie was upset about something that was going on out there. She overheard part of a phone conversation. And then that night, the night he was killed, he had gone to meet someone. Not at the Wagon Wheel, but at their church."

"What's that got to do with Edgemont?" Drew asked, not quite following the gist of whatever Maggie was trying to tell him.

"I don't know. Maybe nothing. Or maybe everything. Maybe Edgemont's the key to everything."

"Is that what you're worried about? That you drove by the waste disposal plant?"

"I don't think the guard noticed me the first time. At least I didn't think he had. Then when I drove back by…I think he might have been watching me."

She made that confession as if she expected him to be angry. And if he were angry about anything, it was that she was taking chances on his behalf. Maybe he had wanted her to at the beginning, but he didn't want that now. Drew mentally reiterated what he had already decided. He had to leave. Just get out and quit putting Maggie at risk.

"And then on the way home, Dalton stopped me," she added.

"Dalton?" Drew said in surprise. If Dalton had already talked to Maggie, then why send his goons up here to search the place? "And you think that was because the guard saw you?"

"I don't know," she said. "I did at first, but… He didn't talk about that. Or about you."

She didn't say what he had talked about, but Drew could guess, based on the previous conversation he'd overheard.

"Then when I got home," Maggie continued, "they were already here. The deputies. I had to let them in, but I thought you'd probably have already gotten out the back. I just didn't know what you had done about—"

She stopped, her eyes falling to the pale blond head that rested on her shoulder before they lifted to Drew's again.

"They caught me off guard," he confessed. "I wasn't expecting company. Laurie and I were watching for you." He reached out and touched the little girl on the back, rubbing his hand comfortingly up and down her spine. "And we were starting to get a little worried."

"What do we do now?" Maggie asked.

He hesitated a few seconds before he articulated the decision he'd made. Despite the necessity of his leaving to keep the two of them safe, he knew walking out Maggie Cannon's back door would be one of the hardest things he had ever done in his life.

"I'm leaving, Maggie," he said softly.

She didn't say anything for a long time, her eyes holding on to his. "Where will you go?" she asked finally.

"I'll take a look at Edgemont. Brundridge worked there. If he thought something was going on, he was probably right."

"Something going on like what?" Maggie asked.

She shifted Laurie a little, settling her onto her right hip, which she cocked sideways with the ease of long practice. The little girl turned her head, cutting her eyes back at Drew. Her thumb had slipped into her mouth, and suddenly she looked a lot younger than she had sitting at the kitchen table coloring this afternoon. He smiled at her, and she ducked her head, turning her face into her mother's shoulder again.

"I don't know," Drew said truthfully. "It could be almost anything, I guess. That's an industry that's ripe for criminal activity. There are a lot of people nowadays with stuff they want to get rid of cheaply. A lot of people who don't care who they endanger in order to do that."

"What kind of stuff?"

"Any kind of hazardous materials. Chemicals, biohazards, radioactive waste."

"Radioactive?" Maggie said, her voice touched with horror.

"Not as far-fetched as you'd imagine. Hospitals use it. Utility companies. Defense contractors."

"And the government," Maggie added softly.

And slowly, thinking about the implications, Drew nodded.

"THIS IS RIDICULOUS," Maggie said, watching him shove things into the backpack she'd dragged out of the top of the closet in her bedroom. It was made of camouflage material and had apparently been on more than a few hunting and fishing trips. "You're leaving, just when we're finally getting somewhere."

"*We* don't need to be getting somewhere," Drew said, steeling himself to reject whatever arguments she made. "I do. And where I need to be getting most of all is away from here. This is nothing to do with you, Maggie. It's my problem, and it's dangerous. And apparently it's getting more dangerous by the minute. The quicker I leave here, the better."

"What if I don't want you to leave?"

"That *is* ridiculous," he said harshly.

There was silence as he shoved the food she had set out on the table into the backpack. He didn't look up to see her face. He was afraid that he wouldn't be able to do this if he did.

"You aren't leaving before dark?" she asked finally as he pulled the zipper around the bag.

"Yeah," he said.

"Yeah, you are or yeah, you aren't?"

"Yes, I am."

"Drew…"

At something in her tone, he finally raised his eyes, meeting hers. They weren't filled with tears as they had been in the hall, and for that he was infinitely grateful.

He knew in his heart that what he was doing was the right thing. The best thing for Maggie. However, he also knew as well as she did that it wasn't the best thing for him. And he didn't need anything, especially Maggie's tears, weakening his resolve.

"Too dangerous, Maggie. And you've done more than I had any right to expect you to do. Far more than I had a right to ask you to do."

"You didn't ask."

"The hell I didn't. I *begged* you to help me. I tried to put a guilt trip on you because of what your husband had done. And that was wrong.''

''What Tommy *did* was wrong,'' she said.

''And you regret it?'' he asked.

His eyes deliberately focusing on Laurie, seated again at the coffee table in the living room, making misshapen animals from colored clay. Maggie's gaze didn't follow his, but her eyes were again touched with tears. *You bastard,* he thought, when his came back to find them there.

''I don't regret that she's alive,'' she said. ''You know that. But…what they did to you was wrong. And if I don't do something to undo it, then I'm as bad as they are.''

''This has *nothing* to do with you. You don't owe me anything. You do owe her, however. You owe it to her to be her mother. And to be here. She's already lost her daddy, Maggie. She can't lose you, too.''

He picked up the backpack and slung it over his right shoulder. He couldn't wear it the way it was intended, and despite how little was in it, he knew it would be awkward to do any climbing while having to hold the pack. Still, he needed the few supplies he'd gathered.

And he needed the map Maggie had carefully drawn for him on the back of one of the pages she had copied at the library. He wasn't sure, given the confusing network of back roads, that he could find Edgemont, but he thought he could get close enough to ask directions. Maybe he wouldn't find anything there. Maybe Nell Brundridge was wrong about what she suspected, but it was somewhere to start. That was more than he'd had a few days ago.

''So you're just going to leave us here to face them alone?''

He turned back, surprised at the tone of Maggie's question. It was definitely accusing. ''What the hell does that mean?''

''What am I supposed to do when Thompson and Emmitt come back and ask me why I was out at Edgemont? What do I say when Rafe Dalton asks why I went to visit Nell Brundridge?''

The questions beat at Drew, troubling his surety. He knew he needed to get away from here. To get out of her life. Maggie couldn't hurt them. Surely they knew that, too.

''They won't,'' he said. ''They've got no way to know about your visiting Brundridge's widow. And as far as Edgemont is concerned, all you did was drive along a public road. They won't ask, but… If they do, just tell them that. Tell them you were lost. Tell them anything, and keep telling them. With me gone, they won't pursue it, Maggie. You didn't do anything.''

''They know about Nell,'' she said. ''They know I was there.''

''How could they?''

She walked over to the counter and picked up two glass jars that were sitting there. She brought them back, holding one in each hand, and set them down with a bang on the table. Then she turned them so that the labels were facing him.

''Another little error I made,'' she said. ''I told you what I had done was stupid.''

''They saw these?'' Drew asked, feeling that things were unraveling out of control faster than he could get a hold on them.

''They could have. They were in the truck. I don't think Rafe could read them. I don't know that Emmitt could, either, but he was close. Maybe close enough to see Nell's name.''

She waited, her eyes challenging. And the certainty that he was doing the right thing, a certainty Drew had felt only minutes before, was beginning to fade.

''They killed Charlie Brundridge to keep whatever is going on out there hidden,'' she said. ''You said they might have killed Tommy, too. To keep him quiet. Whatever they're hiding, Drew, I don't want to be the next sacrifice to it. And I don't want Laurie to be, either.''

"What do you want me to do?'' Drew asked, almost angry at her for terrifying him with those possibilities. And furious with himself over what he had set into motion here.

"If you're going to look at Edgemont, then take us, too. Don't leave us here alone. Grimes and his partner left, but they'll be back. I know it. And I don't want to be here when they come. At least...I don't want to be here alone.''

"You're better off without me,'' he said.

"I don't see how. I know you didn't mean to get us involved in this, but now we *are* involved. I shouldn't have gone out to Edgemont. That wasn't your fault. It was mine. But it's done, and nothing can undo it. I don't know how to protect Laurie from whatever is going on. I don't know who in this county I can trust. There's no one but you to protect us.''

The trouble was she was too right about a lot of that. He had gotten her involved, just by being here. By coming here to find Cannon to force the truth out of him. By asking for Maggie's help. By letting her copy those articles and then go to Brundridge's. Because he had done those, and they had stirred things up, he couldn't desert her and Laurie now.

Maggie was right about something else, as well. There was no one else in this county Drew would trust to look after them, either. "Then we wait until dark,'' he said.

MAGGIE HAD DRIVEN down the mountain with her lights off. She had come up and down the road leading to her cabin so many times she had always thought she could probably do it blindfolded. Before tonight she had never had to put that skill to the test. The moonlight was bright enough, however, that it wasn't nearly as bad as she had expected it to be. And her night vision had always been excellent.

Laurie was sitting beside her, safely strapped in, and Drew was lying flat in the bed of the pickup, covered by an old tarp Tommy had used in the shop. Maggie would have felt better had he been up in the cab with them, but until they could be sure no one had staked out her road, waiting to stop her if she attempted to come off her mountain, it was safer for him to be back there.

She drove the first few miles expecting a county patrol car to appear behind her at any minute. Even after she turned onto the highway, headlights on now, she kept checking her rearview mirror. And there was never anything back there. There was always very little traffic on this lonely two-lane, but tonight it seemed as if they were the only people in the world.

"Where are we going?" Laurie asked.

"Just to look at something," Maggie answered.

She had thought long and hard about bringing Laurie with her. She had a neighbor who occasionally kept the little girl, but Maggie was reluctant to let her daughter out of her sight.

And that's really paranoid, she had thought, even as she had made the decision. She might be putting Laurie into danger by bringing her along, but as she had told Drew, he was the only one she trusted. What she wasn't sure of was how much of that trust was tied up with the other feelings she had for him.

Feelings she hadn't had in a long, long time, she acknowledged. Was part of what she felt for Drew Evans born of her loneliness? Of her physical needs? Or of his?

"Is he going to look at it, too?"

Maggie turned to smile at the little girl. "He's the one who's going to do the looking. You and I will probably just stay in the truck and wait."

"I want to look," Laurie said.

Maggie's lips tilted, thinking of what they were going to check out. Those mountains of garbage loomed in her mind's eye. If what Drew suspected were true, however, then the place where they were headed was a whole lot worse than the normal landfill.

Hazardous waste. Maybe chemicals dumped and seeping into the ground water that fed all these communities. Or disease-infested materials from hospitals. Things that were supposed to be disposed of in some way other than simply dumping them and covering them over with dirt. Such illegal disposals had happened in other places, only to be discovered years later when children sickened and died from toxins that no one knew were in the ground where they lived and played and went to school.

If that's what was going on, then someone would have to be making a hell of a lot of money from it, Maggie thought. Enough to be willing to kill a man to hide what they were doing? Of course, people were killed all the time for nothing more than the change in their pockets. It wouldn't take all that much to arrange a murder.

But were they making enough from taking in toxic waste to pay all that money they had given Tommy to help them cover up Brundridge's death? Or had that come from someone else, someone who had a bottomless supply of taxpayer money? Someone who had used it to frame an ex-CIA agent named Drew Evans?

Maggie took a breath, knowing that she wasn't going to figure out the answers to those questions. Drew would have to do that. Up until tonight, she had been his legs. Tonight she was simply his transportation.

"Mama?" Laurie said, and with a jolt Maggie's mind came back to the present. To the here and now. "Can I have a look?"

"We'll see," Maggie said, not quite sure what Drew intended to do once they got to Edgemont. Not to let Laurie go exploring, of course, but a vague, motherly "we'll see" might satisfy the little girl until they arrived at their destination, which shouldn't be too long now, she realized.

As they approached the entrance to the landfill, Maggie could feel the anxiety building in her stomach, a feeling that was part nausea and part tension. Her eyes made another survey of the road behind her. There was still nothing back there.

At the next turnoff she came to, she pulled off the road, driving far enough down the rutted, unpaved lane for the truck to be hidden from any passing cars. She doused the lights and turned off the engine, sitting in the night-shrouded stillness, watching the empty dirt track behind her for at least five minutes. Then she reached back and tapped with her knuckles on the glass of the back window.

Chapter Twelve

"What did you find?" she asked. As soon as she recognized Drew, Maggie lowered the rifle, watching as he materialized like an apparition out of the thick woods.

After she had let Drew out of the truck, she had settled down to wait. Laurie had finally fallen sound aslccp on the front seat, her thumb comfortingly in her mouth the last time Maggie had checked on her.

Maggie herself had ended up sitting in the bed of the pickup, leaning back against its side, the rifle she had taken from the gun rack beside her. Despite the security the gun provided, she had reacted to every rustle in the undergrowth.

"Not much," Drew said.

He had been gone more than three hours, but he had warned her it would take him a long time to do any kind of survey of the landfill. She had fought a sense of foreboding the entire time she'd been waiting. To discover that his search hadn't turned up anything useful was more discouraging than she wanted to admit.

"Of course," he went on, "I didn't really expect to."

Then why the hell are we out here in the middle of the night? she thought. She didn't ask that question, however, because she knew very well why they were here, wild-goose chase or not. This was the only lead they had. A very tentative one, based on a few words in an overheard phone conversation.

"Whatever they're doing," Drew continued, "*if* they're doing anything, I knew it was going to be carefully concealed."

"What do we do now?"

"I want to get around the back. The area farthest away from the highway. With the size of the site, I couldn't have gotten there on foot and still had time to do any kind of search. Think you can find a way around it?"

"Maybe," Maggie hedged, thinking about the surrounding terrain. The fact that the landfill was in that narrow valley didn't make the prospects of getting around it very encouraging.

She scooted on her bottom over to the tailgate, letting her legs dangle off when she reached it. One of them was stretched a little farther toward the ground than the other, prepared to cushion her jump down. Suddenly, just before she slid off the end of the truck, Drew moved, positioning his body between her thighs, stopping her forward progress.

Startled, she looked up, right into his eyes, which were now level with hers. The dirt he had rubbed over his face before he'd set out made him a stranger, alien and frightening, like some commando rigged up for a secret mission. Like a spy in one of those movies Tommy had taken her to see.

That's exactly what he was, Maggie realized, a little startled by the belated realization. Drew Evans *was* a spy. An ex-CIA agent, who had done things like this a hundred times. He had been doing them while she had gone to high school and gotten married and had a baby. While she had raised a garden and cooked and ironed and cleaned and washed. While she had done all the things normal people do. *Normal people.* Which Drew wasn't.

Drew's arms slipped around her waist, his hands settling over her lower back. His mouth was almost stern, only his eyes moving in that darkened face. They searched her features as if he had never seen her before. As if he were learning them. Learning her.

And when his head began tilt, aligning his lips to fit over hers, the disappointment of tonight's failure, which had been a cold, dead weight in her stomach, became something else. Something sweet and hot and remembered.

She wanted him to kiss her, she realized. She had wanted it since someone had turned the handle on her back door, destroying what had been happening between them. And Drew hadn't really touched her since that night. Not like this.

The kiss in the hallway didn't count. She had initiated it by throwing herself into his arms, so relieved he and Laurie were safe. Maybe his response had been a reaction to that relief.

And that kiss had been nothing like this, she thought, as his lips made contact with hers. That had been about comfort. She knew immediately, from the very first touch, that this one was about something very different. Something they both wanted. Something they needed.

His tongue pushed into her mouth, not waiting for permission. Or allowing her time to deny him. And that was not her intent. Instead, her hands found the back of his head, pulling him to her. Her fingers spread into the thickness of his hair, relishing the texture and feel of it against her skin.

One of his hands moved up her spine, pressing her into closer contact with the wall of his chest. And she realized she had wanted that contact as much as she wanted his mouth over hers. Her breasts were flattened against his shirt, the passion-hardened peaks of them incredibly sensitive to that abrasion.

His hands moved again, pushing under her hips, lifting them off the hard metal of the tailgate and positioning them against a hardness that was far more exciting. In response, she wrapped her legs around him, crossing her ankles to hold them in place.

She used the muscles in her thighs and buttocks to raise her pelvis slightly, rubbing against him. Then she slowly released the tension she had created. Her body moved up and then down, a small, subtle pressure against his arousal.

The groaning release of his breath was encouragement enough to repeat the motion. When she did, Drew broke the kiss, putting his mouth against her cheek instead. His breath was hot on her skin, the sound of it ragged and uneven. His hands pulled her hips more closely into his with an urgency her body echoed.

There were too many layers of clothing between them. She wanted his skin moving against hers. His hardness sliding, heated and heavy, into the slow roiling wetness he had created between her legs. No barriers. No impediments. Flesh to flesh. The way it was meant to be between a man and woman.

The way it hadn't been for her in a long time, she acknowledged, her growing need a clamoring ache, low and powerful in her belly. And then she remembered that for Drew the last two years would have meant an even longer emptiness. A greater need.

Her hands found the buttons of his shirt and, trembling with urgency, she began to unfasten them. She stripped buttons from buttonholes, her fingers frenzied in their haste.

When she had unbuttoned as many as she could, she didn't bother to pull the tail of the shirt out of the waistband of his jeans. She didn't have time for that. Instead, she slid her hands inside the opening she'd created, palms moving against the hair-roughened skin of his chest.

As soon as she touched him, the same guttural sound was torn from him again. His head fell back, all pretense destroyed that what he had wanted when he started this was simply a kiss. His breathing had deepened until it was gasping.

Hearing the sounds of it, Maggie felt a molten, living warmth spread upward into her body from where their hips continued to move against each other. Moving exactly as if the barriers between them did not exist.

Her hands brushed over his nipples, which were pebbled as with cold. She caught them between her fingers, squeezing. Squeezing hard. His body jerked in reaction, and she wondered what he would do if she lowered her head, putting her lips over those small, taut nubs. Or her teeth.

She released them instead, her hands slipping under his arms, one on each side. She ran her palms down the symmetrical rows of his ribs, feeling the strength of his body. The solidness of it. Savoring it.

They slid down to his waist, which was long and narrow, exactly as a man's waist should be. There was not an ounce of excess fat on his lean body, sharp-honed by prison and injury and fever. And then, daringly, she eased the tips of her fingers into the waistband of his jeans. She dragged them along the top, inside his shirt, until both her hands were centered between their bodies, palms against his stomach and the backs of them against hers.

Suddenly Drew moved. His hands, which had been supporting her bottom, pulled out from under her, dropping her onto the tailgate of the truck. It bounced with the impact, and she had a fleeting, troubled image of the child asleep on the front seat.

Some mother part of her listened, alert to any stirring from Laurie. The other part of her, the woman part, followed the movement of his hands as they forced their way between their bodies.

It took only a second for her to understand what he intended. About as long as it took for him to twist the metal button out of its hole and to jerk down the zipper of his jeans.

He leaned back as he did, breaking the hold of her legs around his waist, creating enough distance between them to complete the task he'd begun. As soon as he had, he began to pull his shirt out of the now-gaping jeans. She felt the bottom button pop off with the force of his hands, which were ripping the material apart. The button fell with a small metallic ping onto the bed of the truck.

And then his hands were on top of hers, pushing them down into the opening he'd created. She closed her eyes, concentrating on the sensations of his body in her hands. Coarse hair. Hot, taut skin.

"Yes," he said, his mouth very near hers, his breathing more uneven, gasping harshly in response to what she was doing. "Yes, Maggie. Please. I need you so much."

The whispers were as urgent as his hands had been, working at the opening of his jeans. As frenzied as hers, struggling with the buttons on his shirt. And still, there were too many barriers between them. There always had been.

"Please," he said again as her hands moved over him, caressing. Stroking.

There were so many things in that broken plea that stirred her heart. The echo of two long years of deprivation that Tommy's lies had cost this man. Years of loneliness and a terrible dark despair.

Beyond that was the undeniable appeal of this, the ultimate surrender of control his begging represented. The acknowledgment that this was her choice, her gift. And perhaps, she realized, it would be the only one she would ever give him.

There was no future for them. They both had understood that from the beginning, despite the growing attraction they fought. Drew Evans was a fugitive, a convicted murderer with a far smaller chance of being able to clear his name than either of them had wanted to admit.

And he couldn't stay in Cooper County. Maggie had known that all along. Just as she had known, despite her very real fears about the mistakes she had made today, that she wouldn't go with him when he left.

Her life was here, in this county, just as it had always been. Maybe she would wait until Drew was safely away and then appeal to Rafe Dalton for help. She could make up some story to explain what she had done. Rafe might not believe it, but he would try to protect her. She knew that, because she knew he wanted her. He would protect her even if he were in some way involved in what had been done to Charlie Brundridge.

And besides, she acknowledged even as her hands continued to move lovingly over his body, Drew had never asked her to go with him. He had made no commitment. Drew Evans had no life to commit. Not to her. Not to Laurie.

And he wasn't a man who made empty promises. That was inherent in everything she knew about him. No promises. No future. No guarantees. Nothing really except his need, and her ability to assuage it.

Her hands moved over his body, trying to tell him that she understood all the constraints of their relationship. And all the impossibilities. Only this was possible between them. For now at least.

She knew by the shuddering breath when it began. With her touch she tried to say to him the things she would never say with her lips. Not unless...

Deliberately she blocked that thought. No promises. No commitments. That was the reality. That and the convulsive movements of his body in response to her touch. *Her touch.*

When it was over, his body stilled with a last hard shiver. He leaned forward and stood slumped against her a long moment, his forehead on hers. She put her arms around him, inside his shirt, and held him, feeling his heart thundering against her breasts. It beat wildly at first, then gradually it slowed. As it did, his harsh breathing eased.

After a long time, he straightened, and she released her hold, putting her hands in her lap. And again they were face-to-face. "I'm so sorry," he said softly.

She didn't ask for what. He hadn't touched her except

with his eyes, and so she understood what his apology intended. She nodded instead of answering him.

"I know…" he began, and then his voice faded.

His lips flattened and his gaze lifted beyond her face, staring into the darkness a moment before his eyes came back to hers. One hand lifted to touch her cheek, the palm settling along her jaw, almost a caress. His thumb moved over her bottom lip, pulling the moist skin as it trailed across.

"I wish there could be something more," he said.

She nodded again, holding his eyes. She had no words to express her emptiness. And if she had had those words, there was no point in saying them. They were strangers, brought together by a betrayal. And eventually they would be separated by it.

"I don't have anything to use to protect you, Maggie. And even if I did, this isn't…" He took a breath, deep enough to be audible in the stillness. "You deserve so much better than this."

Better than making love in the back of a pickup parked out on a dirt road. Better than making love in the darkness, hiding from the likes of Emmitt Grimes. Better than making love to a man who could give her nothing except pain when he left. And they both knew he would.

Wordlessly, she shook her head. Her eyes filled with tears, and she blinked, denying them. But he knew. He had to know.

He bent, his lips just above her left eye, his hand still cupping her face. Her eyes closed and her head tilted upward. He kissed her eyelids. First the left and then the right.

And then he gathered her to him, enfolding her in arms that were strong enough to keep her safe. He rocked her a little from side to side, just as she sometimes rocked Laurie. A comforting rhythm as old as time.

She didn't cry, not even when he released her and stepped back, his hands briefly on her waist as he lifted her off the tailgate.

"I'll drive," he said, stuffing his shirt back into his gaping jeans before he pulled up the tab of the zipper and refastened the metal button.

"Okay," she said.

She didn't move, standing in the silence, listening to the night sounds all around them as his long fingers made quick work of the buttons of his shirt.

"Maggie?" he questioned when he'd finished.

"I'm okay."

"Before I leave—"

"Don't," she ordered.

No promises. No commitments. At least not any coerced by guilt or remorse.

"It's…okay," she said, more calmly. "The keys are in the truck."

She walked around to the passenger side, leaving him standing alone in the rutted dirt track. She opened the door, and stepped up into the truck. She lifted Laurie's upper body enough to slip onto the seat. And then she pulled the little girl into her lap, the small blond head lolling against her shoulder. Maggie wrapped her arms tightly around her daughter, holding her close.

Holding Laurie wasn't what she wanted right now. At least, not all she wanted. It was, however, all that she had. All she had had since Tommy died, she admitted bitterly. And whatever she had been hoping for—

The door on the other side of the pickup opened, and she turned toward it. Drew's eyes examined her face again before he climbed in. "Think you can get us to the back side of the site?"

Without speaking, Maggie nodded. She leaned forward, shifting Laurie's weight to rest more against her right shoulder as she did. With her left hand, she pushed the latch on the glove box. She took out the county map she kept there and, working one-handed, fumbled it open.

"I need some light," she said. "Can we risk that?"

Without answering, Drew reached up and flicked the over-head switch. Maggie blinked against it, although it was pretty dim. Her eyes fell to Laurie's face, but the little girl didn't stir.

And then she raised her gaze to Drew. He was watching her, hazel eyes fastened intently on her face. Still concerned. A concern she didn't want, she thought, turning her head to concentrate on the map.

She had gone into this with her eyes open. She had known what she was getting into when she'd agreed to help him. Her decision. Her choices, even those less than brilliant ones she had made today, which might have some pretty far-reaching consequences.

She tried to concentrate on the faint lines on the map that represented roads and creeks and property boundaries. Even as familiar as she was with this county, it took her a few seconds to locate the landfill. She had been right about ev-erything she thought she remembered. The configuration of the narrow valley. The ridges on either side.

"I don't see a road that goes all the way around it," she said, still examining the topography.

"How close can we get? Close enough to get in there on foot?"

Resisting the urge to look at him, she forced herself to calculate distances and terrain. "The closest way is probably straight across the landfill."

"Damn it," Drew said softly. That was a route he had considered and rejected as too time-consuming.

"There *is* a road that goes part of the distance around. And it may go even farther than the map indicates. This shows only paved roads. The one we're on right now isn't marked here, for instance. It's possible there's a track like this that cuts behind the ridge. There are a lot of unpaved trails in these mountains. Even if it is there, whether the truck could make it or not is the question. We'd just have to try."

She finally looked up, meeting his eyes again.

"Are you game?" he asked. "I figure we've got about five hours until daylight. Not much time to do that kind of exploring."

"And if we don't?" she asked. "What then?"

They both knew the answer. This was the only lead they had. And Drew, at least, didn't have the option of not exploring it.

He nodded unnecessarily, and then he reached up and pushed the light switch into the off position, plunging the cab back into darkness. He started the engine and put the truck into reverse. Then he turned in the seat, prepared to begin backing down the dirt road and back out to the highway.

As he did, his eyes touched hers again. They held for a long moment, and his lips tightened. Almost deliberately, he completed the motion he'd begun, looking out the back window instead of at her.

Maggie laid the map, improperly folded, on the seat beside her and put both arms around Laurie, holding her daughter close. All she had, she thought again. All she had.

Chapter Thirteen

"It's no use," Maggie said.

Drew had been trying to ease the truck farther along a narrow trail that had never been intended for vehicle traffic. And as much as he hated to admit it, he knew Maggie was right. After spending the past hour and a half wandering down back roads that looked as if they might end up on the other side of the landfill, they were at a dead end. Another one.

"Damn it to hell," Drew said, not hiding his frustration.

Turning to look over his right shoulder, and avoiding Maggie's eyes as he did, he began to back down the road that in the last few yards had become little more than a path. Too many frustrations. The futility of his initial search of the site. Not being able to get where he knew in his gut they needed to be. And most of all the situation with Maggie.

He had made a decision to leave her alone the first night he'd kissed her. And for two days, he had somehow managed to keep his hands off her. Then tonight, seeing her sitting in the back of the pickup, waiting patiently for his return, whatever control he thought he had had disappeared.

He had screwed up royally, and he knew it. Maggie didn't need to be emotionally involved with him. It wasn't fair to her. He had already decided that, and then he had given in to the sexual pull that had always been between them, from the first few days she had cared for his injury.

Now she thought he had been using her. *And you weren't?* his conscience jeered. The worst part of that question was that he had been. In one way at least. A pretty obvious one. And yet what he felt about Maggie was about so much more than hormones, despite the fact that she certainly got those stirring. A little too powerfully tonight. He supposed he should be grateful it hadn't gotten any more out of hand than it had.

What he had told her was the absolute truth. She deserved better than to be mixed up with him. Wrong time. Wrong place. Wrong woman. Maggie Cannon was too good for the kind of life he faced—a life of running and hiding. She deserved the Norman Rockwell kind of existence he had watched unfold below him during those days when he'd staked out her cabin.

Drew knew he couldn't give her that life. Not now at least. There was no guarantee he would ever be able to. It was better not to suggest anything permanent between them. And he understood that for Maggie any emotional or physical commitment would have to go hand-in-hand with permanency. That was the kind of woman she was. And he wouldn't have wanted to change her.

The truck scraped against something on the driver's side, and Drew slammed on the brakes. Apparently, his attention had wandered too far off what he was supposed to be doing. Maggie put out her hand to touch the dashboard, trying to protect the sleeping child she held from the jerk of that unexpected stop.

There was no need to take his frustration out on them, Drew thought in regret, glancing over at her and Laurie. Or on Maggie's truck, which was their only means of transportation.

He rolled down his window, sticking his head out to see what he'd hit. It was a sapling, the branches dragging against the side of the pickup. Pulling forward again would probably do as much damage as continuing to back out past it. He was on the verge of doing that when he heard the noise. He froze as he listened, trying to figure out where the sound was coming from.

"What's wrong?" Maggie asked.

"Shh," he cautioned, holding his right hand up, the palm facing her. After a moment he pulled his head back into the cab and looked at her. "You hear that?"

After a few seconds, both of them straining to listen to the faint, distant noise in the surrounding stillness, Maggie said, "It sounds like a train."

"Does the map indicate where railroad tracks run?"

She shook her head, the movement visible even in the dimness. The only light was that reflected from the beams of the headlights bouncing off the trunks of trees, which made the whole scene eerie and unnatural.

Drew turned again so he could look out the back window and pushed down on the gas pedal. He began backing again, going much too fast, still listening to the train through his opened window. The click of its wheels was regular and unchanged since he had first become aware of it.

Since his tour of the landfill, he had been trying to figure out how they could get illegal substances to the site in a sufficient quantity to make the dumping profitable. After all, the main entrance was on a public highway. It would be highly dangerous to try to truck in illegal waste via that route, especially if they were doing it in any great amount. If they were shipping stuff in by rail, however, that was another matter entirely. Especially in this location.

Even if you were stopped by a train at a crossing, you didn't look all that closely at the passing cars, at what they held. And the tracks, by design, always ran though the rural countryside, away from prying eyes. If this particular branch ran behind the landfill, where he had speculated anything illegal would be going on, then they just might be on to something.

"What are you doing?" Maggie asked, her hand still on the dash as they careened backward.

"Trying to get to that train."

"Why?"

"To see what it's carrying. And where."

After he'd reached the end of the dirt road and backed out onto the pavement, it took him maybe three minutes to locate the tracks, still working by sound alone. He killed the headlights as soon as he saw the flickering movement of the cars passing behind the trees that screened them. Then he cut across country, easing the pickup over the rough terrain and between trees.

Finally he brought the truck to a stop on top of a small rise that looked down on the tracks. Through the front windshield, he and Maggie watched as the containers rolled by, gleaming white and deadly in the moonlight. There were no markings on them, nothing that would be obvious to someone who might be watching them pass. And of course, no one was.

Not here. Not at this time of night. All anyone who lived in this county would ever be aware of would be the sound of wheels clicking by in the darkness. The same sound that signified the passage of thousands of other perfectly harmless cargos. A train like this, scheduled maybe once or twice a week, always at night, could bring in a hell of a lot of toxic materials, Drew speculated. And no one would ever be the wiser.

Except apparently a guy named Charlie Brundridge, who had seen something that had made him suspicious about what was going on at Edgemont Disposal. Something that had gotten him killed.

The end of the train appeared before Drew had made up his mind what to do. Of course, given his situation, he really didn't have much choice. For a moment, as he tried to decide, he wished he'd never agreed to bring Maggie and Laurie along, but without Maggie's help, he would never have found this place. Without her, he would never have gotten this close.

Last chance, Drew thought, echoing what he had known from the beginning. And he had no choice but to take it. He gave the truck gas again, bouncing down the shallow slope from which they'd been watching the train.

"Now what are you doing?" Maggie asked, her steadying hand again on the dash.

"Following it," Drew answered succinctly, guiding the pickup to the top of the embankment on which the tracks had been laid.

"MY GOD," Maggie said softly.

He hadn't been wrong, Drew thought, feeling a sense of vindication that almost made up for everything that had happened to him during the past two years. Someone had killed a man to keep what they were doing here from being discovered, and then they had framed Drew for that murder. Using Tommy Cannon as their pawn and Drew as their scapegoat, they had made absolutely certain no one would ever investigate Charlie Brundridge's death. That it would never lead back to them. Or back to this.

They had picked Drew because he was a stranger, somebody without ties or resources. Somebody who, if they had done the most cursory background check, would appear to have no past, no family, no friends. Thanks to the CIA's efficiency in destroying his identity, Drew had been the perfect victim. And it had all worked out just exactly as they had planned.

"What *is* that?" Maggie asked.

"If I had to bet…" Drew said, and then he hesitated. He wished he had a pair of binoculars, but the containers themselves were a pretty good clue. As were the protective suits the workers who were unloading them were wearing. "I'd say some kind of radioactive waste."

"They're putting radioactive waste in a landfill?"

"*That's* done all the time," Drew said, his concentration on the scene they were watching rather than on Maggie's questions.

His knowledge about the disposal of hot materials was pretty rudimentary, but he knew this wasn't on the up-and-up or they wouldn't be working at night. The mercury lights right over the unloading ramp and the hooded suits gave the operation a nightmare quality. And if they were doing what he thought they were, it really was a nightmare. Or something even worse.

"Then why did they kill Brundridge?" Maggie asked. "I mean, if this isn't illegal."

"I didn't say that. I said nuclear waste is disposed of in landfills all the time. However, the way they're doing it here almost certainly isn't the way it's supposed to be done."

"How can you can tell?"

"They're bringing the stuff in in the middle of the night. And none of the information posted out front indicates this facility is licensed to handle that kind of waste."

"But if it's put into landfills all the time—"

"In specially prepared landfills. With concrete pits, covered by protective caps. And there are other precautions taken to keep it from leeching out into the ground."

"And you don't think they're doing that here?"

"It's not likely," Drew said softly, watching a worker lift a container off the train with a forklift and set it down on a concrete slab. "Not given the secrecy in which they're working."

"So why isn't somebody out here, following that shipment? Don't they have to keep track of stuff like this?"

"They use contractors," Drew said. "*Everybody* uses contractors. Hospitals. Industry. Even the Department of Energy. They contract with some company to dispose of the stuff, but no one's going to be able to check that all those shipments go where they're supposed to. They put it on a train somewhere, and they trust that the contractor is going to dispose of it properly.''

"And instead they're bringing it here.''

"Ideal location," Drew said, knowing it was. "Rural county. Sparsely populated. Nobody asking any questions.''

"Not even our illustrious law enforcement officers.''

He turned to look at her, knowing that if anything happened to him, she needed to know it all. "They may be in on it, Maggie. The investigation of Brundridge's murder may not have just been ineptly handled. Everybody from Dalton on down may have been paid off.''

"Including Tommy," she said softly.

"Including Tommy," Drew agreed, understanding the guilt she would feel about that. "But…it's possible he didn't know about this. They offered him money to lie in court. He may not have known it was tied to Edgemont.''

"They gave him a *lot* of money to lie. Which must mean there's a lot of money to be made off something like this.''

Drew nodded, his eyes moving back to the workers. "Doing it right is expensive. Doing it wrong is a whole lot less expensive. The contractor charges the waste producer the going rate to do it right, and then he cuts corners.''

"And puts that…junk here. In this county. In our soil and water.''

"For the next couple of hundred years," Drew agreed.

Maggie turned, looking back toward the truck. "I need to check on Laurie," she said, as if that thought had made her more conscious of her daughter's safety.

Drew had parked the truck in the edge of the woods after they'd driven down off the rail bed. Then he and Maggie had climbed this bank so they could overlook the area of the landfill where the train was being unloaded. Maggie had decided to leave Laurie asleep on the front seat. After all, they could still see the truck from up here.

"You aren't planning on going down there?" she asked, suddenly turning back to face him after she'd taken only a few steps. It didn't really sound like a question.

"We don't have enough information to call the authorities in on this. I need to see what they're doing with the shipments."

"Drew," Maggie said softly. Nothing else. Just his name.

He pulled his gaze away from the activity below to find her eyes on his face. She was really looking at him for the first time since they had almost made love in the back of the truck.

"I don't have a choice, Maggie. If I report this and can't give them details, if I can't prove what's going on and that it's connected to Brundridge's death, then I'm going back to prison. If I'm *lucky,* I'll make it back to prison," he added.

He had to make her understand why he was willing to take this risk—and he knew better than she did what a risk it was. *Last chance,* echoed again in his mind.

"Nobody's going to ask these people for any explanation about what they're doing out here based strictly on my accusations," he said softly. "Not without more proof. And nobody's going to find that proof for me."

"Even if you could prove what's going on here…"

Her voice faded, but he knew what she meant. Even if he could prove to someone that they were improperly burying nuclear waste out here, that was still quite a jump to proving they'd framed him for Brundridge's murder.

The ties he and Maggie had discovered between the operation below and his conviction for murder might seem totally convincing to the two of them. There was the fact that Charlie Brundridge, who had been employed at Edgemont, had been concerned about something that was going on here. According to Maggie, Brundridge's wife would be willing to testify to that. And then there was the payoff Tommy Cannon had been given for fingering Drew, which Maggie would confirm. Even the bungled forensics from the crime scene were pretty damning.

Those things added up to some pretty solid evidence of environmental fraud and public corruption, which had ultimately resulted in a murder. In any other county, any other venue, Drew knew he might be able to make a case from them. But could he do it here? And would he be given the chance?

"I've at least got to know what they're really doing down there before I take this to the authorities. And when I do, Maggie, it won't be in Cooper County."

"You think they're all in on it," she said.

"That seems the most likely explanation."

"Then…if they catch you down there, they'll kill you," she warned.

She was right, of course. Drew understood that as well as Maggie did. They would kill him and bury him along with whatever they were planning to bury out there tonight. And this one would be a murder no one would ever know about. Martin Holcomb would simply never be seen again after his escape from prison. The perfect escape. And the perfect murder. They wouldn't even have to find a scapegoat to take the blame for this one.

"If I don't make it back before daylight—" he began.

"Don't," Maggie said harshly. "Damn you, Drew, don't start telling me what to do if you don't show up back here."

He had never heard her voice filled with such anger. Maybe this felt like a desertion to her, he thought. After all, he was proposing to leave her and Laurie alone to go down there. And they both knew what the odds were that he could find out what he needed to know and still get out alive.

"That's a possibility you have to think about, Maggie. Something *I* have to think about. If I'm not back by daylight, then you take Laurie and get out of here."

"And go where?" she asked. "Where the hell can I go?"

He had meant she should go home, but Maggie wouldn't

want to do that. That's why she was here tonight. She was afraid to be alone at her cabin because she thought she had given away her involvement with this yesterday.

Drew wasn't sure that was the case. Maybe the deputies really had received a call about a stranger lurking around. Or maybe they weren't even looking for Drew when they had gone there. Maybe they knew nothing at all about what Maggie had been doing yesterday. After all, they had left the cabin. If they really suspected she was trying to investigate Brundridge's death or that she was sheltering a fugitive, would they have? Would they have been satisfied to go without making a search?

It didn't seem there was any way to know any of those things for sure. Not now. Not until they showed up again at Maggie's. And if he wasn't there...

"I don't have anywhere else to go, Drew," Maggie reminded him as he tried to think. "I've got no money. Everything I own is up on that mountain. I don't have anywhere else to go but back there."

"And you'll be safe. They'll never know you were here. And the other stuff you're worried about is minor, easily explained away. Dalton will buy whatever you tell him, because he'll want to. He'll want to believe you. You're not a danger to them, Maggie, and they have to know that."

"That's easy for you to say. You don't live here."

"I'll be back before dawn," he said, recognizing there was nothing he could say to convince her.

"And if you're not?"

"Go home. Forget about this. Let it go. There's nothing you can do about it."

"Just let them get away with murder?"

By that time, it would be two murders. Drew didn't remind her of that. "You don't have any choice," he said instead.

No choice. Just as he had none. He had to go down there to verify that he was right about what he thought was going on. And he had to find out where they were putting those containers. They were the proof of what he would tell the authorities about Brundridge's murder. They had to be able to come out here and find that illegal waste.

"And what about what they're doing?" Maggie asked. "Even if something happens to you, I can't just let this go on. For Laurie's sake, if for nothing else."

She would never let it go. He knew her well enough by now. Maggie wouldn't sleep at night, knowing what was out here, ticking away like a time bomb.

"Call the CIA," Drew said. "Ask to speak to a man named Carl Steiner. Tell him about this. Tell him about me," he added reluctantly, knowing that would probably be the only way to get someone like Steiner to listen to her.

"Why didn't you do that?" she asked.

"I thought they were the ones who had framed me. I thought everything that happened here was directed at me."

"Then do it now. You know they weren't in on that. Call them now, Drew. Let them handle this."

And for a few seconds he even thought about doing it. But that had been a part of the deal he'd made, of course. He was to have no connection with the agency. No contact. "If you get into trouble, we've never heard of you," had been Steiner's exact words. Drew wasn't sure they would respond to Maggie's appeal for help, but he damn sure knew they wouldn't mount any rescue for him.

"I can't. I broke all ties with them when I walked away. That was the deal."

"Steiner was your boss?"

Drew shook his head, his lips lifting slightly as he mentally compared Griff Cabot and the current assistant deputy director of special operations. "He's the one in charge now. He wasn't when I was there, but you call him anyway, Maggie."

"And he'll recognize your name?"

"If he pretends he doesn't..." Drew began, thinking

about Steiner's possible reaction. Despite the seriousness of the situation, he was almost amused by the thought of the current head of operations fielding Maggie's phone call. "Tell him you know I was a member of the External Security Team. And tell him you know all about what we did."

"But...I don't," Maggie said.

"It doesn't matter. If he thinks you do, he'll listen. Tell him to get somebody out here to investigate Edgemont. Tell him what we saw. Tell him everything you know, Maggie, and then ask the agency to arrange protection for you and Laurie."

"Will they?"

He wasn't sure they would, but he supposed it was worth a shot. If Griff had been there, of course... But Griff Cabot was dead, he reminded himself grimly, and apparently none of the agents Drew had worked with were around anymore. Still, the CIA was the best protection he could offer Maggie if she were determined to pursue this.

"Maybe," he said truthfully. "I don't really know. That's why it's better to leave this alone. Better to forget what you saw tonight."

"And forget you?" she asked softly.

"Especially better to forget me," Drew said.

He looked back down on the scene below. The activity surrounding the train was surreal, like some animation depicting evil gnomes digging in the earth. Except there was no fantasy about this. This was cold, brutal reality, fueled by greed. A reality at least one man had been murdered to protect.

"I won't forget you," Maggie said. "You have to know that."

He looked at her again, and found her eyes steady on his. "For *her* sake, Maggie. Forget me. Forget this."

"That's what Tommy did. He lied for *her* sake. And it was wrong."

''And because he did, Laurie's alive. Would you make a different choice?''

''That isn't fair,'' she protested.

''Nothing ever is.''

There was a long silence, but he didn't pull his eyes away from her face. Finally he said, ''Go home, Maggie. Take Laurie and just get the hell out of here.''

''What would you do if I really did that?'' she asked.

''I don't need you. I don't even want you here. I want you to go. Don't wait until daylight. Just…go home. I'll handle this.''

''Like you handled it two years ago?'' she asked, the edge to the question hard.

''I was operating in the dark then. Now I know what really happened. I know some of the people involved. And I've got contacts. I'll call in some favors.''

He would have, he acknowledged, if he had any idea who to call. Not Steiner, of course. Steiner wouldn't care if Drew Evans rotted in prison, as long as the agency wasn't involved. Steiner had always thought Griff's men were rogues. And when Drew remembered the agents he'd worked with, he couldn't deny that Steiner was right.

''You're lying,'' Maggie said, her eyes searching his face.

''Go home,'' he ordered again, turning his eyes toward the scene below because she could read him too well. ''Go home and forget this. Forget me. Forget all of it.''

She put her hand on his arm, trying to make him turn, but he didn't want to look at her. That's what had happened before. He had looked at her, and all his resolve to keep her at a distance had disappeared. He couldn't afford to let that happen now.

''They'll leave you alone,'' he said, hoping he was right. ''Just go home and stay there for a few days.''

''Will I see you again? I mean if…''

If they don't catch you down there. If they don't bury you with whatever else they're burying out there tonight.

"No," he said. "It's safer that way. Go home, Maggie."

"Drew—"

"It's over. Things will go back to the way they were before."

"Not everything," she said.

"Everything that matters," he said.

He pulled his arm from her fingers and walked to the edge of the rise they were standing on. He didn't look back.

Clean break, he told himself. Like a surgery.

This way, Maggie would never know what happened to him. She would never know whether he had succeeded here or not. Or whether he'd ended up under a few tons of radioactive garbage. And that would be for the best. Maggie could get on with her life. Exactly the way she had been before he'd showed up.

"I love you," she said, her voice pitched loudly enough to carry the distance between them.

He heard the words, felt them in his chest like a blow, but he didn't react. He touched the top of a stump that stood where the land fell off, sloping down to the site and, holding on to it to maintain his balance, stepped over the side and began to carefully pick his way down the incline. And in spite of what Maggie had just said, he never looked back.

Chapter Fourteen

Go home. There had been no equivocation in that command, Maggie thought, making her way back to the truck. *Go home. Forget about me. Forget about this.*

No equivocation and no hint that Drew would give a damn if she did. And she should, she thought angrily. She should just get into the truck and drive home. Put Laurie to bed, like any good mother would already have done, and forget all about Drew Evans. Forget about what was going on out here. Forget about everything except keeping her daughter safe.

That's what Tommy had done, she acknowledged, and it had come back to haunt them. Her grandmother always said you couldn't do a wrong and expect a right in return. Life didn't work that way.

Her mind still on the man who had left her alone at the top of the rise, it took a moment for Maggie to notice that the interior light was on in the truck. She began to run, her heart racing, imagining Laurie waking up alone and frightened, maybe even getting out of the pickup and wandering off into the woods.

Although it was only a matter of a few minutes between the time she first noticed the dim light and when she skidded to a halt beside the truck, a thousand possibilities had run through her head, most of them too horrible to contemplate.

She had tried to banish them, at least until she looked into the cab through the open window and found the front seat empty.

Her eyes sought the door on the other side and found it ajar. She ran around the front of the cab and jerked the door open, as if she believed Laurie might be hiding between it and the seat, which would have been a physical impossibility. Then she turned, directing her gaze to the adjacent woods. The thin light filtering out from inside the truck made little headway against its stygian darkness. She could see the trunks of the nearest trees and the beginning tangle of undergrowth, but nothing beyond that.

"Laurie?"

She tried to keep her voice low, despite her panic. She didn't know how far sound would travel in the breathlessly still heat of this summer night. Besides, she didn't believe her daughter could have gone far. Maggie had looked at the truck only a few minutes ago, right before Drew had disappeared down the slope to the landfill. If the light in the cab had been on then, she felt sure she would have seen it.

"Answer me, Laurie," she ordered, moving on trembling knees nearer the edge of the forest. There was no sound from the darkness. No reply to her demand.

This was the stuff of nightmares. The worst imaginable nightmare for any mother. To have your child disappear. To know that you were responsible for having left her alone.

She should never have brought Laurie. She should have taken the little girl to stay with Amy Burke, who had kept Laurie on those rare occasions when Maggie had to have a sitter. If she had done that, then her daughter would be safe, sound asleep in the same double bed with the Burkes' youngest. And instead...

"Laurie?" she called again, pitching her voice a little louder, despite the fear that someone at the landfill might hear her and come to investigate. That was a chance she would just have to take.

"A long way from home, aren't you, Maggie?"

She whirled at the unexpected question. Her eyes, adjusted to the darkness of the woods, were momentarily blinded by the dim light spilling out of the truck's interior. Unable to see the speaker, Maggie had already made an identification from those few words. And with it, fear unfurled sickeningly in her stomach.

"Rafe," she said, and then she stopped because she couldn't think of anything else to say.

Drew had told her to deny everything, but it was going to be pretty damned hard to explain what she was doing at Edgemont in the middle of the night. And despite the fact that she knew they had killed a man to keep this secret, right now Maggie was more concerned about where her daughter was than about what would happen to her as a result of being here.

"Where's Laurie?" she demanded. "What have you done her?"

"She's asleep in the back of the cruiser. A lot safer than where you left her, Maggie. You want to tell me what the hell the two of you are doing here in the middle of the night?"

There was nothing she could say to Rafe that would explain that. There was no road out here, at least as far as she and Drew had been able to determine. And it would be difficult to claim she had followed the tracks without making any reference to what she had seen being carried on that train. And if she admitted she had seen those containers…

"I guess not," Rafe said when she didn't answer.

He stepped forward, moving out from the shadows behind the truck and becoming fully visible for the first time. His usually pleasant expression was hard, his eyes cold. Despite Drew's claim that Rafe would be more than willing to believe anything she told him, Maggie knew the sheriff's interest would be little protection now. Not in this situation.

"You're in way over your head, Maggie."

"I don't know what you're talking about. Into what over my head?" Her mind was racing, formulating and then rejecting plans to get to Laurie and to get them both out of here. The problem was she knew none of those desperate ideas would work.

Rafe said he had put Laurie in the back of his patrol car. That was where they kept prisoners, which meant automatic locks and metal screens. Besides, the sheriff was standing between his car and Maggie, making it obvious she would have to go through him to get to her daughter. Although he didn't have his gun out, his holster was unsnapped.

"I think you do," Rafe said. "I think you know exactly what I mean."

"I don't care what's going on out here," Maggie said, still trying to think despite her growing terror. "I don't give a damn what you all are up to. Just give me back my daughter, Rafe. Give me Laurie, and then you can do whatever the hell you want."

"*Whatever* I want? You know, Maggie, I swear that sounded like another invitation." There was an edge of amusement in his voice, and she hated the thought that she was this terrified while he was laughing at her. "You wouldn't be offering to bribe an officer of the law, now would you?"

She fought the urge to close her eyes, just to block out the hated image of his face. She knew what he was suggesting. The same kind of bargain Tommy had made. A deal with the devil.

This one had nothing to do with money, however. This one had to do with something Rafe Dalton had apparently wanted for a very long time.

"No," she said softly. Even as she said it, she was unsure if that had been an answer to his question or a refusal of that unspoken, and unspeakable, suggestion.

"'No'?" Rafe repeated, his thin lips tilting into a smile, those clear green eyes locked on her face. "Did you say no,

Maggie? I don't think you're in much of a position to tell me no. Doesn't seem like a real smart move to me.''

"You're supposed to uphold the law."

"I don't need a lecture from you on how to do my job, Maggie."

"Then do it. Give me Laurie and let us go home."

"You've been sticking your nose into things that don't concern you. And that can be dangerous. I'm just trying to look out for you."

"I'll look out for myself. Give me my daughter."

"Why don't you come on over here and get her," Rafe said, the hint of amusement back. "I got no reason to keep you from Laurie. All you got to do is ask me nice. That's all I ever wanted from you, Maggie. For you just to be nice to me. That's not so much to ask, is it?"

The tone of that question made her flesh crawl, but realistically, what choice did she have? She had to get Laurie, and when she did, she'd run her truck over this sadistic, taunting bastard. *When she had Laurie,* she told herself, holding on to the words as if they were a talisman. *When she had Laurie...*

She took a step toward him and realized her legs were shaking. *It doesn't matter. Nothing matters but getting Laurie and getting out of here.* She took another step, concentrating not on the destination—because she couldn't afford to think about that—but on the process. On putting one foot in front of the other. Until finally she was standing in front of Rafe Dalton, looking up into his face.

She fought to hold on to her courage, pretending defiance, working hard to keep her eyes filled with hatred rather than tears. When he saw what was in them, however, his smile widened. He put his hands on her shoulders, running his palms down and then back up her bare upper arms.

"Always did think you were the prettiest woman in this county. I even liked it that you were standoffish. Made me hot just thinking about you. And I've been doing a lot of thinking about you since Tommy died. Thinking maybe you were lonely. Maybe hungry for a man. Aching for a man's touch. You lonely, Maggie, living up on that mountain all alone? Sleeping in that big old empty bed all by yourself?''

As he talked his hands continued their slow glide up and down her arms. From shoulder to elbow and then back again.

"I'm not lonely," she said, her voice tight.

"Maybe you've just forgotten what you're missing. Did old Tommy do right by you, Maggie? Did he give you what you needed?''

"You said I could have my daughter," she reminded him, fighting the urge to raise both fists and batter his leering face.

"You can. Just as soon as you and I take care of some other kind of business here. I been patient for a long time, Maggie, thinking about you.''

"What do you want?"

"Whatever I can get, sweet Maggie. I'm not particular. Not when it comes to you.''

The problem was that she was particular. And when she compared the way she felt about kissing Rafe Dalton to the sweet anticipation she had experienced when Drew's mouth had begun to lower to cover hers, she knew she couldn't do this. There had to be another way.

She stepped to the side, breaking away from his hands and attempting to walk by him. His smile widened again. One tanned arm reached out, his long fingers gripping her elbow. She twisted, attempting to pull out of his hold, and heard him laugh.

"I like a woman who's got spirit. I always suspected that about you.''

"Let me go," she said. She again tried to pull her arm from his fingers.

His free hand came up, catching her behind the neck. He lowered his head, putting his mouth over hers. His tongue pushed against her lips, attempting to force its way inside. Maggie tried to turn her face away, but his fingers on the back of her neck were controlling. All she could do was to tighten her lips and keep struggling to move so that his mouth couldn't connect with hers.

His head lifted slightly, and he looked down into her eyes. Then, without warning, the fingers that had been wrapped around the back of her neck tangled in her hair. He pulled it hard, jerking her head too far back and holding it there. His face revealed his sudden anger, mouth flattened and eyes again cold.

"I've tried to be nice to you, Maggie. I've protected you. All I ever wanted in return was a little thanks. Just a little gratitude."

"Gratitude for what?"

Maggie bit off the words. Her eyes were tearing. She wasn't sure if that was from the pressure on her scalp or from sheer, blind anger.

"You been sticking your nose in things that don't concern you. That's a real good way to get it cut off, and you're too pretty for that."

"And you've been protecting me?" she asked sarcastically.

"There's some people that don't like the fact that you've been nosing around. They don't like anybody nosing around. It's not a healthy pastime in this county."

Emmitt Grimes and his partner? Maggie wondered. Rafe had called them off when they were at the cabin. Was it possible he really had been protecting her?

"You need to leave the investigating to the folks who are supposed to be doing it. You're in way over your head, Maggie," he warned again.

"And *are* those 'folks' investigating?" she asked.

The anger that had caused him to manhandle her had begun to fade from his features, but his grip on her hair had not loosened. Her neck was aching from the unnatural angle at which he had it pulled back.

He smiled again, a slow, almost secretive movement of his lips. "Too many questions, Maggie. Too much concern about things that aren't any of your business."

"Tommy was my business," she said.

"Tommy's dead. It's time to move on."

Move on to him? she wondered. That would be a cold day in hell. "Let me have Laurie," she said, "and I'll go. No one will ever know I've been out here."

He didn't answer, but the hand that had been holding her elbow released it. She took a breath in relief, and then his fingers fastened over her breast, kneading the soft flesh.

"You're one fine-looking woman, Maggie."

His fingers continued to massage. She didn't struggle, refusing to give him the satisfaction and knowing that she couldn't break free of the hold he had on her hair.

She was replaying his words in her mind, trying to decide if he really had been protecting her. Had Rafe been out here investigating or was he as corrupt as those who were bringing in the illegal waste and dumping it? Which side was Dalton on?

"Let me have Laurie," she said.

She knew now that was the only important thing. Rafe was right about that much. Investigating this was someone else's job. Drew's or Dalton's. Her only job had been keeping her little girl safe. Maybe Tommy had been right, and she was the one who had been wrong.

"First you show me how nice you can be, Maggie, and then we'll talk about Laurie."

His hand slipped under the hem of her knit top, pushing it up. The heel of his palm brushed across her bare stomach, and she flinched away from it, provoking a tightening of his fingers in her hair. Then his other hand was cupping her breast again, this time under her shirt.

"I was really hoping you wouldn't be wearing a bra. Why

don't we just get rid of this thing and see what you're really like under all that Miss Prim and Proper.''

Suddenly there was a sound behind Dalton. It was distraction enough that his fingers, which were still tangled in her hair, loosened minutely. Maggie raised her head, straightening her neck as much as she could when he turned to look over his shoulder.

Another patrol car was coming down the gravel embankment where the rails ran. As they watched, it pulled to a stop behind the sheriff's cruiser, which was parked in the shadow of the trees, a few hundred feet behind her pickup.

Dalton's fingers uncurled suddenly, freeing her, and then he turned around to face the car. Maggie, standing behind him, was probably hidden from whoever was in the vehicle.

"Don't move," Rafe ordered, his voice so soft she knew he was talking to her.

She obeyed, but she had to fight the urge to run, just to break away now that she was free and run to get Laurie. However, there was now someone else to consider—whoever was driving that second patrol car.

Its front doors opened simultaneously. The men who climbed out through them were little more than silhouettes, dark shapes highlighted by the overhead light in their car. Maggie held her breath, eyes straining into the darkness as they began walking past the sheriff's vehicle.

As they reached it, one of them hesitated, bending to look into its back seat. He put his cupped hand against the glass and leaned his forehead against his fingers, peering into the car. After a moment he straightened and continued to approach the sheriff, lagging a few steps behind his partner.

"What's going on here?" the officer who hadn't stopped to look in the car called.

It was Grimes. Maggie's identification was instantaneous, and, just as it had when she had recognized Dalton's voice, a surge of fear crowded her throat so strongly it was hard to breathe.

Even when Rafe had detained her, even when he was touching her, she hadn't felt he was threatening her life. That wasn't what Dalton wanted. He wasn't out to murder her. She couldn't be so sure about Emmitt Grimes, however, not based on what she had seen in his eyes when he had come out to search her house.

"Y'all go on about your business," Rafe said, his voice revealing nothing except that familiar tinge of good-natured amusement. "There ain't nothing going on here that needs concern the two of you."

"Who's that you got with you, Rafe?" That was Grimes's partner, Thompson, the one who had looked into the window of the cruiser.

"I don't kiss and tell, boys. My mama raised me to be a gentleman," Rafe said easily, his voice sounding as if he were a little embarrassed by the questions. "And I'm way too old to start making changes now."

"This looks like Maggie Cannon's pickup," Grimes said.

"Is that a fact?" Rafe said, his voice still amused.

"It's a fact," Grimes agreed, refusing to back down, and apparently not intending to leave, despite the sheriff's orders. "What's she doing out here?"

"Meetin' me," Rafe said.

"And what are you doing out here?"

"Meetin' her."

The sheriff's tone was mocking now. As defiant as Maggie had tried to be earlier. And far more successful.

The position of Rafe's right arm was shifting as he talked, moving slowly and very carefully. He was reaching for his gun, Maggie realized, remembering that the holster had already been unfastened. Maybe in the darkness he would be able to get away with doing that. Maybe.

"I wouldn't do that if I were you," Grimes warned.

"You aren't me, Emmitt," Rafe said, his hand still moving.

Suddenly Maggie knew what was going to happen. Knew

it and was powerless to prevent it. She was afraid to run. Afraid that if she did, she would simply draw Grimes's fire.

All she could think of was Laurie. And what Drew had said about her daughter already having lost her father. Maggie was all she had left, and if something happened to her, then Laurie would be alone in the world.

You lonely, Maggie? Rafe Dalton had asked, and she had denied it. But she had been, of course. She and Laurie had both been lonely. Missing Tommy. Or at least they had been missing the third person in what was supposed to be the strong, stable triangle that made a family.

And for the briefest moment after Drew Evans had kissed her, Maggie had allowed herself to dream that maybe they would never have to ever be lonely again. Now she knew that dream was doomed to die here on this humid summer night, as most of the ones she had dreamed in her life had already died.

She watched as Rafe's hand, moving seemingly in slow motion, closed over the butt of his weapon and began to extract it from the holster. Before he had completed the movement, a shot rang out, shattering the quiet. The rear window of the truck exploded behind her, and Maggie flinched from the sound, ducking her head and trying to shelter more of her body behind Rafe's.

The gun he held quickly boomed an answer to that shot, and it seemed that even as it did, he was pulling her down with his left hand. "Get under the truck," Rafe ordered, and Maggie scrambled to obey, sliding under the vehicle and then pulling herself forward with her elbows.

As she slithered toward the front of the truck, a couple of bullets ricocheted off the metal of its bed, pinging away into the darkness. She was aware by sound that Rafe was returning the deputies' fire, but she couldn't tell if either of them had been successful in hitting their targets.

She turned her head, looking toward the rear of the truck. All she could see were Rafe's half boots and part of his trouser legs. He was duckwalking along the tailgate toward the far side of the truck. He was no longer paying her the least bit of attention, his focus entirely on the two men with whom he was exchanging shots.

Despite her fear, Maggie realized that she might never get an opportunity like this again. She turned her head to her right and looked into the same forbidding tangle of woods she had contemplated only minutes before. Now they looked inviting. Safe. At least a lot safer than what was going on out here.

She began to slide sideways, reluctant to leave the shelter under the truck, but terrified that Rafe would be killed, and whatever protection he had offered them would be gone. If she could get into the woods, she could crawl to the sheriff's car. She could get into the front seat, and then figure out how to release the locks on the back doors...

She had reached the edge of the truck. The open space between its protective cover and the beginning of the trees seemed much wider than when she had stood out there. Maybe she should just stay here and take her chances with whoever survived the gun battle. Battle? she thought, realizing that she hadn't heard a shot in several seconds. And unsure what that meant.

As she lay on her stomach at the edge of the truck, desperately trying to think what to do, there was another shot. This one struck something besides metal. There was an outcry, but she couldn't tell which direction it had come from.

She turned her head, searching for Rafe's boots. They were not visible on the other side of the truck. Not visible at the rear, either. Maybe that meant nothing. Or maybe it meant he had been the one who'd cried out. And if Rafe Dalton were dead...

Without giving herself a chance to change her mind, she eased out from under the truck and, trying to keep as low as possible, made a break for the woods. She never heard the shot that hit her. All she felt was the force of its blow, powerful enough to knock her to the ground.

She lay there, stunned by the unexpectedness of it. There wasn't any pain, but she couldn't seem to will her body to move. It required too much energy and a strength she no longer had. Maggie turned her head, the movement almost languid, and looked up at the branches of the trees above her. Their leaves were black against the lesser blackness of the star-touched sky.

Laurie loved the stars, she thought. She loved for the two of them to sit together on the front steps of the cabin at twilight and watch them pop out, one after another.

Laurie. Drew had tried to tell her, and she hadn't listened. Maggie's eyes filled with tears and she closed them, her regret as overwhelming as the pain that burned low in her back.

Laurie and Drew. She had thought for a few days that she had everything. And now... Now there would be nothing. No dreams. No stars. Nothing but the cold black loneliness she could feel creeping over her body, robbing her of feeling.

I love you, she thought, but even if she had been able to articulate the words, there was no one here to hear them. No one but the stars.

She opened her eyes again, straining to see their light through the hot moisture flooding her eyes. It made them dance and flicker more than they ever had before. And when her eyelids fell again, veiling her view, she wasn't even aware that she could no longer see them.

Chapter Fifteen

Drew had started running when he heard the first shot, scrambling to the top of the slope where he had last seen Maggie and then half sliding down the other side. When he had reached the foot of it, he had entered the woods, making his way through them, as silently as possible, back to where they had parked the truck.

Now, from within the cover of the trees, his eyes focused briefly on it and then on the two sheriff's cars parked in tandem a few hundred feet beyond it. He could see nothing besides those three vehicles in the narrow space between the forest and the railroad tracks.

For a second or two, he questioned whether the gunfire could have come from somewhere else. Drew had a lot of experience with that kind of sound evaluation, however. He knew in his heart those shots had come from here. He had known as soon as he'd heard the first of them, even taking into account any distortion caused by the topography. And the gut-twisting knowledge that he had left Maggie and Laurie unprotected had sent the adrenaline roaring.

Surprisingly, no one from the crew unloading the train seemed to be coming to investigate. Drew couldn't figure out why, unless they had been told to ignore anything they heard, content that whatever was happening, the local law would protect them.

And the law was certainly here in force, judging by the presence of those two patrol cars. Anywhere else that might be reassuring, Drew thought. Anywhere but Cooper County.

Where the hell was Maggie? Drew's eyes searched the clearing around the pickup. His eyes lifted again to the two cruisers, parked farther back.

Despite the fact that the area appeared to be deserted, they had to be somewhere—Maggie and the drivers of those cars. Or had there been a third patrol car? One that had taken her and Laurie away before he could get here? *Damn it, Maggie, why didn't you go home like I told you?*

Even as he was assessing the situation, Drew was moving soundlessly from the protection of one tree to the next, edging closer to the strip of land between the tracks and the woods. His gaze was still searching the darkness, Maggie's revolver held before him in the traditional two-handed grip, its muzzle raised slightly.

Maybe Maggie had managed to get the little girl out of the pickup before the shooting had started. Were they hiding in the woods? he wondered, his eyes no longer focused on the clearing, but trying to penetrate the blackness between the trees.

He didn't dare risk calling to them. If she'd had time to get into the woods, then whoever was shooting might not even be aware Maggie and Laurie were here. He didn't want to lure them out of hiding and into the path of a bullet.

He needed to know that Maggie and her daughter were all right, and he needed to know if whoever had been shooting minutes ago was still here. He supposed there was only one way to find out.

He took a step forward, out of the woods and toward the pickup. A bullet slammed into a tree above his head. A small explosion of bark and splinters rained down almost before he heard the whine of the shot. He had ducked instinctively, his eyes sweeping the cleared strip.

There had been movement from across the railroad tracks,

parallel to the first of the sheriff's cars. Nothing more than a shifting of shadows, but Drew kept his eyes fixed on the spot, crouching motionless below the tree where the bullet had struck.

His patience was eventually rewarded. Whoever had fired couldn't resist raising his head to try to determine if his shot had been successful. Drew took aim, carefully aligning the muzzle of Maggie's revolver on the dark blob that emerged from the shadows. Then he hesitated, his finger on the trigger.

He had no idea who was out there. Rafe Dalton? Or his deputies? Or was it possible that was Maggie, who must have known Drew would come when he heard those shots, trying to see if he'd been hit. Reluctantly he lowered the revolver.

Maggie and Laurie were somewhere in this moon-shadowed darkness. Until he located them, he couldn't afford to just shoot at anything that moved. And in this situation, there seemed to be only one way to draw out the people who wanted him dead. Only one way to differentiate between them and Maggie.

Transferring the gun to his left hand, he fumbled around on the ground with his right, his eyes never leaving the place where he had seen that movement. Eventually his searching fingers closed around a short, thick limb. Probably dead fall and rotten, but at least it was heavy enough to serve his purposes.

He hefted it a couple of times, considering targets. Not the truck, where Laurie might still be sleeping. *Might,* he acknowledged. Because even if he didn't know where Maggie was, knowing her as he now did, he believed Laurie would be with her.

The muscles in his legs tightened, preparing. And then he threw the stick as hard as he could. At the same time, he charged to his left, away from the bullet-scarred tree. The limb he'd thrown struck its target, the hood of the first patrol car. It drew fire, as he'd hoped it would. A bullet ricocheted off the vehicle, singing away harmlessly into the woods.

Even as he had sprinted to his left, shifting the revolver back to his right hand, Drew had kept his eyes on the place where he believed that first shot had originated. And right after the piece of wood he'd thrown had struck the car, he'd been rewarded with a visible flash from that location. He fired on the run, aiming for that spot and hoping for an outcry that would indicate he'd struck what he was aiming at.

For several long seconds there was no sound at all in the clearing. Drew had stopped, his back against the shielding bulk of an oak. Finally, as the silence lengthened, he peered cautiously around it.

The dark shape he had targeted had disappeared. Which didn't mean a damn thing, of course. Except maybe that whoever was out there might know as much about this kind of night fighting as Drew did. At least enough to know to change position after you'd fired and revealed your location.

He moved behind the tree again, his back pressed against the solidity of its trunk. He held the gun in both hands once more, standing motionless, breath held, straining to hear any sound in the surrounding darkness.

There was a faint rustling to his right. Toward the patrol cars. He looked in that direction, but couldn't see a thing.

He eased to his left, shoulders rolling over the roughness of the bark behind them. He checked out Maggie's truck one last time, hoping that if she were in there with Laurie, she would do something to let him know. Blink the light in the cab or flash the headlights. *Just do something,* he commanded her silently.

There was nothing. Mouth tight with frustration, Drew rolled his shoulders around the trunk to the other side of the tree. His eyes searched the clearing again. Still nothing moving there. No more sounds.

Where the hell are you, Maggie? Fear for her and Laurie

was building because he knew her. If she could, Maggie would have done something to let him know where she was. *If she could,* he repeated, picturing Rafe or one of his buddies holding a gun on Laurie, forcing Maggie to silence, while the others were out there in the darkness stalking him.

One thing at a time, he told himself, fighting to control emotions that had no place in this kind of situation. He knew that. He had had enough experience at this not to let his fear for the two of them get in the way of doing the job. *Take care of whoever is out there with a gun and then find Maggie and Laurie. One thing at a time.*

He began to move, working his way closer to the first of the patrol cars, trying to draw his opponent away from the truck where he and Maggie had left Laurie. He moved silently, as he'd been trained, using the trees for concealment.

The moon slipped behind a cloud and recognizing his chance, Drew left the edge of the woods and covered the short span between the trees and the cruiser parked closest to Maggie's truck at a dead run. As soon as he reached the protection of the car, he stooped down, keeping the vehicle between him and the last known location of the shooter. Which might not, of course, be anywhere near his present location.

Fighting to silence his labored breathing, he listened for any noise. And was again disappointed. He eased up, trying to look through the back windows of the cruiser and over to the railroad tracks. As he did, the moon came out from behind the cloud again, its faint light pouring in through the window on the opposite side of the car he was hiding behind. It illuminated the back seat, shining on the soft blond hair of the little girl who was sleeping there, thumb in her mouth.

Drew's heart stopped, and he closed his eyes, remembering with horror that he had thrown his decoy at this car rather than the truck. He had no idea what the child was doing in one of the patrol cars, but despite everything, she seemed to be fine. And totally undisturbed by what was going on around her.

He took a breath in relief, the steady rhythm of his heart resuming just as a bullet struck the glass of the driver's side window. Drew threw himself to the ground, scrambling under the car. As he did, he squeezed the trigger of Maggie's revolver, and continued to squeeze off shots, shooting under the chassis.

He didn't have a target. He was simply trying to keep whoever was shooting from beyond the tracks from firing any more bullets at the cruiser where the child slept.

Apparently, however, one of his wild shots struck home. He heard the howl of agony and deliberately aimed his next shot right at the sound. Then he waited, listening as silence settled once more over the clearing.

Finally, after it seemed he had waited an eternity, he crawled out from under the patrol car on the side next to the woods. Cautiously, he raised his head far enough that he could see into the back seat. Despite the bullet that had starred the front window, Laurie was still asleep, mouth working steadily at the comfort of her thumb.

Drew tried the handle of the back door and found it locked, which put an end to his idea of getting the child out of the car and into the relative safety of the dense woods behind him.

He still had no idea where Maggie could be. And no idea how many of Cooper County's finest were out there in the darkness. He eased toward the front of the cruiser, trying the passenger side door as he did. It, too, was locked, which was what he'd expected. The windows had all been left open a crack, but not enough to allow him to get to the interior locks.

When he reached the front bumper, Drew searched the ground around him again. He wasn't as lucky this time. He couldn't find anything with enough weight to carry very far. He slipped off his shoe and, leaning out as far as he dared, threw it toward the pickup. There was a satisfying clamor when it landed inside the bed. And then there was nothing.

No response. Not from the woods or the other patrol car. Not from beyond the protection the raised railroad bed offered. No reaction at all to the noise the shoe made striking the truck.

Emboldened, Drew eased forward a little more, still holding Maggie's revolver before him. Crouching, he made his way around the front of the car until he could see the space between it and the tracks. Despite the shifting clouds, which intermittently obscured the moon, he could make out a darker shape lying on the ground on the far side of the cruiser, nearer the graveled rail bed than the woods.

Maggie? Fear that it might be turned his knees to water and crammed his hammering heart into his throat. And it destroyed his caution.

He moved away from the cover of the patrol car and made a run for the shape, keeping low. Every second he expected a bullet. He knew he would feel its impact before he heard it, and the whole way across the clearing, his muscles were clenched in preparation for the blow.

And then, as he got close enough to see details, he realized this wasn't Maggie. *Uniform.* Whoever this was was wearing a pale uniform. Dalton or one of his deputies. *Not Maggie.* He fought the urge to close his eyes in relief. *Not Maggie.* Despite that surge of emotion, Drew held the revolver on the still form, ready to shoot if it displayed any sign of life.

Cautiously, he stooped down next to the body, still alert to any threat from the darkness around him. He reached out with his left hand and gingerly patted the pockets of the uniform pants, trying to determine which one held the keys to the cruiser where Laurie was locked up.

When he discovered the unmistakable shape of a key ring in the pants pocket on the right hand side, Drew switched Maggie's revolver to his left hand. As he did, the moon made one of its periodic reappearances, revealing the face of the man whose pockets he was searching.

It was Rafe Dalton, a dark bloodstain spreading into the dirt around his head. And Drew still had no idea who had been shooting at whom before he'd arrived. All he knew for certain was that he hadn't heard Maggie's rifle, so she hadn't been involved.

Had what happened here been a falling out among thieves? Or a fight between the honest and the dishonest elements of the Cooper County Sheriff's Department? Or a fight with some outside agency, who had stumbled, as he and Maggie had, onto what was going on in this county?

Whichever it had been, it was nothing to him, Drew decided. Figuring out what was going on at Edgemont, attempting to separate the good guys from the bad, even clearing his name had suddenly slipped way down on his list of priorities. All he wanted to do was find Maggie and get her and Laurie out of here.

Edging closer to the sheriff, Drew reached into the pocket where he had felt the keys, fishing for them. As soon as he did, the man on the ground exploded into motion.

Dalton's legs locked around Drew's body, which had been highly vulnerable as he stooped, slightly off balance, to reach for the keys. Using his legs, the sheriff threw him to the ground and held him there.

He followed that initial move by rolling over on top of Drew, his right hand closing around Drew's left wrist. Fingers like talons, Dalton slammed the hand that held Maggie's gun again and again against the hard-packed dirt of the clearing.

If Drew had been holding the weapon in his right hand, Rafe might not have been successful. Eventually, however, the weakened muscles of Drew's injured left shoulder succumbed to those repeated blows. His fingers loosened against the barrage of pain, despite his efforts to hang on to the weapon.

The entire sequence occupied a few seconds. During that time, the shock of a seemingly dead body coming to life had given Dalton the advantage. As soon as Drew realized he was losing control of the revolver, he concentrated on pounding his right fist against the side of the sheriff's head.

A couple of those blows landed, but Dalton got his left arm up to fend them off. And as soon as the revolver fell from Drew's fingers, the sheriff was able to bring his right up to trade punches with the man he was holding on the ground.

Drew fought with a desperation compounded of fear for Maggie and the knowledge that he wasn't back to full strength. If he didn't defeat Rafe Dalton soon, he wouldn't be able to. With that realization, somehow he got his knees up under the bulky body and threw the sherrif backward. He staggered to his feet in time to find Dalton was coming at him again.

Obviously the head wound hadn't been serious. Maybe a graze, just enough of a blow to the skull to render the sheriff briefly unconscious. Any head wound, no matter how minor, bled profusely. He should have remembered that before it was too late, Drew acknowledged, meeting Rafe's charge with a right cross that had every ounce of power he could muster behind it.

The blow stopped Dalton's forward motion, sending him to his knees. Drew kicked out, aiming for his opponent's chin. Rafe got his hands up in time, grabbing Drew's foot instead. He jerked, and Drew went down, his back and head hitting hard enough that the air thinned and blackened around him, and he fought not to pass out.

While Drew struggled just to remain conscious, the sheriff got to his feet. He kicked out, catching Drew in the side with his booted foot. The pain took Drew's breath, and he felt a rib snap. *Now or never* echoed in his head, as the strength seemed to seep out of his muscles.

He rolled, putting his hands over his head and gathering

his body into a ball to protect vital organs from the next kick, which he knew was coming. As he rolled, he felt the unmistakable shape of a fallen limb under his hip. Probably as rotten as the one he had thrown, but still he reached down and grabbed it with his right hand.

He rolled again, freeing the limb, which he now clutched in his fingers. He tightened them around it, as the sheriff followed him, aiming kicks at Drew's retreating body. A couple of them made contact, but none with quite the same nauseating force of the first.

Crab-crawling and rolling, trying to dodge those brutal blows, Drew mentally gathered the last ounce of strength. *Last chance* beat in his head like a refrain, just as it had from the time the bus had wrecked, freeing him to begin this quest. Now that chance had all come down to this last battle.

When he realized he was beside the patrol car where Laurie was asleep, Drew reached up, the fingers of his left hand locking on the door handle. He was still in the process of pulling himself upright when Dalton arrived.

Drew jumped to the side, barely avoiding the toe of the sheriff's boot, which slammed into the metal of the door instead. Rafe's expletive was loud and colorful as he hopped backward on one foot. And this time it was Drew who charged.

He raised the branch he'd picked up and brought it down on the side of the sheriff's head with a satisfying thwack, like a baseball bat makes meeting a fast ball. Without another sound, Rafe went down, the blow driving his upper body backward as if he'd been shot.

Swaying drunkenly, gasping for air, Drew stood over him for a few seconds until he was convinced the sheriff wasn't going to get up again. He rolled Dalton onto his stomach and used the handcuffs from the sheriff's own utility belt to fasten his wrists together behind his back. Then he bent and dragged the car keys out of the sheriff's pocket.

Before he went over to unlock the car, he stopped to find the revolver Dalton had beaten out of his hand. This had all been going on too long. Someone from the landfill would eventually get curious when no one from the county showed up down there to explain the gunshots.

Get Laurie, find Maggie, and then get the hell out of here, he told himself again.

Fingers shaking with exhaustion, he tried all the keys on the ring in the lock. None of them fit. Cursing in frustration, he threw them against the side of the car.

And then, trying to be rational, despite his mushrooming fear about Maggie, he examined his options. He could try to shoot the lock, but with the mechanism protected by the metal of the door, that seemed a pretty good way to get hit by his own ricocheting bullet. He could go back and search Rafe again, assuming the car keys were on a separate ring. Or he could find something and try to break out the safety glass of the window, already weakened by the bullet hole.

His first thought was the limb he'd used on Dalton, which had certainly seemed solid enough. And then the image of Maggie's rifle was suddenly in his head.

It would be in the pickup, either in the bed or in the cab. And because he hadn't searched the truck, there was always the possibility that Maggie would be with it, hopefully cowering, her head down and protected.

Please God, let her be cowering somewhere. Even as he prayed that quick prayer, he knew in his heart that Maggie Cannon wasn't the cowering kind.

When he reached the pickup, he put his foot on the back bumper, lifting enough to see into the bed. It was empty except for the tarp he had hidden under. He jumped down and started around the passenger side of the truck toward the cab.

He hadn't taken three steps when he stumbled over Maggie's outstretched legs. He hadn't seen her before because she was lying in the shadows cast by the truck itself, no more than five feet away from the safety it would have represented.

Her upturned face was pale, and her limbs lay in a boneless sprawl Drew had seen too many times. Seeing it now, his heart stopped. Everything else, even Laurie, was forgotten as he knelt on the ground and put trembling fingers against the artery in her neck. He closed his eyes, fighting the bite of tears of relief as he felt the reassuring pulse of blood beneath them.

He laid the gun on the ground beside her, and began to run both hands over Maggie's body. Her shirt was wet on the lower right side. He held his hand up to the faint moonlight and saw the dark smear of blood on his fingers.

He slipped his hand under the cotton knit shell and found the wound. Not the small neat hole a bullet makes when it enters flesh. Exit wound, he decided, trying to keep his rising panic in check as he made the critical assessments.

He moved his fingers around to her back, gently slipping them under her side and working strictly by feel. There was blood there, too, and finally his fingers found the puncture-type wound he had been seeking. She had been shot in the back and the bullet had passed through her body.

And what the hell kind of damage had it done on the way?

He had to get her to a hospital, and he had to do it fast. He slipped his right arm under her shoulders, lifting her upper body. Her head lolled lifelessly, and the cold, sick fear lurched inside his chest again. He got his left arm under her thighs somehow, even remembering to grab the revolver he'd laid on the ground before he attempted to pick her up.

Using the muscles in his legs and buttocks, he managed to lift her off the ground, despite the pain in the damaged muscles of his chest. Her body was far heavier than he had expected. *Dead weight.* He regretted those unthinking words as soon as they had formed in his brain.

Hospital. That was all he needed to be thinking of now. Just get Maggie to the hospital. Give her a chance. Give the miracle workers in the ER a chance. He started praying that he could find his way back to civilization through that maze of dirt roads they had traveled tonight.

He started toward the pickup, staggering a little under his burden, and found the deputy who had testified at his trial standing at the back of Maggie's truck, the barrel of her rifle propped on the far side of the bed, aimed straight for Drew's heart.

"Far enough," Emmitt Grimes said softly. "Martin Holcomb, ain't it?"

Chapter Sixteen

"Maggie's been shot," Drew said, ignoring the deputy's question.

The rifle Grimes must have acquired by reaching into the open window of Maggie's truck didn't waver. For the first time, Drew noted the dark stain on the shoulder of the deputy's uniform. Was Emmitt Grimes the man he'd shot? If so, whose bullet had grazed the sheriff's skull?

Grimes's, perhaps? Because Dalton was in on whatever was going on at the landfill? Or because the sheriff was the one who was clean and Grimes and his partner had killed Brundridge?

The fact that Emmitt had the drop on Drew and hadn't shot him, at least not yet, seemed to indicate he might be on the right side of the law. There was no proof, however, one way or the other. Nothing for Drew to go by, except his instincts. And everything he felt about Rafe Dalton was colored by the fact that the sheriff had made his attraction to Maggie so damned obvious.

The important question right now was not who was guilty or innocent here, but whether if he dropped the gun, Drew could trust Grimes to see that Maggie got medical care. Even as he wondered that, Drew knew he really trusted no one but himself to look after Maggie.

"I'm taking her to a hospital," he said. It was not so much a threat as a determination. An announcement.

"What you're gonna do is drop that gun," Grimes ordered.

Drew hesitated for a heartbeat, evaluating the demand. He had actually been a little surprised to realize he was still holding the revolver. It was gripped awkwardly in his left hand, not even in a position to be fired. The weight of Maggie's lower body was draped across that arm so that Drew doubted he could even get the weapon up, given the damaged muscles in his chest.

Despite his vow not to go back to prison, Drew knew he couldn't kill an innocent man, which Grimes might be. And if he shot at the deputy and Grimes returned fire, Maggie would be in the way.

"I'll see to it that Maggie's taken care of," Grimes said. "I swear to you I'll get her to the hospital, but you have to throw down that weapon before we can do anything else."

Drew didn't know whether he could believe that promise. He couldn't even know for sure that Grimes wasn't the one who had shot Maggie. Given Rafe Dalton's obvious infatuation, it seemed unbelievable that he would have gunned her down. Of course, in that exchange of gunfire, Maggie could have been hit accidentally. Drew had no way of knowing about that, either.

"Drop it," Grimes urged. "Do it now, Holcomb. Don't make me do something we'll both be sorry for."

Maggie. She was all that mattered now, Drew realized. He had gotten her into all this. She was here because of him. And she was hurt. How badly hurt he couldn't know, but he did know that the longer treatment was delayed, the less chance she had.

Even as the emotional side of his brain was considering that reality, all his years of training were presenting alternate options. Demanding that he take some action. Do something besides giving up control to Grimes. The instinct for survival clamored fiercely for his attention, and the words ''last chance'' echoed one last time.

Maggie's last chance, he thought, rejecting the realization that had driven him throughout this hopeless journey, from the moment the bus had careened off the mountain road and burst into flames until now. *Maggie's last chance.* Drew Evans opened his fingers and let the revolver fall into the dirt.

''Get her some help, damn it,'' he said. Even in surrender, the words sounded like a command.

Grimes held his eyes a long time, and then, again using the barrel of the rifle, he motioned Drew away from the truck and toward the cruisers.

WHEN MAGGIE WOKE, Emmitt Grimes was standing beside her bed, his left arm in a halter sling. Beside him was her neighbor Amy Burke, holding Laurie in the crook of her right arm. The little girl's wide blue eyes were clouded with anxiety as she looked down on her mother.

Maggie automatically found a smile for her, despite the dryness of her lips. She lifted her left hand to reach out to Laurie and realized there was a wire connected to her finger. Seeing it, she stopped in confusion.

It was only then that she remembered what had happened, and why she was in this hospital bed. She fought the urge to close her eyes against the painful reality of those events, fought the temptation not to face them. It would be easier just to let her mind drift back into that peaceful, uncaring cloud of drugs and unconsciousness. No worries there, and no regrets.

This, however, was the dear reality, she thought, as Laurie leaned forward in Amy's arms so that her small fingers made contact with Maggie's. A reality that she needed to come back to, and suddenly, despite everything, there was an overwhelming gratitude in her heart that she had.

"Hey," Maggie said softly, surprised at how much effort the single syllable required.

"Hey, Mama."

Maggie smiled at her again, letting her hand fall because she was literally too weak to hold it up. Laurie straightened, putting her arm around Amy's neck again. At least she knew that her daughter was safe, Maggie thought in gratitude.

"They say you're going to be all right, Maggie," Emmitt said, drawing Maggie's eyes back to his face. "Nothing wrong that the surgeons and a little time can't fix. Laurie's staying out at Amy's until you're better. We wanted you to see her, so you'd know she's all right and is being taken care of. I guess she needed to see you, too."

Maggie nodded, wanting desperately to ask him about Drew and afraid that if she did, she would give something away. Maybe they didn't know Drew had been with her that night. Last night? she wondered.

"Holcomb came back for you, Maggie, as soon as he heard the gunfire," Grimes said, as if he had read her mind. "I guess you need to know that, too. He deserves some credit. If he hadn't found you…" Emmitt paused, glancing at Laurie, who was still watching her mother. "I didn't even know you'd been hit."

"Where is he?" Maggie asked.

"The state picked him up as soon as I got the paperwork done."

"But…" For a moment she felt almost too weak to keep going. What would anything she said matter now? Drew was already back in prison, and she didn't know who could help her prove his innocence. She didn't even know what had gone on at the landfill after she'd been shot. Or why Emmitt Grimes was the one who had brought Drew in and why he seemed to be looking out after Laurie.

"What happened that night, Emmitt? Why were you and Thompson there? Why would Rafe pull a gun on you? Did you kill him?"

"Rafe's in jail, Maggie. Edgemont was paying him to make sure nobody discovered what they were doing out there. I got suspicious because he always changed the assignment rotation on certain nights. It seemed like he was trying to keep the rest of us away from the landfill."

"You were out there to investigate *Rafe*?"

"And whatever they were doing at the landfill. I'd already contacted the EPA, and we thought if we could see where they took the stuff when they unloaded it—"

"Rafe's the one who killed Brundridge," Maggie said, cutting off Emmitt's explanation.

"Dalton was the person Charlie had been meeting that night at the church. If you thought something illegal was going on, who would you turn to? And trusting the sheriff had cost Brundridge his life."

"Whoa, Maggie. Slow down a minute. That's a mighty big leap from Rafe being in on an illegal dumping cover-up to murder. A murder somebody else has already been convicted of, if you remember. Unless you got some solid proof about what you just said…" Emmitt shrugged.

"No blood," Maggie said, knowing, just as she had when she'd told Drew, that she was right about the importance of this.

"What?"

"There was no blood at the Wagon Wheel. You should have noticed that, Emmitt. Rafe sent Tommy there, all primed with the lie he wanted him to tell and the promise of enough money to save Laurie's life if he told it. Then he killed Charlie and brought his body there and dumped it out."

"You're saying Rafe framed Holcomb?"

"With Tommy's help. And then…" She took a breath, remembering what Drew had suggested about Tommy's death. Something they would probably never know for sure. "It's even possible Rafe killed Tommy because he was afraid Tommy was finding his role in framing an innocent man hard to live with.''

Emmitt said nothing for a moment, but she could tell he was thinking about that.

"Truth be told, Maggie, a couple of things Tommy said sometime after the trial made me wonder. 'Course he'd been drinking when he said them. And you know what Tommy was like when he was drinking. I know for a fact Tommy avoided Rafe when he could. I thought that was because he knew the sheriff was interested in you.''

"Tommy knew that?''

"It wasn't exactly a secret. I thought that's why Rafe started acting so weird when Holcomb escaped. Because he was concerned about you living up on that mountain by yourself. Like sending us up there that day to search your house and then calling us off. I thought he figured Holcomb would come after Tommy. And I guess he did,'' Emmitt finished.

"He's not Holcomb.''

"That's Holcomb all right. I was at his trial. We even checked his prints because that's procedure. There ain't no doubt about who that man is, Maggie.''

"That's an identity they made up,'' Maggie said.

Drew had given her the information she needed. Now she just had to make Emmitt believe her. At least to believe her enough to make one phone call.

"They?'' Grimes repeated dubiously.

"The CIA.''

His eyes changed. The growing willingness to consider what she had said about Rafe and the framing was suddenly replaced by skepticism. She couldn't blame him. She had been just this skeptical.

"His real name is Drew Evans. Rafe picked him because he was a nobody. No ties. No family. And no background,'' she added, ''because the CIA had just created a new identity for him and destroyed the old.''

"Now why would the CIA want to do that?" Emmitt asked. His voice was condescending, as if he were humoring a sick child.

She shook her head, the small motion setting off a dull ache centered above her eyes. Or maybe that had been there all along, and she just hadn't been conscious of it until now. Because suddenly everything seemed too hard to explain, the task overwhelming. Drew hadn't told her enough that she could convince anyone that's really what had happened.

He hadn't been trying to explain the change in identity. He had simply been trying to give her a place where she could get help if something happened to him. For some reason, he was convinced the CIA wouldn't respond to any request for assistance made on his behalf, but it seemed to Maggie there was no way to be sure of that except to try.

"I don't know," she said. "He said he belonged to something called the External Security Team. He said to tell them that. And to ask for a man named Steiner. Carl Steiner."

"That's a bunch of crap, Maggie," Grimes said. "Some story he made up to get you to hide him when he was on the run."

"One phone call," she urged softly. "Just ask them. Ask to speak to Steiner and tell him what I told you. You were Tommy's friend. Help me undo what he did to that man. You know he'd want that. Let Tommy rest in peace and let this finally be over. One phone call, Emmitt. What can it hurt?"

"YOU HAVE A VISITOR," the guard said, unlocking the door of his cell and sliding it open.

For a minute Drew's blood froze, considering the remote possibility that this could be Maggie. Not that he didn't want to see her. Not that he wouldn't have given a year of his life just to hold her again. To make sure she was all right. He just didn't want to see her here. He didn't want her to see him like this.

"Who is it?" he asked.

"The guy didn't give me his business card," the guard said sarcastically. "You coming or not?"

Guy. The surge of adrenaline began to fade and his heart rate steadied. The thought of Maggie being here was foolish. After all, Drew had only been back in prison a week. Maggie was probably still in the hospital.

Guy. Drew didn't have any idea who might come to see him. Maybe Emmitt Grimes? If so, at least he could find out about how Maggie was doing.

The deputy had let him know that she had come through surgery okay, but Drew hadn't heard anything else. And he really hadn't expected to. Maybe Grimes was more compassionate than he had given him credit for, or maybe…

Drew's breathing faltered as he realized for the first time that this could be bad news. That would be far more likely to bring the deputy here than just a progress report.

"I'm coming," he said, pushing up off the bunk despite the fear that was stirring in his gut.

They didn't take him to the common room, which was always loud and crowded with people on visiting days. Instead, they led him into one of the smaller rooms where prisoners were allowed to meet privately with their lawyers.

Drew took that to mean he would be meeting with someone official. He hadn't even contacted his lawyer yet. He wasn't sure he wanted to continue with the one who had represented him before. And he wasn't sure that what he had found out while he'd been outside would be enough to justify asking for a new trial. It took a lot of evidence to get a murder conviction overturned. Hard evidence. The kind Drew didn't have.

Grimes had admitted that he had suspected Dalton was engaged in whatever was going on out at Edgemont for a long time. His actions the night Maggie had been shot seemed to prove the deputy had been right. It wasn't proof, however, that Dalton had had anything to do with Brundridge's death. Drew pulled out a chair and sat down at the table, wondering if Grimes was even considering that angle.

Despite the fact that he now knew it wasn't the agency who had framed him, Drew hadn't revealed his CIA connections to the deputy. After all, he couldn't prove he wasn't Martin Holcomb. And he certainly couldn't prove he was an ex-CIA agent named Drew Evans. Whatever proof that might have existed was buried within the bowels of an agency where he, along with everyone else who had been a member of Griff Cabot's team, was persona non grata.

To the agency, he was no longer even alive. For all practical purposes Drew Evans was a dead man. And as far as anyone in authority was concerned, Martin Holcomb was still a convicted murderer.

The door to the room opened, and Drew looked up. Right into the eyes of another dead man. A man who had died in a terrorist assault at Langley more than two years ago. A man who had once been his superior at the CIA and the head of the elite External Security Team.

"Hello, Drew," Griff Cabot said, smiling the same enigmatic smile Drew remembered so well. "You're a hard man to track down. And believe me, we've all been trying."

JUST BEING ABLE to tell Griff everything that had happened seemed to have made the years they had been separated disappear. Cabot's dark eyes had rested on his face, just as they used to, as he patiently listened to the whole story.

This was, of course, after Griff had explained his own agency-engineered death and his on-going efforts to reassemble the members of his team, which the CIA had deliberately scattered when their mission had been deemed politically undesirable.

With the death of Jake Holt, the team's computer expert, the task of locating those agents whose identities had been destroyed had proved almost impossible. If it hadn't been for Emmitt Grimes's call, Cabot explained, and Carl Steiner's friendship, and maybe even Steiner's guilt over what had been done to the External Security Team, he might never have discovered Drew's whereabouts.

"You've talked to Grimes?" Drew asked.

"And to the warden and the attorney general. At least long enough to assure all of them that you have friends with…some influence," Griff said carefully. "Dalton is still denying everything, of course. He's claiming he pulled his gun on Grimes and Thompson that night because he believed they were involved in the illegal dumping. To be truthful, unless Dalton breaks, it isn't going to be easy to connect him to that murder, Drew."

Cabot didn't throw his connections or his wealth around, but he still had an enormous amount of both. And it seemed he was willing to use them on Drew's behalf. Which shouldn't have surprised him, Drew acknowledged, but after the friendless despair of the last two years, Griff's commitment moved him as much as Maggie's belief in his innocence had.

"There's a woman," he said softly.

"Maggie Cannon. I know all about her," Griff said. "She's the one who made Grimes contact the agency. If she hadn't…"

"Is she all right?"

"The official word is stable. Grimes says she's going to be fine. Do you want me to visit her?"

Drew thought about it. About the implications if Griff did. About what Maggie might think. "I want you to make sure she has everything she needs, and that may include taking care of her medical expenses. At least until…"

Drew hesitated, knowing that even with Cabot's influence, overturning his conviction was going to be difficult. Tommy Cannon, the chief witness against him, was dead. What he knew about Dalton didn't lead him to believe that he would implicate himself in murder. And the only other people who could testify to having any knowledge about Brundridge's death could offer only circumstantial information.

Unless they could find some kind of hard evidence, that wouldn't be enough to set him free. And if that were the case, the less contact he had with Maggie, the better. He had told her the truth that night. She deserved better. Better than waiting on a man who was still locked behind bars, and who might remain there for the rest of his life.

"Just see that she's taken care of," Drew said finally. "Grimes will help find out what she needs."

"Any message you want to send her?" Griff asked, his eyes betraying an unspoken empathy.

Not yet, Drew thought. Maybe never. Not unless he could go to her a free man. The man he had been before all this had started. And so, holding Cabot's eyes, Drew Evans shook his head.

Epilogue

Six months later

IT'S GOING TO SNOW AGAIN, Maggie decided, looking up at the darkening sky. There was no mistaking those clouds.

She closed the door to the hen house and started back toward the cabin. Although she and Laurie had spent a couple of hours this morning filling the wood bin inside, if she were smart she'd pick up an armload of logs on her way. It was going to be another cold night. *Another lonely night.*

She heard the car coming up the mountain before she reached the front door, and despite everything, a surge of hope tightened her chest. Hope that after all this time she surely knew didn't belong there.

And so she told herself again what she had repeated over and over for the last six months. Forget what had happened. Forget the man who had spent a week in her cabin and every minute since he had left it in her heart. Forget...

Except that was easier said than done, she admitted, watching the car top the rise and start up her drive. Not a car she recognized. It was a big, dark green sport utility vehicle. Obviously new. Obviously expensive.

Standing on the porch, she crossed her arms protectively

over her chest as the wind whipped across the clearing, its damp chill cutting through the thin coat she wore. The SUV entered the yard and came to a stop at the end of the drive. As soon as it did, the driver killed the headlights, which had pierced the gathering twilight, illuminating her figure.

She could see nothing through the tinted windshield, however, and a touch of uneasiness stirred in her stomach. After all that had happened to her six months ago, perhaps she had a right to that anxiety, but she didn't like feeling it.

She shivered with the force of those memories, her eyes straining to see through the fading light. She thought about going inside and getting Tommy's gun, but something, perhaps nothing more than the tradition of hospitality or maybe her own determination not to let those events turn her into a coward, kept her standing in the cold as the long seconds ticked by.

Finally, the driver's side door opened, and a man crawled out. Before it seemed her brain could have registered a recognition, her heart began to race. There was something about the shape of his head. Or maybe the heart-stopping familiarity of his wide shoulders. There was something…

"Hello, Maggie," Drew said, his deep voice carrying across the distance despite the efforts of the wind to sweep it away.

Maggie knew she should answer him. At least acknowledge his greeting. Acknowledge that something she had dreamed about for the last six months had finally happened. She fought the burn of tears instead, reminding herself that it had been six months, and during all that time she hadn't heard one word from Drew Evans.

Not until he'd uttered these two. And she couldn't—she shouldn't—read anything into those.

"May I come in?" he asked.

She wished she could see his face or read his eyes.

Wished she could see something in either that might give her a clue as to why he was here. Obviously, since he *was* here, his conviction for Charlie Brundridge's murder had been overturned. She had hoped for that, of course, but Emmitt had warned her that accomplishing it would be difficult and prolonged.

In the meantime Drew hadn't called her. Or written. And then suddenly, she thought, resentment building, he just shows up. Just as if those long empty months had not been there, between that night and this.

''What do you want?'' she asked.

The tone of that question was wrong. Maybe because of the constriction in her throat. Or the fear that she might be reading into his presence things she shouldn't be. He hesitated before he answered her, and when he did, she knew no more than she had when he had first stepped out of the car.

''To talk,'' he said. ''I'd just like to talk to you, Maggie, if you'll let me. Explain some things.''

She took a breath, wondering why she was debating the right or the wrong of this. She could never turn him away. Maybe the things Drew wanted to say weren't the things she needed to hear, but she'd never know unless she let him say them.

''Come in,'' she said, turning to open the door behind her.

As she did, a wave of warmth from inside the cabin, scented with the fragrance of the cookies she and Laurie had baked this afternoon, welcomed her. She could see Laurie sitting at the kitchen table, her head bent over one of her coloring books.

She glanced back toward Drew's car and realized he was taking something out of the back. Something that looked like a shopping bag. Christmas, Maggie thought, a cold stab of disappointment inside, despite how hard she had been working at having no expectations.

That's what this visit was all about. A token visit. A token offering. A thank you. Fighting despair, she stepped inside and closed the door against the wind. She pulled off her coat and threw it over the arm of the couch.

She felt a momentary flash of dismay as she looked down on what she was wearing. Jeans and one of Tommy's flannel shirts, which she had found on top of the sewing machine. She had replaced its missing button and had been wearing it for warmth. But now...

The tap on the door pushed that concern from her mind. She wiped her hands down the sides of her jeans, as if preparing for some household task. Then she wrapped her fingers around the knob, closing her eyes for an instant before she opened it.

She had been right about the presents. Brightly wrapped boxes were visible at the top of the shopping bag. Her gaze had fallen to that first, and she deliberately reminded herself of their probable significance. *Thanks and goodbye.* And when she thought she had accepted that, she raised her eyes to his face.

He was different, she realized, almost with sense of wonder. The hazel eyes were no longer cold or distrustful. And his mouth wasn't tight. It didn't seem that those things, nothing more than a relaxation of the wariness his previous situation had demanded, could cause such a change.

As she watched, his lips relaxed even more, tilting into a smile. Her eyes came back to his, and again, in spite of all her self-directed warnings about why he was here, her heart jolted at the impact of what was in them.

Then he stepped into the room, brushing her out of the way, and closed the door. The sudden silence after the low moan of the wind was disconcerting—to Maggie, at least. Drew didn't seem to notice. He set the shopping bag down and shrugged out of his leather jacket. For the first time she was aware of a subtle and very pleasant aroma. Some kind of cologne or aftershave, but very masculine. Probably as expensive as the car he was driving.

"Something smells good," he said.

Startled that he had just echoed her own thought, Maggie looked up, straight into his eyes, and realized he was smiling at her again, perfectly at ease, in spite of the length of time since they had seen one another. Of course, he hadn't spent that time engaging in fantasies about what this would be like. About what it would feel like to be with him again.

"Cookies," she said. Her voice sounded thready.

"Any left?" he asked.

Cookies, gift-giving and then goodbye, Maggie amended.

"Probably a few," she said, her tone thankfully more normal. "If Laurie hasn't managed to finish them off."

"Hi, Laurie," Drew said, looking across the living room and into the kitchen.

The little girl lifted her head, considering their visitor without a trace of excitement, or welcome, in her eyes. "I thought you were gone," she said.

Me, too, Maggie thought, realizing for the first time that her daughter might have had the same foolish expectations about Drew she had felt. And her heart contracted because she hadn't even known Laurie needed her comfort.

"I was," Drew said softly. "Now I'm back."

"You want to color?" the little girl said.

"I'm not very good at staying in the lines," Drew said, his eyes again considering Maggie's face. There seemed to be a hint of amusement in their depths. "I never was, I'm afraid."

"That's all right," Laurie offered. And then she spoiled it by adding, "You can color in one of my old books."

"Laurie," Maggie corrected.

Drew's laugh overrode the admonition. "I'll settle for

some of those cookies," he said to Laurie. "Did you help make them?" He had walked across the room and stood by the table looking down on the coloring book.

"Uh-huh," Laurie said. Her eyes, too, considered whatever she had been working on. "It's not very good," she said, her voice soft, perhaps tinged with hope.

"I'd say it was excellent," Drew said, putting his hand on the top of her head.

It looked big and dark and a little awkward resting there. As if he weren't quite sure what he should do next. And again something stirred in Maggie's chest. Maybe nothing more than the same breath of hope she had just heard in her daughter's voice.

"I brought you something," Drew said, removing his hand.

Laurie's eyes lifted to his face. "Something for Christmas?"

"Something for *you*," he said.

"Is it a secret?"

Drew's eyes found Maggie, questioning.

"She means can she have it now," Maggie explained.

"I don't see why not. I'm of the opinion that Christmas should be stretched to last as long as it can. What do you think, Maggie?"

"I don't think anyone here would argue with that."

"Laurie's presents are the ones wrapped in red," Drew said, indicating the shopping bag with a shift of his eyes.

Instead of separating the packages, Maggie picked up the bag and began to walk toward the kitchen. She was annoyed to find that her knees were shaking. She put the bag down on the kitchen table, automatically straightening the scattered books and crayons to make a place for it.

Again, she was aware of Drew's aftershave. Aware of everything about him, from the rough texture of the wool sweater he wore to the way the leather strap of his watch fit around the strength of his wrist. Aware of everything.

Drew reached into the bag and began laying presents in front of Laurie. There must have been half a dozen of them, department store wrapped and dazzling. As each one was taken out of the bag and laid on the table, Laurie's eyes widened.

And she had had little enough of this kind of excitement in her life, Maggie admitted. Little enough spoiling. Maggie couldn't have begrudged her this gleaming overabundance of gifts, even if she had wanted to. And she wasn't sure she did.

"Are they all mine?" the little girl asked.

"All yours, sweetheart," Drew said softly. "And your mama probably thinks I'm spoiling you."

Again he had turned to look at Maggie. She couldn't tell what was in his eyes, so she allowed hers to fall to her daughter's. "What do you say?" she prompted.

"Thank you," Laurie parroted obediently.

"Open them," Drew suggested.

There was no hesitation on the little girl's part. As she tore into the wrappings of the first, Drew reached into the shopping bag and took out another present. This one was very small, and in contrast to Laurie's, it was wrapped in gold foil.

The size of the box was incredibly suggestive, but Maggie denied the hope that had exploded in her chest when Drew had pulled it from the bag. *Not wrapped in red. Not for Laurie. And obviously...*

"This one's for you, Maggie," Drew said. "If I can possibly talk you into accepting it."

He held the box out, and for the first time, Maggie realized that the tanned fingers were trembling. Just as she knew her own would be. A necklace, she told herself. Something impersonal. Meaningless. When she raised her eyes to his, however, what she found there was not impersonal. Or meaningless.

"At least open it, Maggie," Drew said.

She wasn't sure she was physically capable of doing that. And for a long time she simply looked at the box, resting on those outstretched fingers, which were still vibrating slightly.

Finally, her own closed over the box. She fought the urge to bring it to her chest and hold it against her heart. That would be too revealing. *And this could be anything,* she reminded herself doggedly. *Anything.*

She found the end of the foil paper and pulled the tape apart, sliding a small black leather box out of its wrappings and onto her palm. She glanced up again at Drew's face again before she found the courage to lift the lid.

"You were the only one who believed me, Maggie. The only person in all that time who believed *in* me. I hope you always will."

Fighting tears, she lowered her eyes. She lifted the lid of the box, her own fingers trembling now. And then her eyes rose once more to his.

"If you'd rather have a diamond..." Drew began.

"No," she whispered, but with those words the last doubt disappeared. "It's perfect," she said.

Drew took the box from her hand, removing the ring and slipping it on her left ring finger. Automatically, she turned her hand so that the emerald-cut sapphire caught the light, flashing blue fire.

"Should I take that as a yes?" he asked, his voice teasing now. Relieved.

Had he been as doubtful as she had been? Maggie wondered.

"I don't think I ever heard the question," she said, looking up from the ring to smile at him.

"Will you... Will both of you," he amended, glancing

down at Laurie, the fairy princess doll she had found in the first box she'd unwrapped still clutched in one hand. Her own sapphire-blue eyes were locked in fascination on the two of them. "Will you marry me?"

"Yes," Maggie said. No equivocation. And no doubts. "Oh, yes, we will."

She stood on tiptoe, her arms finding their way around his neck as if they had done this a thousand times. And somehow, in the course of that kiss, the loneliness of the long six months she had waited for Drew Evans disappeared, never to be thought of again.

"WE CAN WAIT, if you'd rather," Drew said, slipping his arm around her shoulders and pulling her into his chest.

After five hours, Maggie was almost accustomed to having him here. Almost accustomed to the thought that he had come back for her. That he wanted her. Wanted both of them.

"Because of Laurie?" she asked, almost amused by the offer.

"Because of any reason you might have to want to wait."

"I *have* waited," she said.

"I was so afraid you were going to let somebody sweep you off your feet before I could get here."

She laughed.

"That's good," Drew said, his mouth finding her temple, his lips trailing against the thin skin there.

"What's good?" she whispered, turning so that her body was against his chest. She laid her cheek on the wool of his sweater and savored the smell and the feel of him.

"That you laughed."

"It would have served you right if I'd found somebody else," she said.

"Maybe, but still…I'm glad you waited, Maggie."

"Why didn't you ask me to wait?" she asked, almost an accusation. The closest she had come to making one.

"Because there was never any guarantee that anything would change. Except the length of my sentence."

"Because of the escape?" He nodded agreement, his chin moving against the top of her head. "But it's over?" she asked, a touch of anxiety in the question.

"Definitely over. They found enough of Charlie Brundridge's blood in Rafe Dalton's car to reopen the investigation. Some friends used their influence on my behalf to see that the rest of it happened as quickly as possible. One of them, a man named Griff Cabot, has even offered me a job. But I told him I had some unfinished business I needed to get back to before I could accept."

She smiled, the movement of her mouth hidden. "Then…let's get back to it. Laurie's asleep. Sound asleep. And anybody who could sleep through all that out at the landfill that night isn't going to be awakened by two people making love."

"I wouldn't be too sure of that, if I were you," Drew said, and without giving her time to protest, he bent and slipped his left arm under her knees, picking her up, just as he had before.

"NOT VERY SEDUCTIVE," Maggie said breathlessly, looking down to watch those same long, tanned fingers, that had trembled as they'd held out a ring to her, deal competently with the buttons on her flannel shirt.

"I don't think you have to worry about seducing me, Maggie."

"What does that mean?"

"That I was effectively seduced a long time ago," Drew said, sliding the shirt off her shoulders and moving forward to put his mouth over the hollow of her collarbone. "Too damn long ago," he breathed, his breath warm and moist against her cold skin.

Cold from the temperature of the small bedroom, which was frigid despite the fire in the living room stove? Maggie wondered. Or chilled with anticipation? Shivering with the thought of Drew's hands finally moving over her body?

She shook the shirt off over her wrists and hands, letting it drop to the floor. As Drew's lips continued to caress her shoulders, his fingers worked at the fastening of her jeans, and after a moment or two, she stepped out of them, too, standing before him in only her serviceable white bra and panties.

Neither had been chosen for sexual enticement, and she couldn't prevent a frisson of unease at the thought of Drew comparing her to the other, undoubtedly more sophisticated, women he had known before. And then, as his fingers found the fastening at the back of her bra, she pushed that fear from her mind. Drew had chosen her, and he had known all about her when he had.

All about her, she thought, as his hands disposed of the bra and then cupped possessively under her breasts. His head lowered, and his mouth and tongue explored her sensitized nipples, hardened with cold and excitement.

"I'm sorry, Maggie," he said softly, raising his head and looking into her eyes. "I want this to be perfect. I want to show you...I want to make you know how I feel. And I'm afraid..."

And suddenly, hearing those broken sentences, Maggie was also afraid. "What's wrong?" she whispered, putting her palm under his chin to lift his head so she could see his eyes.

His skin was clean-shaven, almost smooth, despite the lateness of the hour, and she knew that he had shaved tonight. Obviously, shortly before he'd shown up out here.

"What are you afraid of?" she asked.

"That this is going to go a lot faster than I mean for it to," he said, the admission touched with amusement, perhaps even a hint of embarrassment. "It's been a long time," he added softly.

"For me, too," Maggie said, smiling at him as she said it. "Maybe we've forgotten how to do this."

"Not a chance," Drew whispered.

Kneeling, he disposed of the last of her garments, peeling the panties down over the length of her legs with a practiced economy of motion. Putting the tips of her fingers on his shoulder for balance, Maggie stepped out of them and pushed them out of the way with her bare toes. And then she stood before him totally nude.

His eyes lifted slowly, studying every inch of her body on the way up. He raised his hand, touching her throat with a gentleness she hadn't expected. Long fingers trailed down the center of her body, holding her eyes as they did. She shivered in reaction. Seeing the chill bumps on her skin, he stood, taking her hand and leading her to the bed she had turned back when they had first entered the room.

The sheets were so cold. She lay on her side, shivering, and watched him undress. This wouldn't be the first time she had seen him nude, of course. She had a quick vision of the night she had found him naked and injured in her bathroom.

That had been a different man from this, she realized. That man had been wounded. Hunted. Despairing. The man who had slipped a ring on her finger tonight and had made promises to her and to Laurie was none of those things. He was strong and confident. And his lovemaking, no matter the caveat he had just issued, would be nothing less than that.

Even if this were the quick, passionate coupling he had promised, she realized, it would still be exactly what she wanted. This affirmation, the admission that he wanted her too much to wait, was almost as important as the one the ring had represented. And they had all the time in the world for slow and seductive.

Drew slipped into bed beside her, pulling the tumbled quilts up over them both. His body, despite the chill of the room, was warm and hard and hair roughened, a perfect contrast for the textures of hers.

"Not slow," she said.

The movement of his hand against her breast hesitated, and he leaned back, studying her face in the dimness.

"Not slow," she repeated. "Not...deliberate. Or seductive. Not any of those things you think this should be. Nothing but what it really is."

"And what is that?" Drew asked.

"Something we've waited for long enough. Too long. Something I want as much as you possibly can. I don't need to be seduced either."

As she whispered the last, she moved her hips into his, feeling the heated strength of his erection with surge of excitement. She touched him and felt response shudder throughout his entire body. As ready as she was. As hungry.

She pushed him onto his back and put one leg on the other side of his hips, so that she straddled them. And then, guiding his erection, she slowly lowered her body over his. Drew's hand found her breast, long fingers caressing, as she straightened her knees, raising her body slightly away from its contact with his. She held his eyes in the intimate dimness, smiling at him as she lifted, almost too far, and then began again the slow descent.

"Maggie," he said, her name a breath, spiraling away in the cold, his breath whitened like fog.

Then he closed his eyes, his lips tight, fighting against

the too-quick release he had warned her about. Her lips curved in loving amusement at his dogged determination to prolong this until she, too, reached fulfillment.

She was the one in control here, however. And it was a control she relished. She lifted her hips again and then lowered them, millimeter by millimeter, savoring the hot strength of his arousal. Savoring the shuddering breath he took as her body slowly descended. Savoring the touch of his fingers against her breast. And the fact that he had come back for her.

The memory of all the long, lonely nights she had spent here alone, thinking about him, drifted away in the darkness. Forgotten in the reality of this. Everything forgotten except the exquisite sensations which had begun to build in her own body as it lifted and then lowered again and again over the incredible hardness of his.

Her control. And suddenly she knew that she wanted her own fulfillment as much he wanted it for her. She wanted release as desperately as she wanted to give to him. There had been too long a denial, not just for him, but for her as well.

She wanted to feel again that shivering ecstasy which was part physical, part emotional. Tied inextricably, for a woman, to her feelings for the man who made love to her. Or to whom she made love. As she was making love to Drew.

Her lips parted, her breathing gradually increasing in relationship to the ever-quickening movement of her hips. Seeking to bring them both to the end of that long loneliness. And to bring them there together. Together for the rest of their lives.

At that thought, the shimmering heat exploded, running upward from where their straining bodies were joined, fingering out into every nerve and muscle in her body. Her head fell back, breath releasing into the dark, frigid air as a low moan. Her hands clutched at Drew's, trying to hold on to him as the present faded in that all-consuming flood of sensation.

His hips, jerking spasmodically, rose in response to what was happening within her body. On some level, she heard his gasp. Then, as the quivering force of her climax fell away, leaving her almost painfully sensitive to his every movement, his body convulsed again and again within her. Filling her with the hot sweet liquid of his seed.

His seed. Even the words were erotic. She had wanted this for so long. Wanted his body, one with hers. Wanted the possibility of Drew's baby, growing as Laurie had, below her heart. Drew's baby and hers. Their child. Just as her daughter would be.

And somehow, with the secret knowledge that women sometimes possess, Maggie knew that was far more than a possibility now. And the knowledge filled her heart to overflowing, as the convulsive movements of Drew's body slowed and finally stilled, his face relaxing, his fingers once more soothing against her skin.

After a moment or two, she rolled onto her side, lying beside him in the crook of his arm, leaving one leg across his thighs. "That was good," she whispered.

He had turned his head, his lips stirring against her hair as he spoke. "It seems I shouldn't have worried about being too quick," he said, amusement clear in his whisper.

Maggie smiled again, hidden in the darkness as she hugged her secret to her heart. "Next time we'll do it slow."

Next time. So many years of their lives left for living. And for loving. For lying exhausted in the arms of the strong man who loved her and who would take care of them both. Who would take care of all of them, her and their children.

And Maggie's dreams—like Laurie's beloved stars, forever spangled against the night sky—were all back in her heart.

*   *   *   *   *

Don't forget MIDNIGHT REMEMBERED,
the last in the series of SECRET WARRIORS,
is coming in August.

SILHOUETTE

INTRIGUE™

AVAILABLE FROM 18TH MAY 2001

INNOCENT WITNESS Leona Karr

After witnessing a murder, Deanna Drake's four-year-old daughter was traumatised into silence. With the help of Dr Steve Sherman her daughter found her voice—and incited the killer to attack again. But to get to Deanna and her daughter, the felon would have to go through Steve first...

URGENT VOWS Joyce Sullivan

Quinn McClure had no right to show up on Hope's doorstep after five years, looking sexy and desperate with two tiny orphaned children in tow, asking her for an impossible favour: marry him. He was in danger and had to stay alive for the children—and for Hope, who loved him as only a true wife could...

THE STRANGER NEXT DOOR
Joanna Wayne

When a beautiful woman with amnesia became Langley Randolph's neighbour he was surprised to find this mysterious woman fighting tears. Danielle needed to unlock the secret of her memories...before whatever she was running from caught up with her!

UNDERCOVER PROTECTOR Cassie Miles

Lawman Lover

Intelligence agent Michael Slade feared his enemies had found his one weakness. Officer Annie Callahan, the woman he'd loved and left years ago, was being stalked. And Annie was the one thing Michael would protect...at all costs.

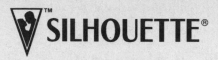

Silhouette Special Edition®
and
bestselling author

Susan Mallery

present

Desert Rogues

*A sensuous new mini-series
set under the hot desert sun*

Meet Khalil, Jamal and Malik—strong, sexy,
impossibly stubborn princes who do as they
see fit. But life in the royal palace is about to
change when they each claim a tempestuous
American bride!

THE SHEIKH'S KIDNAPPED BRIDE
(May)

**THE SHEIKH'S ARRANGED
MARRIAGE**
(June)

THE SHEIKH'S SECRET BRIDE
(July)

*Escape to El Bahar—a majestic land
where seduction rules and romantic
fantasies come alive...*

0401/SH/LC13

Silhouette Stars

Born this month.

Bing Crosby, Tammy Wynette, Michael Palin, Glenda Jackson, Sid Vicious, Salvador Dali, Janet Jackson, Gabriela Sabatini, Toyah Wilcox, Priscilla Presley.

Star of the Month.

Taurus

The year ahead is full of challenges and although you normally resist change you should feel ready to move on. Relationships are strained in the early part of the year but once you understand what you need from those close to you life will become easier, with someone surprising you with their depth of commitment.

SILH/HR/0501a

 **Gemini**

Relationships are the focus of this month and some of you will be making a stronger bond with that special person. Home matters are also highlighted with a change of scene looking likely.

Cancer

Your energy levels are high and it seems there is little you can't achieve. Success brings its own rewards and you will be in demand both socially and at work.

 Leo

Personal relationships need to be handled carefully to avoid conflict as it may be that you are not communicating your true emotions. Any new activity will reduce the stress and help you find a positive way forward.

Virgo

Romantically an excellent time and you will realise just how important those close to you are. Finances are still improving and you may make plans for a trip away, possibly further afield than normal.

 Libra

Energy levels are high and you need to find creative outlets in which to express yourself. Mid-month relationships prove difficult and you may need to step back for a while.

Scorpio

There are many opportunities to further your career and increase your personal finances. There may be some domestic upheaval but the outcome should lead to greater understanding and happiness.

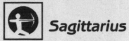 **Sagittarius**

A social month but be careful not to overcommit yourself as you may need some time out to restore energy levels. Romance is well aspected and there may be someone new in your life.

Capricorn

Romance and travel are well aspected so take the time out to indulge yourself and your spirits will be lifted. Finances receive a welcome boost towards the end of the month.

 Aquarius

You may be open to disappointment and expecting too much of yourself so try to be more realistic about what you can expect to achieve. A letter brings the chance to travel late in the month.

Pisces

Socially an excellent month and as finances are looking good you may take the opportunity to entertain in lavish style. Romantically towards the end of the month there could be a chance to improve relationships.

 Aries

Life is about to take on a new and exciting meaning with personal luck putting you on course for success. Romance is just around the corner and may be found in the most unexpected places.

Look out for more
Silhouette Stars next month

FREE!

2 Books
and a surprise gift!

We would like to take this opportunity to thank you for reading this Silhouette® book by offering you the chance to take TWO more specially selected titles from the Intrigue™ series absolutely FREE! We're also making this offer to introduce you to the benefits of the Reader Service™—

★ FREE home delivery
★ FREE gifts and competitions
★ FREE monthly Newsletter
★ Books available before they're in the shops
★ Exclusive Reader Service discounts

Accepting these FREE books and gift places you under no obligation to buy; you may cancel at any time, even after receiving your free shipment. Simply complete your details below and return the entire page to the address below. **You don't even need a stamp!**

YES! Please send me 2 free Intrigue books and a surprise gift. I understand that unless you hear from me, I will receive 4 superb new titles every month for just £2.80 each, postage and packing free. I am under no obligation to purchase any books and may cancel my subscription at any time. The free books and gift will be mine to keep in any case.

11ZEB

Ms/Mrs/Miss/Mr ....Initials ....
BLOCK CAPITALS PLEASE

Surname ....

Address ....

....

....Postcode ....

Send this whole page to:
UK: The Reader Service, FREEPOST CN81, Croydon, CR9 3WZ
EIRE: The Reader Service, PO Box 4546, Kilcock, County Kildare (stamp required)